When ... ... evil rise up,
only angels can save the Earth

the angel prophecy

MELANIE REDMOND

When the forces of evil rise up,
only angels can save the Earth

MELANIE REDMOND

MEREO
Cirencester

Prologue

Millions of years ago, before humans walked the Earth, the planet was a land free from evil, a beautiful world with only simple animal life. Peaceful and tranquil, it was covered by clear blue waters, unspoilt green fields and stunning deserts and mountains.

One morning, over the region of the Kabiri Mountains, a large ball of fire, wind and water collided together, creating an almighty bang. The animals fled, the birds flew away and the insects disappeared underground.

Moments after the collision, four creatures fell to the Earth. Four naked newborn babies lay on the soft grass in silence. One boy and girl lay fifty yards from the other boy and girl and they were shadowed by two large cloud-shaped objects hovering in the air. One of the clouds was white and lit gold by beams of sunlight, while the other was dark grey with speckles of fire burning within it. Each cloud stayed close to the children it had created.

Hours later, two large figures appeared on top of each cloud. The figures were as if made from thicker cloud; they were blurred silhouettes with white, shining eyes.

'This Earth does not need you to create anything evil, it was meant only for my two creations' said an echoing voice from the white and gold cloud, pointing with what appeared to be a hand made of misty smoke.

Then, with a crash of thunder, another voice was heard. 'My creations will stay here on Earth and they will rule, I will encourage them to be evil!' it said.

'You will not devour my planet with your souls, for I am the almighty and you Satan will be overpowered!' said the first voice as he bent forward to look down at his newborn children, Adem and Hawa.

Satan likewise bent forward, laughing and looking down at the two children he had placed on Earth. 'I call mine Ibli and Sari, and I can tell you that when the evil is embedded into their souls it will stay and spread' he said. 'Then you will never see peace on this land!'

The four infants were oblivious to what was happening around them. Although the children created by God were to be good humans, those created by Satan would have evil qualities within their souls; they could grow to be good, but they could easily fall into the hands of anything evil because of their weaknesses. All of them, however, were innocent children and knew nothing of the world around them.

God feared Satan's children would destroy the world, but he knew that at present they were just young and could still end up growing to be good people if they were around his own children for long enough. Satan, on the other hand, wanted his children to be the only ones, and felt they would have to fight for who was to stay on Earth.

Thunder started to sound and lightning appeared in the skies above.

'We can end this here, if I have to I will battle with you' God said, and he held out his fist and opened his palm. Satan also held out his fist and opened his palm, and each created a fireball, ready to strike the other.

'We will battle for this, and when I destroy you, your creations will be destroyed also' replied Satan.

Hovering over the children, they started to hurl beams from their hands. God sent a gold and white mist shooting towards Satan, but Satan held it back with beams of fire and dark streams of cloud.

The two struggled and the Earth quaked around them. Bursts of fire and lightning came from the airborne battle as they fought, but the clash of the beams stayed in between them, directly over the children. Then suddenly there was a loud bang and an explosion in front of them and the battle stopped. Slowly they watched a stone they had just created from the clashing beams fall to the ground where the children lay.

'The stone has fallen' said Satan. 'We now have no say in what is to happen.'

'You see that stone?' replied God. 'If it lies untouched the fate will lie in our children as to how they decide to take on the world. But if it is touched by Ibli and Sari, because they have your soul, evil will prevail. They must leave it be, because the only thing that will stop it is the message on it.'

"This stone has the power of evil and it will bring evil into the world when it is held, but it can only be destroyed by the chosen Custodia or whoever has its heart – 12/12/12".

'Your children could well leave the stone and live as normal' said God in his deep voice.

'I have faith in my children. They will pick up that stone one day and you will then see that we will be the rulers of this world' Satan snarled.

'If they do touch the stone, the Custodia, or angels as we call them, will make it their job to find it' answered God. 'When they have it they will end the lives of all evil. It may take years, decades or millennia, but the angels will grow stronger every time they reappear. By destroying the stone, your devils will slowly die out and you will be wiped off the planet. And I can assure you, this will happen.'

'That's where you are wrong, my friend' said Satan, laughing loudly. 'If my creations touch the stone they will bring evil into this world, and it will never be destroyed. We will overtake everything and there will be no stopping us. We will kill anything that gets in our way, and there will always be many others like us. You won't stand a chance.'

Then God and Satan disappeared into the air, and were never seen again.

Years passed, and the stone lay untouched as the children were growing up. All four had to learn how to find food and water, build shelter and get by in a world where they were all alone to fend for themselves – but they knew no different. Neither of Satan's children showed signs of evil, nor did God's children act in any way differently from their fellow humans, but Adem and Hawa stuck together, as did Ibli and Sari.

By the time the children had reached the age of ten, they had built their own homes in caves and learnt how to hunt for food. They had all grown into beautiful children, each with a different skin tone and different features as if they had a mix of Asian, European and Afro Caribbean in them. God's child Adem had a head of curly black hair with olive skin and European features, while Hawa was very pale with long chocolate-coloured hair and cat-like green eyes. Ibli was the tallest of the four with long fair hair, eyes as dark as the night sky and tanned skin, and Sari had fuzzy thick red hair with dark coloured skin and blue eyes. Adem and Hawa felt a strong bond towards each other as they grew up, as did Ibli and Sari, who often kept themselves apart from the others.

Another year passed. One dark evening as they all left each other to make their way to the caves they called home, Ibli and Sari stumbled across the stone. They knew at once it was no ordinary stone. As the moon shone down on it, it sparkled. They looked at each other, confused as to what it was. They had never before seen such a strange-looking stone.

Ibli bent down to pick it up, but before he could do so a voice came from the sky above. The voice was soft and pleasant. 'Child, do not touch the stone' it said. 'Leave it be and you can decide your own fate in the world.' The children looked up, but could see nothing but clouds.

'Take it, pick it up!' shouted another voice, and there was a loud rumble in the skies, followed by a strong wind. 'Pick it up and you will have powers greater than anyone!'

Sari looked at Ibli and her eyes widened. Ibli looked excited and stared at Sari as the wind became heavier. 'I am drawn to this stone, I need to touch it!' he shouted, as the wind blew their hair into their faces.

'I too want the stone, we should pick it up together' she agreed, shouting over the wind.

'Leave the stone!' said the voice of God. 'You can live your lives as good people, but if you take it you will follow in Satan's footsteps. My children will be able to extract that evil when they turn to angels but that means you will be removed from this land. If you touch the stone you will never be helped unless you are destroyed.'

'Do not listen, take the stone. I am your creator and you should obey me' said Satan.

The children did not know who to listen to, but they felt more of a connection to Satan, and after that they blocked out the voices from above. All they could hear were mumbling sounds at the backs of their heads.

They picked up the stone together, and as they did they felt it tremble in their hands. They held on tight to it, and heavy rain started to pour down. The thunder and lightning became louder and took over the skies, and the voices disappeared.

Ibli and Sari ran to a nearby cave, where they inspected the stone further. Neither could work out the markings on it. They knew it must have had some sort of meaning, but they didn't care; they felt excited about what they had just done.

They slept that night, but throughout it they felt strange, as if they wanted to go out and destroy everything around them. They felt as if their souls were being controlled by the stone.

As morning broke they felt a little more in control, so when they returned to Adem and Hawa they did not tell them what they had done. They placed the stone in a hiding place and left it there so it would never be found.

When the children reached the age of 12, Adem and Hawa did not like the company of Ibli and Sari, so they all kept their distance from each other, only communicating whenever necessary.

One afternoon, on the 12th day of the 12th month of the 12th year, Adem and Hawa suddenly started to feel strange sensations all over their bodies. The pain worsened as the time went on, and within an hour they found they had large feathered wings extended from their backs, both had no idea what had happened to them. Over the next hours and days their wings appeared and disappeared randomly and after a while they also realised that they had developed great strengths and their minds went into overdrive discovering things they had never thought possible. They now knew they were different, and because of this they took the role as leaders.

When they had told Ibli and Sari of this, the two became jealous of the newborn angels and wanted them dead. However, because of Adem and Hawa's newly-acquired strength, they had no idea how they could possibly kill them.

* * * * *

By the ages of thirty Adem, Hawa, Ibli and Sari had produced many children, and all their children mixed together and produced more children. The world slowly started to become more populated.

Ibli and Sari became more evil, killing animals for fun and destroying every area they lived in, including the trees and crops. They would beat all the others, including their own children, but they were unable to hurt the two angels, Adem and Hawa. This frustrated them and they spent their days working on how to become stronger, hoping that one day they would become the most powerful in the land. They couldn't take the fact that the other two had been given their wings and their powers, when they had not. They began to plan various ways of destroying the two angels.

One day Ibli was out walking when he came across some old bones that must have belonged to an animal. The bones were large and sharp, as if they had been split down the middle. Ibli had a vision; he thought that by using one of these bones he would be able to kill Adem and Hawa. He was used to killing animals by slitting their throats before they had any time to fight back. When he returned home to Sari, he conferred with her and they decided that they would go ahead with a plan to kill them whilst they slept later that night. First they would have to go back and collect the bones, then sneak back to their caves to shape them into deadly scythe-shaped weapons. Then they would then travel to where Adem and Hawa lived.

As midnight approached Sari got herself ready as Ibli paced the front garden, thinking of the best way to catch Adem and Hawa when they least expected it.

'Come on Sari, we must go, we must hurry because we have three miles to walk' shouted Ibli.

'I'm ready, my love' Sari replied, and after collecting the shaped bones they set off. Approaching the area where Adem and Hawa lived, they found the two sleeping in their small cave. Ibli looked again at the weapon he had created. It was twelve inches long, and rounded with a rough but sharp edge to it.

'Right, this is what we will do' he said. 'We will slowly creep into the cave and stand behind where they are. Then when I look at you, we are to do it without any hesitation whatsoever. Do it whatever way you wish, but just be sure to get her neck, I will get Adem. You are clear on that, yes?'

Sari nodded, and they proceeded into the cave. It was small and dark and the only light they had was the fire, now almost extinguished. By its light they could see the two wrapped in each other's arms.

Sari was jealous of Hawa's beauty. She longed for her pale skin and long smooth brown hair. Her skin was always glowing and her body was in perfect shape. Sari also hated it that she was so pleasant and always there to help the others before she helped herself. She wondered how they had ever got on when they were children, but that had been a long time ago, and she needed this to come to an end.

Ibli was the same. He hated Adem's handsome features, and especially his strength. Ever since they had been boys, Adem would always win when they played games, and whenever he attempted to fight with Adem, Adem would just turn the other cheek.

They now stood over the two sleeping angels. They both took a deep breath, then Ibli gave Sari the nod and slowly they bent forward, holding their newly-made weapons up high. Then together they grabbed the angels' hair, pulled their heads up and rapidly slashed their throats. The scythes were sharp and ragged, making the pain unbearable as they dragged the reconstructed bones through their necks, roughly ripping skin and flesh.

Adem and Hawa didn't know what was happening. They did not have any time to get up or move. By the time they knew what was going on they were only able to give short, gurgling screams. They looked at each other in agony and sadness, for they knew their time had come to an end and that they would be dead within the next few seconds.

Before they let themselves slip away they slowly turned around to see who it was doing this to them, and to their shock they saw the two people they had grown up with. Then they slowly slipped away from life, thinking of the families they had left behind and hoping they would be safe.

Ibli and Sari barricaded the cave and walked off without looking back. They were proud that they were finally the most powerful beings in the land. From that moment, there was no chance their evil could be undone.

As the bodies of Adem and Hawa lay lifeless by the burnt-out fire in the cave, their spirits slowly escaped from their bodies and rose up and out of the cave, going higher and higher into the skies above.

After the murders Ibli and Sari carried on as normal. No one ever found out what had happened to Adem and Hawa. This was the first sign of evil on Earth, and the beginning and the birth of it.

Ibli and Sari decided that they would need a name for the evil force they had created. They decided on Iblisari, their names joined together, meaning 'People of Satan'. The Iblisari founded a cult of devil worshippers, those who believed in Satan and evil. Not everyone followed them, and they could not force other humans into being evil-minded. But as time went by and the world became more populated, their small group of followers grew larger and larger, with perhaps one person in ten on the side of evil.

Years after the deaths of Ibli and Sari, the Iblisari cult carried on. Whoever was evil was drawn to it. Meanwhile the stone was left untouched, hidden in many places over the years and lost and found many times.

By the time the date of 12/12/12 came round once again, thousands of years after Ibli and Sari had lived and left their evil legacy, the Iblisari had greatly increased in power. They had far more followers, and the power of evil had grown throughout the world.

The Iblisari had studied the stone and spent years working out what it actually meant. They knew they had to destroy the angels if they reappeared, so that they could carry on living their evil lives as they wanted to.

True to the stories of the Iblisari, on the due date of 12/12/12 the angels emerged. This time there were twelve of them, but as soon as they appeared an evil prince named Tobias led the way to the angels and twelve of his men slaughtered them, exactly as Ibli and Sari had done to Adem and Hawa so many years before.

The Iblisari had not yet worked out how and when more angels would appear, but the date of 12/12/12 gave them a good idea. They would not appear every time that date came by; there would have to be four or more millennia in between. They made their plans.

CHAPTER ONE

New York, May 2012

'Get out of bed you, guys!' Amy shouted as loudly as she could. Rushing around looking for a pair of matching socks was a regular occurrence in the Carter household. 'Why can't you look after things?'

A normal Monday morning in a small house in Massapequa, Long Island, New York State, and Amy as usual had a hundred and one things to do before she set out to work. She always had her three-mile morning jog, despite having to get the kids out of bed for school, walk the dogs, make the lunches, and get herself ready for work, the same routine she'd had for the last 15 years.

Amy lived with her two children, Jake, 15, and Scarlett, 14, and their two dogs in a nice part of the town, just a few miles from Manhattan.

'Hurry up, breakfast is on the table and I'm off to work now!' she yelled. 'Have a good day, love you guys'. She slammed the door and could hear the kids shouting 'love you too ma'.

Amy set off on her usual journey to the railway station. From here she took the LIRR train into Penn Station, Manhattan, where she worked on Fifth Avenue in a big insurance company. She had worked there for 17 years since after relocating from San Diego with a few of her friends, she was happy enough with the job as it paid the bills, and having been there for so many years she got some perks, and it had security, which is what she needed as a single parent.   Over the last year Amy craved change in her life, but nothing exciting or different ever happened to her.

Amy had been single since the day she had told the kids' father, Joe, she was pregnant with Scarlett. Neither she nor the children ever heard from him after that day, but she never dwelled on it, because in her view he had been a complete waste of space. Not only that, he often became very abusive to her and arguments would usually end up in violence. When she had met him he seemed a happy, caring, considerate and an all-round good person, but that didn't last long. The problems started off when he was made redundant shortly after she became pregnant with Jake at the age of 20, from then on the relationship went downhill. He became depressed, lazy and worst of all possessive and abusive.

Amy worked a ten hour-day and would come home, heavily pregnant, to a messy house and an aggressive man.

'Why are you wearing those dresses to work, why all the make up?' He would yell at her the moment she got through the door. 'I know you've been seeing someone! That baby's not mine!' He always accused her of going off with other men, but Amy had been faithful to him from the day she'd met him.

'I am sick of going out to work all day long and coming home to this mess' she would say. 'Goddam it I'm pregnant and tired, you can at least make the dinner. I don't give a shit if you think I am having an affair, think what you like and if you don't trust me, then leave!'

She would tell him to get out and he would usually go off for a night or two, then return with a sorry story. 'I'm so sorry, I didn't mean to say those things' he would say, 'I'm just feeling the pressure with no work and a baby on the way, and I promise I'll change'.

Amy would force him to go out to work and he would agree.

Then she would forgive him, and a week later it would be back to the same thing.

Weeks went by and Amy stayed at work for as long as she could to avoid him, or go and stay at a friend's house, because when she did go home she would again have to go through the usual crap. She'd confide in her friends and family about it all the time, but however much advice they gave her telling her to leave him, she didn't listen. She always thought he would change, and maybe after the baby arrived he would even be back to what he was like when they first met.

Jake arrived three weeks early. He was a healthy, beautiful baby and Amy loved every minute of being a mother. She wanted to stay off work for at least two years, but Joe being Joe he didn't bother looking for work and they needed an income. She had just four months off work and during that time Joe had changed a little, well for the first three months anyway. It was not long before she again was the one who had to clean, shop, get up in the night to feed the baby (which she didn't mind) and then go out to work every day, and she would usually pretend he wasn't there at all, there was no point in him living there. He also became abusive to her, punching and hitting her in places where no one would notice the bruises.

When she returned to work after the fourth month, Joe told her he would be happy to take care of Jake in the daytime, but that changed within weeks. 'I'm not looking after this child while you're at work flirting with men all day' he told her. 'You'll have to get a minder, because I will be out job hunting.'

Luckily she had her friends Henrik and Barbell next door to look after him two days a week, and another friend to take him for one day, so Joe had no choice but to do something useful for the other two days. Yet Amy became worried that if he could hit her, what would he do to Jake when he started to cry?

Just weeks later she had to use a nanny for the two days, because Joe had started to become worse, drinking every day, constantly moaning at her every minute they spent together, and calling her every name under the sun. She had no idea how she'd ever deserved a life like that, and she needed to change it.

'Joe, like I said before, go and never come back, we don't need you here' she would often tell him. When Jake was six months old they started sleeping in separate bedrooms. After eight weeks apart she knew the relationship was over. She didn't love him anymore, and something had to be done.

Two more weeks passed, and Amy was so busy she did not notice her missed period. On the way back from work one evening she plucked up the courage to buy a pregnancy test, then stopped off at her friend Millie's house, where she took the test; positive. Millie had always advised her to get rid of Joe, and told her many times that it would end up a lot worse if she carried on the worthless relationship.

'I can't believe this has happened, we have had sex twice since Jake was born and we used precautions. What am I going to do?' she cried.

Millie told her what she had been telling her for the last year. 'Leave him, kick him out. He does nothing to help you, he treats you like shit' she said. 'Get rid of him!' Amy agreed, but was scared of what he would do when she told him, though he hadn't been violent for a few weeks.

'I know, I know, I can't trust him with Jake and I don't love him, so I know I have to do this even though there is another baby on the way. I need to do it for them if anything.'

The next evening after work she arrived home as early as she could. Jake was at the neighbour's house and wasn't due to be collected till six thirty. She opened the door to a gloomy house and a messy kitchen. The plates Joe had had his breakfast, lunch and dinner on were all lying on the sitting room table, and Joe was lying on the sofa.

She stood in the doorway of the messy living room of what

had been such a lovely, bright house and knew there and then that it had to end. This life was not for her. However this conversation ended, she knew she would end the relationship.

'Joe, I have something to tell you' she said in a scared tone. 'I think we have a lot to talk about and sort out.'

'What the hell is wrong with you now?' he replied.

Amy was so nervous she just shouted it out, without hesitation. 'I'm pregnant' she said.

'How the fuck did you get pregnant again? Get rid of it!' he shouted back at her. He got up and walked towards her. 'How?'

She feared at that moment he would attack her, but she didn't move back. She had had enough, and was no longer scared of him. 'I am keeping this baby, get out of my house and never come back' she shouted. 'We don't need you here, you are a waste of space and I can do this alone! I've been doing it alone for the last few months anyway so there is no point in you being here.'

He shouted back at her 'Yes I will get out of here, I'm not hanging around you! That child and the one you are carrying are probably not even mine. I ought to punch you in the stomach right now!'

She stepped back, starting to fear him a little and worried for the child she was carrying. She ran upstairs to collect some clothes and toys for Jake.

'I'm going to pick up my son and then we'll be going to stay with Millie for the night, and I want you out of here for when I return' she said. 'This is my house, my name is on the deeds so you have no right here!' She walked down the stairs and slammed the door.

Joe ran upstairs in a rage. As she walked out of the front gate he looked out of the window and shouted 'I won't be here when you get back, I'll be taking my stuff and leaving for good.'

She looked up at him. 'Well I hope so, because another thing I didn't mention was that I don't love you any more, I haven't for months.'

She felt suddenly overcome with relief, even though it was the last thing she wanted and to be left bringing up two children on her own was something she had never expected, especially with the fact that they had once been in love.

Amy felt safe, but then at the back of her mind she didn't want to think too far ahead in case he was still there when she arrived home.

When she returned home the next day she brought her two friends Millie and Harriet, in case he was still there and started any trouble. When she opened the front door the place looked exactly as it had done when she'd left the previous day, but this time it was empty.

When she walked into the house she found he had completely trashed it. He had put a knife through the sofas, thrown milk all over the floor, smashed plates and smeared the walls with smashed jars of jam and sauce.

There was a note lying on the kitchen worktop.

Amy,
I am glad to be leaving this house and leaving you for good.
You have done nothing but put me down over the last few months,
I am excited to start my new life in America with someone I have
been seeing for 6 months.
You think you are smart emptying and closing your bank account, so
I have taken $2000 from your emergency cash savings you hid in the
attic. I need this to start my new life.
Enjoy your depressing life. I hope our paths never cross again.

Goodbye.
Joe.

Amy was a little stunned at the note, but she reflected what a good thing it was that she had emptied out her account and transferred all her money to another account. It was all her money anyway, and even though he had taken her cash savings, wrecked the house and gone off with another woman, she felt a weight had been lifted from her shoulders and she could now start a fresh new life. She did feel scared at the thought that she would soon have two babies to look after, but she was free and that felt good. She knew she could do it. And even if he did return there was no way she would let him in.

Millie and Harriet comforted her. 'This is the best thing that can happen to you I promise' said Harriet. You have a beautiful baby and another on the way, you can so do this'.

'We will be here for you whenever you need us' said Millie. 'Once we get this placed cleaned up we should get ourselves to the supermarket to stock up on food and get some champagne in. We're celebrating your new life here. And it will all be on us, you just relax.'

Amy had to be strong about this. There was a lot to sort out. She needed to do a bit of decorating and to get rid of the old rubbish and anything that belonged to Joe, so she booked the next two weeks off work. Life was about to get very busy and stressful, but she smiled at that thought. All she needed was her friends and her children.

★ ★ ★ ★ ★

Years passed, and luckily for Amy, Joe never returned or tried to contact her or the kids. She had given birth to Scarlett and her house now looked like new.

She had tried her best to bring the children up as well as she possibly could. Jake and Scarlett were great kids, friendly, caring, helpful, clever and popular at school, but of course they were regular teenagers – stroppy, moody and messy. The three of them got on well together and were able to talk to each other about anything and everything.

Amy never remarried, nor had a long enough relationship to be able to bring anyone home to meet Jake and Scarlett. As they grew up they would often ask about their father, but she waited until they were older to tell them the truth about him. When they reached their teenage years she explained from start to finish everything about Joe, from when they had fallen in love to when and how it had ended. It shocked them a little, but being the kids they were they managed to shrug it off pretty quickly.

Having spent years concentrating on bringing up the children, Amy thought it was about time she got herself out there and did something interesting with her life. The kids were older now and in a few years they would be going off to college. She wanted to maybe go away on trips with her friends a bit more and see the world and in five years or so she could find a good man to settle down with, but she definitely wasn't ready for that, yet even though Jake and Scarlett always expressed their concerns about her being on her own. There was no way she wanted the hassle of a relationship at the moment.

She did enjoy life. She felt she had missed out on certain things, but she would never change what she had for the world. Her problem was that life was pretty basic and dull and nothing exciting ever happened to her.

At 35 Amy didn't look a day over 30. She had amazing skin, long honey-coloured hair and big hazel eyes. She looked after herself well and it showed. She certainly turned heads wherever she went, and she wasn't short of attention from guys. She was always there to help others and always had time for everyone else before herself. After finishing her relationship with the Joe she became a stronger person. She would never let anyone walk all over her again and over the years she had short relationships here and there with guys, but when things got too serious she would run a mile becoming scared when someone wanted to get too close to her.

Most of her friends were married, some with children, her closest friend Millie was also single but not interested in a relationship or children, so it was good to hang out with someone who had no responsibilities. Her other good friend, Harriet, was married and had a 12-year-old son.

Luckily for Amy, she also had her good friends and neighbours Henrik and Barbell next door. They had been neighbours for the last 17 years and were always there to help Amy when she was stuck. They were always happy to look after the children when she had to work late or had a night out in town, and the children loved them like their own grandparents.

Amy had been born and raised in San Diego California. After leaving school to travel across America on a road trip at 18 with her friends they had decided they loved New York so much that they moved over. Her parents still lived in San Diego, and even though they regularly visit each other it was still the other side of the country and she often missed having them close by.

CHAPTER TWO

Henrik Orsson was a 70-year-old retired history teacher from Sweden, and he and Barbell spent a lot of time travelling and exploring the world. Henrik looked older than his years, but his energy levels were as high as those of a young man. He had long messy silver hair which he had kept since he had grown it as a hippy in the 60s. He always wore heavily-patterned shirts with trousers and sandals. He had far more intelligence than most of the people around him. He was a slightly strange and eccentric man, who loved history and had great interest in dates as far back as far as 4000 BC. He had delved into history a lot more in the recent years due to his retirement. He had always thought there was some kind of magic within the human race, and because of this he believed there were many secrets hidden in the years of history before Christ.

Just a few weeks earlier he had set off on the start of five months of travel to study a few countries and find out more about their history. On his trip he visited the Middle East and Iraq, Egypt, Rome, then the Greek islands. In particular he wanted to search into a date that had come up in some of the history books he had read over the years, especially one written by Zaid, a prince who had lived more than 4000 years ago. Zaid's book had mentioned a date and some codes for the date which must have had a deeper meaning, and Henrik wanted to investigate.

He decided to visit the historic cities mentioned in one of Zaid's books and search for some answers. Although Zaid was only vaguely mentioned, he tried his hardest to put the pieces together, but it always led to nothing more than a dead end. However Henrik knew deep down there was more, and insisted in carrying on with his search.

In Iraq he stumbled across an ancient are which had once been called Urak when the country had been Mesopotamia. On the edge of this area he found the small derelict village of Vuoil, and at the centre of the old town up at the top of a hill stood an old ruined ziggurat temple which had once been a tourist attraction; thousands of years ago the palace had belonged to a royal family. In recent years it had been forgotten about as the temple and surrounding village ruins were very slowly sinking underground, but the history enthusiasts still visited the ruins as often as possible and all for the same reason, to find answers.

Henrik had heard from a source a few years back that there were many small temples below the ground which contained tons of old books and papers dated as far back as 2100BC. Very few historians knew of this, and those who did were too scared to go and investigate because they had heard that when others had entered the temples they had been crushed by falling debris or fallen down deep holes under the small tombs. Henrik knew there was more from certain things that were written in books he had come across around the world, and especially ones written by Zaid, which gave clues for further investigative work.

He had found out that the many historians who had gone missing searching for clues or had been crushed to death had been trying to get closer to finding out other historic information, but there was never proof of this.

Henrik found a very interesting story written by Zaid which highlighted the date 12/12/12. He wanted to find out more about Zaid's life and found it intriguing the way he and the people he had written about and described certain occurrences and their life stories. However these were only extracts and he knew there was a lot more behind the stories and that he would not be happy until he found out.

On his final day in Iraq he knew he had one last chance to attempt to get into the lowest parts of the small temples lying under the old palace temple. He was well aware about the dangers of this and what it would do to his wife if he did not arrive home safely, but being the inquisitive person he was, nothing was going to stop him and he was going to get down there whether it was closed off or not.

At five o'clock, fifteen minutes before the daily closure of the temple ruins to the public, there were just a few tourists heading towards the exit. He found himself alone at last, hiding behind the small entrance to the back of the ruins but inside the compound. He could see in the distance security guards leading the last groups of people away to the small bus that would take them back into the city.

Henrik hid for a further thirty minutes behind one of the high walls and waited until there was no one in sight. By half past six the security guards had done their rounds and closed up everything and were waiting for the night guards to arrive. The sun had just gone down and the blue sky started to darken and fill with stars. He stopped and started to work out which direction was the best way to go, as he took his torch from his bag he sneaked around to another entrance, which led further into the ruins and the old underground tombs. The gates were on latches that were easy to open, and he had brought tools to open the gate at the entrances of the older temples and tombs.

The ruins were stunning. The high walls were smothered with fresh green plants running up to the top, while the ground had a light layer of sand spread over ancient tiles. Beautiful statues were scattered around on podiums, and although very old with parts crumbled away, they looked real, as if they had a purpose there and were guarding the place with their eyes following every move.

There were stone benches around the pretty stone fountains, which were surrounded by flowers. Henrik felt as if he were in a dream at the breath-taking beauty of the place. He had been to the temple before, but only passing by, so he had never seen it like this.

As Henrik walked further into the temple ruins he felt as if there were silent, invisible people beside him, but nothing was to be seen. As he reached a dark entrance leading into the first set of temples, in front of him he saw an old rusty gate which had an engraving of an angel at each side and a strange creature lying under each angel. He clipped the chain that was wrapped around the gate with a bolt cutter, and then pushed it open. The gate was at least twenty feet tall and looked thousands of years old, yet it had been preserved to perfection through the rust. He stared up at it mesmerized, and wondered about the story behind the engravings.

As the skies started to get darker, Henrik prayed. Suddenly he had the feeling that he was slowly being guided somewhere by the wind. It felt calming and reassuring, but frightening at the same time. Was this the way the other people had died?

The sense of being guided continued. He shook himself and carried on through the dark tunnels. Soon he had left the daylight behind. As he walked further inside he came to beautifully-tiled courtyards and dark corridors which went slowly downwards. It was now completely black and the temporary lighting had been turned off. He had an idea of the way to go with the map he carried.

Then he came to another large gate which led to some stairs. This was not on the map. These, he knew were the stairs from which no one had ever come out alive. Standing at the gate, he saw that it was locked a little more securely than the other one, but Henrik had his tools, so he placed his bag on the floor and took out a saw. Then he started to cut through the bar and chains around the gate.

He had great difficulty with this gate as the chains were thicker and heavier than the last one, but after fifteen minutes he had finished cutting and opened it up. He stepped over the gateway, and suddenly felt a push on his back.

'Who's there?' he shouted quickly turning around and facing his torch towards the gate he had just come through, but there was no one there. 'Show yourself!' he called, but no one answered. He presumed it must have been a bat or some kind of underground creature, so he carried on further, even though he had no idea which way he should go.

He again felt something on his shoulder. He shuddered and shook himself, but this time the feeling stayed, as if a warm fleece had been placed around him. It was a gentle feeling, as if someone was softly stroking his shoulder blades. He knew no one was there, yet instead of feeling scared he felt surprisingly at ease.

The strange force continued to guide him deeper and deeper, until he came to a group of dark rooms. Here the force left him to carry on alone.

The first room he walked into was dusty and full of old wooden and stone boxes, some square, some circular. The room looked to be about four square meters, from what he could see with his torch.

He opened some of the boxes. The first few were empty, but the final box he looked at had a map inside it, drawn on some form of ancient parchment. The map had a strange code written upon it. It was very hard to read, but Henrik had studied codes before and knew something of what had been written on it, so he roughly knew what direction he should take next as he left the first room.

The map showed the area of a tomb furthest from where he was standing, so he walked over to it. It led to another room which was about 10 square meters in extent. The map now seemed to be telling him to go ten feet towards the corner of the room. As he stepped forward he fell over something. He looked down to see some old bones surrounded by debris and wood, and when he shone his torch on it he saw what appeared to be a skeleton.

He jumped back. Was this one of the lost explorers? But it was too late to turn back now.

As he reached the wall he found a latch. He slowly twisted the latch, to find that it opened up a small door on to what looked like a black cavity. He shone his torch inside he saw a flight of narrow winding steps leading downward.

Leaving his bag, Henrik stuffed the map into his jacket pocket and climbed down the steps; there were about twenty of them. At the bottom a small corridor led him to another room filled with more boxes. One of them, nailed to the stone wall, was marked 'Zaid 12/12/12'.

This was what he had come here for. He wondered what he would find inside it. It appeared that no one had been down here for thousands of years.

He took his gloves from his pocket, sat down by the box and slowly prepared to open it. It was covered in thick dust, which he carefully wiped aside.

Inside the box was a large and ancient book. It was falling apart, so he gently placed it on his lap. There were different-sized pages. The first page had a list, from which it appeared that the book contained stories written in it by different people. There was also diagram of a winged creature on the first page, and again he saw the numbering 12/12/12.

He carried on flicking through the book. It appeared to contain at least a thousand pages. Henrik got himself comfortable and started reading.

In the year 2042 BC, the world population was around 70 million. The largest civilised place on Earth was Urak. It was a beautiful land, unspoilt with lush green fields, beautiful beaches and stunning palaces.

On the edge of Urak, a few miles from the coast in a town called Vuoil, lived the royal family, in the largest known palace on the land.

They were known, loved and praised by all their people on Earth, and many travelled daily to show loyalty and love to them, for they had been loyal and caring to their people.

King Gabir and Queen Amira were in their late twenties. Gabir was a short man at just five feet five, but he was very handsome and had a strong toned olive-skinned body. His eyes were dark brown and his hair short and black. Amira was taller than Gabir and was as pale as a ghost, but she too was very beautiful with emerald green eyes and long dark hair.

They had married when they were both 18 and had many happy years together, but for years they tried for a child and always failed. They both kept diaries so that they could note down steps of their lives and kept them in secret hiding places.

One afternoon whilst eating their lunch Amira seemed a little frustrated and upset. 'My love is there a problem? You appear a little unhappy' Gabir asked her.

'Gabir' Amira sighed, 'I cannot go on being childless. I need a child to love and care for. I need to give you the family you deserve and we need an heir to the throne.'

For years she wept over this, but Gabir was not so bothered. He was happy to spend the rest of his days with his queen, whether it was alone or with a family, however knowing how much this upset her he suggested alternative ideas like finding a motherless child and bringing him or her up as their own, or finding a couple who could not keep their child, but Amira wanted a child of her own.

Slowly as the years passed she knew conceiving naturally was unlikely to happen, so she accepted Gabir's idea of adopting an orphaned child. A year down the line, they decided it was time to do this. One Wednesday afternoon in June 2038 BC, the King and Queen sent out their close and faithful servants and soldiers to start their journey in search of a child who had the misfortune of being without a parent.

Henrik then came to the second part of the book. He settled down to make himself a little more comfortable.

At the other side of the town, in a village called Goaz, a slightly poorer place on the edge of Vuoil, lived Viola, a plump and pretty fourteen-year-old who lived with her parents and seven younger siblings.

One spring morning in 2038 BC the family were getting ready for school and work. They were about to leave when Viola started to feel extremely ill.

'Mother, I feel so terribly sick today' she said. 'Please may I stay here in bed for the day to recover?'

Her mother checked her forehead and agreed she seemed very hot and poorly, so she put her to bed with some hot water, honey and a warm blanket.

'I will be gone for five hours my love, so have some rest and I will return to look after you' her mother told her. Viola said that was fine and waved goodbye to the family, then walked over to her bed to rest.

As she was lying on her bed the pain became more and more frequent. A sharp pain struck her abdominal area and she felt a heavy weight on her stomach.

'Help, someone help me, please!' she screamed, but there was no one anywhere near her house. As the pains got worse she felt herself going in and out of consciousness. She screamed louder and louder, praying she would not die.

'What is happening Lord, what is happening?' she shouted angrily. 'I am only young! Please do not take me to my death!'

Two hours later the pains had worsened into a deep heavy pain everywhere around her lower body, and especially her abdomen. It made her curl her body up. Sweating profusely, she suddenly she felt the urge to push on her stomach, but this felt worse. She tried not to do it, but couldn't help doing it again and again. As she pushed she groaned loudly to disguise the pain, but it did not work.

Viola tried to raise herself up from her bed to look out of the window and see if there was someone nearby to help, but as she stood up she felt faint and had to throw herself back down on to the bed, still crying with pain and trying to make herself comfortable.

She lay back with her knees up. 'Why is this happening, am I dying?' she thought to herself.

Pushing down on her abdomen again she felt her legs spreading by themselves, so she placed her hand on her crotch area, where it hurt the most. Then she screamed. Something was coming out of her. At that moment she knew exactly what was happening; she had seen her mother go through it. Viola was about to give birth.

As she screamed more and more and pushed more and more, she was worrying about what her parents would say, how the community would treat her, how she was going to bring up this child when she was only 14. She cried and gave one last long and hard push.

Suddenly the sound of a crying baby echoed in the room, and this scared her more than the pain had. She looked down and there in a pool of blood in front of her was a baby boy. She turned away from him and cried. She had never known she was pregnant.

Her thoughts now went to the baby's father, Guilliam, who lived at the other end of the village. He was 18 years old and married, and his wife Anya was expecting their own first child in a couple of months. He had seduced Viola nine months before when he was helping her father build a shed in their garden. They had seen each other for three months after that, until he had found out his wife was pregnant.

He told her they had to end the affair. Upsetting as this was to Viola, she accepted it and moved on with her life, as she knew she was too young for such a relationship, and especially for a married man who was about to have a family of his own.

Viola jumped up from her bed with blood dripping from her and the umbilical cord still attached. She grabbed the nearest sharp object and ripped the cord in half. Still feeling sore and faint, she pulled the placenta out, gritting her teeth and closing her eyes.

She did not yet touch the baby that lay there screaming. She was so very scared, but she had to think about what she needed to do. She felt guilty that she would have to give the baby away and could not bear the thought of living a life knowing her son was out there somewhere. However she did not want the child growing up in a life where he would have nothing, and she certainly did not want her parents finding out, because if they did she would have been disowned, sent away or even stoned if anyone found out who the father was. She had to think quickly.

She remembered her mother would be back in two hours, so she grabbed some towels and linen sheets and slowly picked up the little boy. As she cleaned him off she noticed a long brown mark on his forearm which was presumably a birthmark. She thought that one day, if they ever crossed paths, she would recognise him from this mark.

Viola washed herself down and put on her clothes, though she was still in pain and bleeding heavily. She dumped the blood-soaked sheets in a stream at the back of the house, then ran two miles towards the village church, her body aching. She knew she should have stayed in bed, but she had to get this over with and hoped she wouldn't collapse before she got there. The church would be the only place safe for the child. She knew the nuns there would look after him well and tend to his medical needs.

Finally she reached the church and walked towards the door. Slowly and quietly she crept around the back where the priest and the nuns lived. The light was on and there was a smell of cooking, so she placed the baby down on the step with a vague note explaining where the child had come from and why she had had to give him up. It also said she was going to take her own life, so there would be no point in mentioning this to a soul, or looking for her. Then she ran away weeping as fast as she could, not looking back once.

Henrik stretched his shoulders and rotated his neck; he was feeling a bit stiff. He had an idea what might happen next. Shuffling about, he noticed a small door behind the box, but the box was bolted to it. He tried to unscrew the box from the door so he could push the door inwards slightly, it seemed to be very secure. There had to be some reason why it was hidden and bolted, but he wanted to get on with the book, so he decided to check it out later after he had read through the text thoroughly. He carried on reading.

It had been five days since the royal soldiers had left in search of a new-born child. Before they had set off, Queen Amira had stopped Felix, her most loyal soldier, and begged him, 'Please try not to return without a baby for us. But most importantly, you must not force a mother to give her child to you. I trust you and I know you will not let me down' she softly whispered into his ear.

'My lady, I will try my best not to let you down, my men and I will work hard to make our King and Queen happy' Felix replied, bowing his head.

The soldiers searched for days. They travelled to every town and every village, but there was no sign of anyone who was willing to give up a child, nor could they find a child of a suitable age for the King and Queen.

'We have done all we can, Felix.' said Omar, one of the soldiers. 'We need more rest, food and drink, as do our horses. We will need to stop at the next village before we proceed home'.

Half an hour later they came to the village of Goaz. It was a Monday afternoon on the first day of spring. The sun was shining and the air was crisp and clear. The men had an hour to rest and eat before they made their way back to the palace just a few miles away, so they searched for a church to see if the nuns would be able to feed and water them and their horses.

Omar saw a church in the distance and tiredly directed their horses towards it. When they arrived one of the soldiers knocked on the door of the church but there was no answer. However the men could hear singing and talking from the back and they could smell cooked food.

Felix walked around to the back of the church to find someone to open the door and ask if he and his men could be fed. He could hear the banging of pots and pans, so he walked further around to find the back door. Then he heard a soft moaning sound.

Felix turned the next corner to find two wild dogs sniffing at a bundle of sheets. He heard the sound again; it sounded like a small animal, maybe even a child. He quickly shooed the dogs away and looked closer into the sheets.

There, to his amazement, lay a tiny baby wrapped in linen. There was a note among the sheets. Felix took the note and unfolded it; it appeared to have been written by a desperate woman wanting a better life for the child she had just given birth to. After reading her words he didn't think twice. He scooped the child up, placed it in the bag wrapped around his neck and walked back to the other soldiers, who were now talking to the priest at the front church doors.

'Come on over Felix, the priest has invited us in for food and drink' said one of the soldiers, but Felix answered, 'I must proceed with my journey. You enjoy yourselves here, and I'll meet you back at the palace when you are done.' As quickly as he could he ran back to the horse jumped on it and cantered back to the palace, gently holding the child.

Queen Amira was waiting patiently in the palace, spending most of her time looking out of the small apertures in the walls they used as windows. The palace had many of these small windows scattered around it to let as much light in as possible. The floors were made of the finest tiles and the stone walls were decorated with paintings and pictures and surrounded with plants. There were candles in every corner and by every step, and long chiffon curtains woven with gold thread were draped from the ceilings to the floors. Amira wanted her home to look as bright and homely as possible and she had succeeded; it was the most beautiful palace on Earth. Even the outdoor areas and gardens were of the finest taste and design.

As she walked to the highest floor of the palace she went over to the outdoor rooftop area with the best views. In the distance she saw a man on his horse; it looked like Felix. She shouted for Gabir and turned back to go inside, for she couldn't bear to see him return with no child.

'Gabir, there is a soldier approaching, I think it is Felix and I cannot bear to look' she said. Gabir ran down to greet Felix, and saw that he was carrying his bag very carefully.

He shouted, 'Any success?' Felix dismounted and walked over to Gabir.

'I bring joy, my Lord!' he said smiling as they both heard the crying of the child. Gabir held out his hands for the child. 'You have done well, my soldier!' he said. 'How did you find this child, where did it come from?'

They walked into the palace to see Amira, and Felix explained to Gabir how he had come about the child. Amira was too scared to run down to greet Felix in case he had no child for her; she didn't want to go through any more disappointment. So she went straight to her bedroom, where she paced the floor back and forth until she heard a knock. The door swung open and Amira walked over to find Gabir holding the bundle of white linen sheets with Felix behind him. Peeking through the sheets, she saw a beautiful baby.

She fell to her knees and cried. 'I knew we could trust you to find us our child, thank you so much, Felix!' she cried. 'You are an honour to us and we will never forget this. You will be rewarded well!'

As she held the baby, Gabir explained that it was a boy and told her how he had been found. They knew this child would bring them great joy and pleasure and decided his name should be Zaid.

Later that day she asked to speak to Felix to find out if he was telling the truth about exactly where and how he had found the baby and what had happened. Felix explained everything, and gave her the note that had been left with the child. It seemed a sad story, but it made Amira happier knowing she could take care of a child who had been given up by its mother in such circumstances. She offered Felix a place in the palace, away from the workers' quarters, and asked if he would be godfather to the child. Felix agreed.

CHAPTER THREE

Henrik had wondered earlier what relevance this story had, but now he knew it was Zaid's explanation of how he was brought into the world and what his life had been like. He carried on reading.

Two years passed and Gabir, Amira and their son Zaid lived a happy and fulfilling life. Zaid had brought great joy to them, and was to them the perfect son.

One morning the sun was shining brightly over the city of Vuoil.

'I think we should go out for a walk to the ocean together as a family, don't you?' Amira said.

'It sounds like a good idea but I do have a lot of work to do here' Gabir sighed then paused 'But I suppose I could delegate it to Felix.'

'And I also think it would be nice to go without being followed by servants and soldiers.'

'I guess so, it's been years since we have been out all day alone' he replied.

They agreed and prepared themselves to go straight after lunch. As the three of them sat down to eat, Gabir was called by Felix to attend to some urgent business,

'Cant this wait, Felix?' he said angrily. 'We are about to eat!' But by the look on Felix's face this could not wait, so Gabir jumped up and followed Felix into another room, leaving Amira with a grim expression on her face.

'We may as well pack this food up and go on a little picnic of our own, Zaid' she whispered angrily. Just then Gabir walked back in.

'Amira, we must postpone this trip for another day my love, there is trouble in Siex', he said firmly. 'I promise you if the weather stays we can go tomorrow'.

'What is happening, it sounds serious?' Amira asked.

'We do not know what exactly this trouble is yet, but I must attend immediately to see what is going on' said Gabir. 'There have apparently been some unexplained attacks on the local villagers.'

Annoyed Amira turned, shrugged her shoulders and carried on packing up the food, but Gabir told her to stay at the palace. He explained he would be back as soon as possible. Amira agreed, but she was very annoyed at this. She had been looking forward to this trip and the weather would probably not hold up for another day. After Zaid had left, she paced the grounds of the palace gardens until he was out of sight.

'Right, we will go out for the walk anyway Zaid' she whispered. 'But do not tell your father.'

It was only a three-mile round trip and there was nothing much else for her to do around the palace. She grabbed Zaid and a picnic basket full of the food they were about to eat earlier and set out.

The walk was peaceful as they strolled through the lush green countryside and on into the dusty, sandy roads, all lined with beautiful tall trees swaying in the breeze with a clear blue river running alongside heading out towards the sea. Zaid ran alongside her, but then he demanded to be carried. Finally they could hear the ocean and knew they were close.

She carried on walking with Zaid in her arms as she saw the ocean. It was the first time Zaid had ever seen the sea so she placed him down so he could run towards the golden sand. The sea was a bright turquoise colour and the breeze was cool and light. The place was completely empty; not a human in sight and not a sound but the ocean.

The two walked to the water's edge and put their feet into the cool water. Amira ran through the water while Zaid sat playing in the sand. She had never been alone like this away from her husband, family and maids, and it felt good, but she wished Gabir had been with her.

The heat from the sun was unbearable, so the two of them made their way over to a large palm tree to relax in the shade. They soon fell asleep.

A few hours passed and Amira woke up to see the sun setting. She jumped up, realising it was getting late and that she would need to get back before dark or she would lose her way home. She picked up her basket and they started their journey back to the palace.

Walking back in the same direction, Amira noticed a man walking towards her. Strangely, he was wearing a long dark cloak in the heat. And the road to the sea was usually empty.

'Good Day' she said nervously as she walked past him. He did not reply, and it appeared he did not recognise her as the Queen, but Amira didn't look back.

As she walked on she suddenly heard rapid steps behind her. Quickly looking back behind her she saw the man walking fast towards her.

He shouted at her 'Show your wings!' but she didn't understand what he was saying, so she just carried on walking. It was approaching darkness now.

The man shouted at her again. 'Are you one? Show your wings!' he said. His tone was scaring her,

'I do not understand what you mean' she said, and started to speed up. But he ran after her at an impossible speed and stood in front of her again. She trembled and cried, 'I mean no harm! Please let me pass, my son is tired and hungry, I must get him home'.

Ignoring her, he took down his hood. His face was strange. His eyes were a weird dark shade. His nails were long and dark and he was extremely tall and scary, but at the same time he was quite handsome.

He stared at her as if she were filth. 'I see you are not one' he said. 'You are very beautiful, but you are weak.' He knew that the date mentioned in the Iblisari stories meant that the angels were not to appear until the 12th day of the 12th month of the 12th year, yet he had thought this woman was an angel. Clearly she was not.

He then directed her to put her son by the tree. She grabbed Zaid tighter, but as she did so he grabbed her arm and angrily pointed again.

'Place him by the tree!' he shouted. He looked very angry, so she placed Zaid near to the tree and stood a few meters from him. The man walked towards her and grabbed her, his nails digging into her skin.

'Who are you? I mean no harm!' she cried. 'I want to go home with my son, please, please let me go!'

But the strange man did not listen. He dragged her to a rock, throwing her against it. He carried on shouting in a strange language that sounded to her as if he was worshipping the devil. She had no idea what he was going to do to her and wept uncontrollably.

Hearing a noise in the bush behind them, he stopped for a moment and went to have a look. While his back was turned Amira grabbed a rock lying on the ground next to her. She waited for him to walk back to her, then quickly smashed him over the face with the rock and attempted to run back to Zaid.

But when the rock hit him, the man did not move. It was as if he had not even felt it. However this made him angrier, so he grabbed her and dragged her over to a crevice between the rocks. There he ripped off her top and forced her towards him, kicking and screaming. She managed to push him away, but he laughed grabbing her hair, pulling her head back. With one hand pulling her hair and head back he used his other hand to pull up her long skirt. Then he pressed himself towards her and violently kissed her neck whilst placing his hand in between her legs. She kicked and screamed, but there was nothing she could do. He was far too strong and she was way too weak.

Crushing her between himself and the large rock, he entered her forcefully and thrust himself in and out of her, still holding her head back with her hair. This carried on for three long minutes until Amira's body turned numb and she gave up screaming and just kept still, praying the nightmare would end quickly so she could get back to Zaid.

When he had finished he threw her to the ground and fled.

Trembling, she jumped up and ran over to the tree where Zaid sat and to her relief he was still there, safe and sound. She hugged him, picked him up and ran home as fast as she could.

Just half a mile from home she could see the lights of the palace, so she slowed down and tried to tidy herself up. She did not want to tell a soul about what had happened, and she especially did not want Gabir to find out, because she felt dirty and used. She also felt the attack had been her fault, because she had gone out when Gabir had told her to stay at the palace.

She managed to tie her shirt together so the rips were not noticeable and dusted her skirt off. Then she tidied up her hair. She just hoped Zaid wouldn't mention anything of what happened and she hoped he did not realise what this man had done to her.

Arriving home feeling sick and dizzy, Amira tried to block the day's events from her mind and to focus on the nicer parts of the day – the beauty of the ocean, the scenery and the time spent with Zaid. But it was hard to forget the man's face and what he had done to her.

She put Zaid to bed as soon as she arrived back at the palace and went to her room to lie down with her diary. She always wrote everything in her diary, bad or good. She wept as she wrote of the day's events. Then she locked the diary away in a wooden box and hid it under a stone slab which covered a hole in the corner of the room. Finally she returned to her bed and fell asleep.

CHAPTER FOUR

Henrik felt a tear trickle down his cheek after reading that. He felt Amira's pain. He took a deep breath and pulled himself together, stretched and read on.

The following evening Gabir returned from his journey, exhausted and bloody. He hugged Amira and sat down to tell her what had happened to him and his men.

He had been to visit the places where there had been news of attacks on the local people. Five tall, dark-cloaked men had been terrorising the people of the nearby cities and villages, attacking and killing men who got in their way. Amira started to tremble. The description matched the man who had attacked her.

'What is wrong, my love?' he asked, looking worried.

'Nothing really, I just feel a little tired' she explained. She sat back down on the edge of her bed. Gabir carried on, 'We were in search of these men, but what or who they were was unknown to any man. No one understood the language they spoke.' He looked confused. 'However, they said the word 'angel' a few times and they were the only words we could understand.'

Amira now knew it was definitely the same man, because he had asked if she had wings.

Gabir proceeded with his story. He told her that he and his soldiers had scoured the area in search of the evil creatures that were doing these things and creating such havoc and fear.

'Five hundred of my soldiers went on the journey with me' he said. 'We were all armed with two or three weapons each. We were unaware of what we were about to deal with and did not know if there would be more of them, or how powerful they would be.'

The previous night at around midnight, they had caught sight of four hooded men wandering through the forest at the edge of the village of Halditi. Gabir had told his men a hundred of them would go in first while the rest stayed behind. They went in search of the evil people and within an hour they caught sight of a few of them in the distance. They sneaked up closer to them, surrounded them at a distance as quietly as possible and prepared for conflict.

As the king and his men made their way towards the strange men, they could see that they had sat down around a bonfire and were chanting as they welcomed a fifth member; they appeared to be devil worshipping. 'They will appear, they will appear, the angels will appear and they will die!' the men chanted louder and louder, but as Gabir and his men attempted to get closer, one of his soldiers fell in the dark, making a loud crunching noise. Startled by the sudden sound, two of the cloaked men turned around and stood up. 'Who goes there?' one of the men shouted.

The others also rose from around the fire. 'We are the Iblisari!' they said. 'Why do you hide from us?' The taller of the men spoke in a deep voice. As he stood up to face the soldiers, many more men behind him raised themselves up, all chanting in a strange language, then one by one they saw more of the devils.

Gabir shouted and took a step forward shouting. 'We come to kill those who have caused death and chaos to our land'.

'Ha, but there are almost a hundred of us here' replied the man. 'We are the Iblisari! We are the devils! You will need more than one hundred soldiers to defeat us. We have great fighting powers; you would need double or triple the men to kill us all.'

Felix walked forward, smirked and replied, 'We will worry about that when it comes to it, my friend'. They gave each other one long stare and both armies prepared to run forward for battle. Gabir gave the order to fight and battle began.

Running as fast as he could, Felix took the first devil on. He ran towards him with his sword. The devil pushed the sword away with his bare arm and punched Felix in the face. Felix fell to the ground but was able to jump up straight away and kick the devil in the stomach, making him fall to the ground. Felix stamped on his head, killing him.

Another devil ran at Gabir, but he managed to strike the creature in the face first, slicing his cheek. As he fell Gabir ran his sword into the eyes of the creature. Blood sprayed into the King's face and the cracking of the devil's bones was so loud over the shouting and fighting that some of the other soldiers turned to look.

The soldiers could see the devils were strong and prepared to start fighting for their lives. One of the King's men was taken on by two devils. They knocked him down with swift punches to the face and chest, and then one placed a knife into his neck and slit his throat while the other thrust his knife into his heart and dragged it down towards his stomach. This happened to many more. The battlefield was loud with the screams of the soldiers. The devil men were strong and hard to beat, and there were soon at least thirty of the King's men on the ground, dead or dying slow and painful deaths. Some had hands cut off, while others had gashes so deep in their necks that they appeared to have been beheaded. This was something the King had not seen before in any kind of battle, but he had no time to stop and worry. He needed to carry on with the fight, so he shouted for all his men to come forward.

As Gabir moved forward he was pushed from behind. He fell to the ground and felt a spike going into his skin. Quickly he moved away and jumped up, pushing the man behind him and making him step back. Gabir had dropped his sword. He didn't even have a minute to think, and now they were fighting again. One of Gabir's men stepped in to help. He took the devil from behind and put his hands around his neck, attempting to break it, but the devil managed to slip his head a little further down until his mouth was level with the soldier's arm, then opening his mouth he sank his teeth deep into the arm. The soldier screamed and tried to throw the devil to the floor, but his arm stayed in the devil's mouth. Eventually he freed himself, in great agony. He looked down at his arm and saw the broken bone protruding from his flesh. The devil turned to him, grabbed the soldier's head with his two hands and within a second he had bitten his nose from his face with his teeth and spat it back out at him.

The King's man fell to the ground. His pain ended only when the devil thrust a knife into his chest to finish him off.

The King saw this and tried to help, but was being held back fighting another devil. The devil stabbed him in the chest, but Gabir had such anger raging through his veins that this barely hurt him, so he turned back to him with his two swords and stabbed them into the devil's ears.

It was the worst scene Gabir had ever experienced. He started to worry about the future of the kingdom, with these devils in it. They needed to be destroyed.

By now all the other soldiers had come forward, as their army was disappearing fast. The devils were far more powerful than the King had imagined, but Gabir and his men put up a good fight.

The barbaric battle went on for a further thirty minutes and by the end of it, blood and limbs lay all over the clearing and woodland. Dead bodies had heads hanging off, some had missing fingers and hands, and men lay dying with huge gashes in their bodies.

As time passed the King's army started to rally, killing at least five devils every ten minutes. Before long it was down to the King with five of his men along with thirty devils, all still with their cloaks on and ready to finish the battle. There had been five times more men than devils at the beginning of the battle, so the odds were now reversed. However, although they were tired, the soldiers Gabir had left were the best of his fighters. There was little time for thinking, they had to just go for it and hope for the best.

'You need to be protected, my Lord' one of his men advised him. 'You should stay put while we take them on.'

'No, no, no, I will hear of no such thing!' the King replied angrily. He pushed them out of his way and started to fight with one of the nearest devils. They fought with long swords, going back and forth, both struggling to drive their swords into each other. Weapons had been lost, so they had to scour the dead bodies for knives, most of which were embedded in the skulls and bodies of their own soldiers. Finally, after a grueling battle, the only ones left standing were the King, two of his men and one devil. The King was proud, but devastated at the loss of his loyal soldiers.

Unknown to Gabir, the last remaining devil was the one who just hours before had raped his queen. The three men surrounded the devil. One soldier had a large spiked club in his hand, while the other had two short, sharp knives. The King held a short sword.

'You will not get away with this!' hissed the devil. 'There may be none of us Iblisari left here, but I assure you there is still evil on this Earth. We will be back within days, and our legacy will continue. The devils are all around, but there are few that take their powers seriously. I have left a trace, my friends. When the next devils come into the world they will know, and they will keep the Iblisari going forever. Should our followers be removed by humans they will appear again and again, and once the stone is found only the angels can destroy us. But this will never happen, because we will destroy them first'.

The King and his men did not know what he meant, nor did they listen.

'The angels will be removed when they arrive!' the devil said in his slow, deep voice. 'They will appear one day soon, we do not know when nor where, but they are humans until the day in question, when their powers will become known to man, unlike us devils who are always around, true to our faith. You see, we are evil from birth. Our darker powers are trained into us by our leaders, we have a bloodline. You need know nothing further. Now take me to hell!' he said, as he bowed his head.

'There are no more of you on this planet, so how do you expect to live on?' Gabir snarled at him.

'You will be able to spend every day with your leader in hell' growled Felix.

Felix lifted his knife to kill the devil, but he did not move. With his head bowed he awaited his fate. His death was as gruesome as the bloody scene in front of them.

The battle had finished. Every devil had been killed, but sadly so had nearly five hundred of the King's army.

Amira wept as she heard Gabir finish the story. She was praying for the families of the men lost in the battle.

'I was so very worried about you' she said softly. I am so happy you have come back safe and well but so sad for the men that have lost their lives fighting for peace. I hope this is the end of all the fighting so we can get on with our lives as before. I could not bear it if you were to go back out to fight again.'

Gabir stood up, 'I can assure you my dear, there will be no more battles for as long as I am King' he said. 'We are free from all that is evil on this land. It will no longer come back to haunt us and we can relax. I have great respect for the soldiers who have perished and they will be remembered always as strong brave fighters.'

They smiled sadly at each other, and Amira told him to get washed and have a good rest.

CHAPTER FIVE

A few weeks passed, and everything seemed to be going well for the King, the Queen and little Zaid. They spent more time together as a family, doing things they had wanted to do as a normal family would. She had blocked out the last few weeks as best she could but still found it difficult and often had nightmares about her attacker.

One evening after dinner Amira felt poorly, so she decided to go to bed early. On her way upstairs she collapsed and fell to her knees, holding her stomach. As she blacked out and fell to the floor, two of her maids ran to her rescue.

'Find the nurse!' one of the maids yelled, 'Hurry!'

Gabir ran out to see what the commotion was. 'My god, what has happened?' he said as he ran over to her, 'is she OK? Amira, can you hear me?'

She slowly came back to consciousness.

'What happened to me? I must have fainted', she said softly as she tried to get up. The nurse came running over and ordered the two maids to help her to her bedroom to allow her to rest. After they had checked her out they confirmed she had just blacked out, but they wanted to test her further just in case there was a more serious problem. Gabir waited outside the bedroom for the nurse to finish her tests on Amira. Half an hour later the door opened and the nurse came out with a grin on her face.

'She is fine my lord, she may need some rest' she said. She winked at him and walked back to her quarters. He walked into their bedroom where Amira lay in bed. 'What is it, my beloved?' he asked.

She smiled at the King and told him the news the nurse had just given her.

'I am with child Gabir, I can't believe it, it has finally happened' she said. 'It must have just been time that was waiting for us.'

Gabir looked stunned at the news, 'I can't believe after all these years this has happened, how?' he said, looking confused.

'I have no idea, but it has happened, and now we shall be able to give Zaid a brother or sister.'

'This is great news, how far gone are you?' he asked getting excited.

'Nurse told me around seven or eight weeks, so it is very early days'.

'This is wonderful!' said Gabir, leaning over to hold her in his arms. 'You do know this child will have the right to the throne? He or she will be our blood child.'

'Yes I know, but I don't think Zaid will be bothered too much about this at the age of two now, do you? As we bring him up we shall explain it to him.' They smiled again and lay down together to sleep.

Amira had worried when she was told of the pregnancy until the nurse had advised her how many weeks she was gone. If it had been only five weeks or ten weeks she would have known the child was not Gabir's, as they had not made love two weeks either side of the rape by that evil monster. But she was seven or eight weeks gone, so it could have only been the King's child. However, much as Amira tried to reassure herself, she still had a worrying feeling that something wasn't right.

When eight months had passed, no child had arrived, 'He or she should be here by now' Gabir said to Amira.

'Well I presume nurse took a guess at seven or eight weeks. I did not bleed so I cannot remember' she told him. 'Be patient, it will be any day now'. If the child did not arrive soon, Amira knew its father would be the devil who had raped her. She thought long and hard about this, but she decided that whoever had fathered the child she would still love it, and Gabir would bring it up as his own, for she could never tell him of the rape.

A further four weeks passed, and nine months to the day after Amira had been attacked, a baby boy arrived in the world. He was large and heavy with thick black hair. The King and Queen were delighted with the child and called him Petrus.

Deep down Gabir felt there was a possibility that this was not his child, but he never mentioned that to Amira, for he could not bear the thought of being told such a thing. He loved her and trusted her, so he quickly shrugged these thoughts off.

Amira knew this child could not be her husband's, but she could not tell him this. She used the excuse that he had just come into the world late.

As she gave birth she worried about how this child would be. Would he be evil, a monster like the man who had attacked her. But once she held the child she knew he was innocent and should not be treated any differently. He was hers, and she hoped that she and Gabir would bring him up to be a good person and teach him right from wrong, because one day Petrus would have the throne.

＊ ＊ ＊ ＊ ＊

Five years passed, and the two brothers Zaid and Petrus were turning out to be very different. Zaid was a good, easy-going, well-behaved young boy, but Petrus was badly behaved. He never did as he was told and his only interest was killing things. He would often bring birds, rabbits and even dogs into the house which he had slaughtered. His parents now knew there was something wrong with him.

Although he was two years younger than Zaid he was taller and stronger and often attacked Zaid when his parents weren't around. He would always blame things on his older brother and plant evidence on him, leaving his parents not knowing what to make of the situation.

Another couple of years passed and his behaviour became even worse. Amira began to worry about what they should do with him, but Gabir believed he was a normal young man, because he would behave like a normal child in front of his father. Amira, however, knew he was possessed by something evil, and she knew exactly why he was like this. She was trying hard to bring him up as best as she could, but it was not working.

On Zaid's eleventh birthday Petrus attempted to push him off the top floor of the palace, over the balcony. Zaid fought back with great courage and finally managed to beat Petrus, and after that Petrus changed his mind about his brother. He still didn't like him but felt as he was his brother maybe over the years he could talk Zaid into being more like him.

However, from that day Zaid kept his distance from his brother. He hoped he would grow out of the bad behaviour, but even after Petrus started being nicer to him he still didn't trust him. Zaid was very close to his parents and was able to tell his mother everything Petrus did, but Amira always told him not to worry about it and to ignore him, telling him it was just a phase he was going through. She listened to Zaid and understood and always took precautions when they were together, but this was always kept from Gabir. Amira didn't want to worry the King with these problems, and she was worried that he would find out that the child was not his biological son.

Petrus was always a well-behaved, sweet boy for the King, but a completely different child with his mother.

Amira knew this child's evil was going to get worse and there would be little chance of him getting any better, because of the person who had impregnated her. Year after year she became more and more guilty and depressed about it. Hiding it from the man she loved ate her up inside and she became a different woman.

At 13 years old Petrus was the same height as Gabir, and it was increasingly obvious that he was not his child. Every day when Amira woke up she would prepare to tell Gabir about the rape, but she always ended up being too scared to go through with it.

CHAPTER SIX

One autumn afternoon when Zaid was out riding with Felix, Gabir started constructing a tree house at the end of the palace gardens for the boys to play in, along with their nephews and the other children. Amira was in her room having an afternoon nap when she was woken by a knock on her door. Petrus stood in the doorway with his head down and his eyes up, staring at his mother in a strange way.

'Mother', he shouted at the door.

'Come in', Amira called. 'What is it, son?'

'You have lied about my father, Gabir is not my father!' he said in a dark tone.

Wondering how he had got this information, she jumped up and asked him

'What are you talking about, Petrus?'

'You are a whore! I read your diary. I read it all, and you are lying to all of us'.

'Petrus, how dare you speak to me in that way! That is just a story, nothing in it is true. How did you get to read it? I have my diary locked away at all times and there is only one key for my box and the cupboard I keep it in, and I keep the key around my neck at all time. There is no way you can get into my private things!'

'Oh, but I can do anything I want' he replied to her. 'You lied to us, and I have already told my father'.

'What?' she shouted. 'You should not have told him this, you stupid boy! How can you do this? Where is he, where is Gabir?'

'Well that's the thing, you see when I told him of your lies he hit me' Petrus said cheerfully, and laughed. 'He struck me around the face and then he told me that it was foolish rubbish and I should stop lying. I told him you whored yourself to the devil because you did not love him. It is obvious though, is it not? I am already way taller than him with a different face, skin tone and different hair colour, and I was born on a day that would not tally up with when you were together. Your diaries confirm that, Mother.'

'Where is he?' she cried. 'Fetch him for me!'

'Oh I cannot do that' replied Petrus. 'He struck me, remember, so I killed him. I put an axe to the back of his head. Go and have a look.' He spoke in a normal tone, showing no remorse whatsoever.

'I don't believe you!' she screamed at him, 'You are evil to say such things, you do not belong here with us!'

'Well it's too late for that, mother' he said. She pushed passed him, crying hysterically, as she ran down the corridor towards the stairs and out to the gardens, all the way to the bottom where the tree house was being constructed.

'Gabir!' she called out. 'Gabir, where are you my love?' But there was no answer. She called his name again, crying, and ran further around the back of the tree. And there she saw him, face down on the ground, blood everywhere and the blade of a large axe in the back of his head.

Amira didn't scream, although Gabir's head was almost split into two pieces. She kneeled down beside him, weeping and holding on to him.

'What have I done?' she cried as she looked up at the sky. 'What have I done?' Then she laid her head on his back, this man she had loved for so many years, the man she had spent every day with loving and laughing together. She thought to herself that if she had been honest in the first place, or if she had given birth to the child and left him with the nuns, would that have made things different? But it was too late. This was her doing, and she would not be able to go back on it, nor go on with her life.

Amira looked up at the tall tree which had partially been converted into a tree house and stared at it for five long minutes. Then she picked herself up, fetched a long rope and climbed up the ladder to the first level. Slowly she walked to the edge of the thick branch, and then carefully sat on the edge. She started to sing a song she used to sing with Gabir to relax him. Her eyes closed, and with the light breeze she took deep breaths in between each line of the song. She tied the rope to the middle of the branch and the other end around her neck. Then, after finishing her song, she stood up. Once more she looked up and whispered softly to the sky, 'I am sorry I have sinned my lord, and I am sorry to my child Zaid. I know Felix will look after him. I will be no good for him, living with the pain of what has happened'

Then, taking another deep breath, she stepped off the branch.

Amira had told Felix months before that if anything ever happened to them he was to look after Zaid. He was also to take the key and the chest with all her and her husband's possessions and hide them away for Zaid until he was old enough. Felix had agreed happily, as he and Zaid shared a special bond and got along like brothers.

After the death of King Gabir and Queen Amira the land mourned deeply, and everything stood still for many months. It appeared to many of the people that Amira had killed her husband before taking her own life, but the people close to her did not believe this. They knew someone else was involved, but no one ever found the culprit and no one ever imagined it was the royal couple's own son, Petrus.

Petrus was given the throne on his sixteenth birthday and from then on everything went downhill. He was given help and guidance by a distant cousin of the late King on how to rule for the first two years, but Petrus didn't take anything in. He had his own ideas, and as he grew older he became more ignorant and dangerous. He praised Satan and became the leader of the devil worshipping cult, the Iblisari. He believed this was his life and that it was what he was meant to do.

Zaid could only sit back and watch his brother ruin the world. He felt alone. Felix had died from a mysterious poisoning a few months before, so Zaid kept himself to himself and just concentrated on his studying. He distanced himself from his brother and they only spoke when they needed to. They hated each other deep down, and constantly argued when they were together about how the land and the people were not taken care of properly.

Zaid often wondered about his brother being the killer of his parents and Felix, but if that was the case why would he not try to kill him?

Zaid had his own quarters in the palace, where he lived and kept all of his work. He spent all his time there, and Petrus spread the rumour that he was a crazy recluse. Some believed this and some did not, but it didn't faze Zaid. He loved his own space. He especially enjoyed history, and spent most of his years delving deep into it with help from various teachers and tutors.

Before Felix had died he had hid away Gabir and Amira's private boxes and left a note for Zaid about where to find them, telling him not to open them until he was older, so he could add new stories.

Petrus had been given the throne at too young an age. He did not become the king everyone had hoped for but a jealous, immoral, corrupt, depraved, sinful and evil young tyrant. He always had his face covered in a dark hood. As he turned into a man, he became worse.

Years passed and Petrus just lazed about the palace without caring at all for things that were going on around him in Vuoil. People were starving and living in squalor, because he made everyone pay him a tax for the upkeep of the palace, even though it was not needed. He enjoyed seeing people suffer and often made children as young as eight work as his slaves. He beat and assaulted his workers and raped the women.

Petrus was bored and constantly thought of things he could do to disrupt the world. All he had was the growing devil-worshipping cult he led. There were several cults around the land, but Petrus led the main one, the Iblisari, and worshippers came from miles around to see him. Zaid didn't know a lot about the cult as he did not wish to have anything to do with it; all he knew was that it was evil.

One afternoon while Zaid was out, Petrus broke into his quarters to see what he could find and what things his uninteresting brother had there. He rummaged through his papers, hoping to come across some of his mother's things, but all he found was historical documents, all of which looked very boring to him. But as he was about to leave he came across an animal skin scroll, tightly tied up with a piece of string. He sat in Zaid's chair and carefully opened it out,

What he read was the most intriguing and interesting piece of information he had ever read, something that he had thought about for many years. It excited him greatly. He knew this was the beginning of something big.

CHAPTER SEVEN

Thick dark clouds filled the evening skies of Urak, obscuring the beautiful purple and pink sky and sunset. King Petrus paced the square stoned path of the palace courtyard with his head looking at the floor. His long black hooded cape was flowing in the wind, barely showing any part of his face or body. Angrily he yelled 'Fuverus, Fuverus, where are you?' demanding his most loyal servant appear in front of him immediately. Fuverus arrived looking scared and disorientated, trembling with a fake smile on his face,

'Y- yes my lord? Fuverus stammered as he walked over to where his king stood, his white toga style cape draped over his shoulders with streaks of fresh dark blood on it.

'We got them all, we got them all! 102 of them, come see the proof' he whispered to his lord in a low croaky voice.

Fuverus was a very simple man and a devil-worshipper. He idolised his lord, and did whatever he was asked and told to do. He feared Petrus above anyone else in the world, as did many other people.

'Can I put my black cape back on now?' he said. 'This white one does not go with what we are about, my lord' he asked.

'Do as you wish once I have seen the proof, but we still have work to do with the missing ten angels' Petrus told him. He marched towards the main courtyard where the party had taken place.

Twelve days before this, Petrus had found some vital information from searching through his brother's belongings. He had learned that in a matter of days a miracle was due to occur on the planet and that 112 chosen humans would shed their disguise and be unveiled as possessing powers greater than any other human on Earth. They would be strong and wise. Thanks to the document his brother had kept, he knew this day was to come soon. He now knew exactly when they had appeared before and what date they would appear in the future.

Petrus, being the King and the most powerful man on Earth, did not like this; he abhorred the idea of any creature more powerful than he was. However he had also learned that these creatures were vulnerable to curved weapons, especially when put straight to their throats.

These creatures would have intelligence and beauty that went way beyond anything else on the planet. They would change suddenly from human form into the winged creatures known as angels. However their wings would not always be visible; they would appear and disappear at random until the angel learnt how to control them.

Petrus told the whole land of this story, but people thought it was too ridiculous. How could ordinary humans suddenly appear as angels? It was hard to understand how this would happen.

Zaid had learned this information only three weeks before from an old man who lived on the edge of the city. He had visited this man over the years and treated him as a friend as well as a teacher. The man had various books and stacks of old stories in his cellar, and Zaid would have a good look through them on many occasions.

Zaid had worked out by linking the stories that angels had existed on the planet many years before. He had also discovered the story about the stone, and to his great surprise, the old man knew the whereabouts of it.

The story he had heard was that on the 12th day of the 12th month on a year ending with 12 four millennia ago, 12 humans had been revealed as angels. What happened to them was still unknown. Some said they were slaughtered by the Iblisari; some said they had taken their own lives. There was evidence that the date would occur again, but only after 4000 years, and the number of angels would rise in proportion to the population.

Zaid, along with other historians, believed after reading these stories that after four more millennia, when the date of 12/12/12 came round again, 112 angels would appear on Earth. Then every four millennia the numbers would rise, so in another 4000 years 1112 angels would appear. Rumour had it that this would only happen to certain humans, ones with special qualities and abilities whilst in human form, and they did not need to be related to another angel; the selection was random.

When that day came for the chosen few, great wings would break out from their backs. They would become inches taller, their skin and hair would glow, and they would suddenly become more beautiful. They would have great strength and the power to levitate up to ten metres off the ground. They would also have an excellent vocabulary and be able to speak every language known to man.

A few days after finding the document in Zaid's possessions, Petrus told him what he had done. He began to hassle him for other information that he might have had or was hiding, but Zaid told him there nothing else.

Petrus did not believe his brother, and ordered his men to turn over his quarters daily, which they did, but as the days went on they could never locate any other documents or items, including any belonging to the King and Queen. Zaid had found the boxes for which Felix had left him the key. His parents' personal stories and diaries were too personal to him, and because of this he had taken them to a hiding place far up in the mountains at a secret location a good distance away from Petrus. Zaid had never looked through these items. He wanted to wait until he was older and more mature, so he could understand everything better.

He could not believe his brother had spread the word about the angels, let alone gone through his private possessions, but he had been silly to leave things lying about, especially this story. Fortunately, before his brother could speak publicly about the angels, Zaid was able to spread the word to the people that this was not a bad thing. These angels were good beings and no one should fear them, nor worry should they become one.

A few days later Petrus suddenly decided to be nice to his brother, apologising for being so intrusive and going through his private things. Petrus thought that by being nice he could get Zaid to help him out when it came to luring the angels to the palace.

CHAPTER EIGHT

Finally, to the excitement of King Petrus, the day came. On a warm winter's evening, after everyone had heard what might happen, all 75 million of the world's population gathered in their towns, villages and cities so that they could see who among them would turn into angels. Even the people who dismissed the prediction as nonsense were summoned. Everyone had to be out in public, but little did they or Zaid know that Petrus had serious plans for them if this story were true. Not only did he want to see what humans had these powers, but unknown to his brother he wanted them executed.

True to Zaid's belief, as 12th December 2012 BC dawned, 112 chosen humans turned into angels. The sounds of screams were heard all over the cities and surrounding villages as they slowly and painfully went through the change. They all fell on to their knees shaking. The pain looked excruciating to onlookers as the new angels tried to feel their backs with their hands. They could hear the skin on their shoulder blades splitting and then the sound of ripping clothes. Emerging from their backs were lumps of feathers followed by large bones, and every second they were getting larger, brighter and fuller.

The families who saw this happening before their eyes didn't know what to do. They were speechless to see their loved ones in so much pain and agony. Some ran from them and some tried to hold and comfort them, while others just stood still in shock.

By nightfall the cities, towns and surrounding villages on the land were quiet. For days after, the world was at a standstill. The chosen angels were a mix of ages from seven to 70 years old; exactly half were male and half female.

A week after the change, Petrus sent an invitation to all 112 angels, summoning them to the palace for a dinner party to celebrate this miracle. Zaid was surprised that Petrus had become so pleasant over the last few days, especially towards the angels, he feared there might be something behind it so he wrote letters to the angels explaining to them that they should flee, as there was a chance they could be in grave danger if they went to the palace for the welcoming dinner party, he also advised them that they would need more time to work out how to deal with being angels. The letter also had details of where to go and gave more information about the stone. He told the angels to memorise and destroy the letters there and then, for their own safety.

Many people thought Zaid was a little crazy, so they were not sure whether they should listen to him. Zaid confronted his brother to ask how he felt about the angels and what he intended to do to help them have the normal lives they had had before they turned. Petrus started off by saying he would give them all the help they needed, along with new homes for them and their families, and that they were to be treated like royalty. However, the day before the event Zaid walked in on a conversation between Petrus and a handful of his men. He heard a few words mentioned about a trap, so he barged straight in. When Zaid asked his brother what was going on, Petrus decided to lie no further. He told Zaid that the angel creatures would become aggressive and hungry and end up killing everyone on the planet.

Zaid knew it was just jealousy. They started to argue aggressively about it. Zaid did not want these innocent people killed and explained that they posed no danger to anyone or anything, but Petrus said he was sick of listening to his whining. He was worried that Zaid would spread the word about this, so he ordered his men to take Zaid down to the dungeons until after the dinner party for the angels.

'You cannot do this, let me go!' Zaid shouted as he struggled.

'Brother, you are in my way and this is for the best' Petrus replied in a calm voice. 'I will get you released just after the big event and you will be free to do and say whatever you like. You will be treated well down there I promise.'

'No, this is wrong, these angels are harmless and will cause no harm to anyone or anything, please let me go for the good of the world, let me go!' Zaid begged.

'Lock him up and return the key to me' Petrus said. He turned away and left Zaid to be dragged down to the dungeons.

Through the underground corridors of the palace Petrus' men dragged Zaid deeper and deeper to the darkest depths. They finally stopped in a small heavily-gated room. Although it had no windows it was fully furnished, with a comfortable bed, desk and chair, and there were candles scattered around it, as if it had just been set up expecting someone. The men threw him into it and slammed the gate shut.

'You can't leave me here, you foolish men!' shouted Zaid. 'Can you not see what he is about to do? You will end up in here one day too!' But the men just told him dinner would be delivered in two hours, and walked off without another word. After shaking and banging the gate for a while, Zaid fell to his knees, hoping and praying that the angels would take note of the letters he had sent out.

Fortunately, not all the people trusted their King, nor believed his lies. A handful did not plan to attend the party because they had taken note of the letters Zaid had sent them and prepared to leave their homes to escape to the island of Krobir, as urged by Zaid.

Most of the angels had decided to go to the party. They knew it could be dangerous, but they believed that with their new skills they would be able to deal with any problems they came across.

CHAPTER NINE

As they waited for the day to come, Petrus, his faithful servant Fuverus and 112 other men, all of whom were part of the Iblisari, prepared themselves for the slaughter. They knew that the angels had not had time to get used to their new powers and that if he and his men acted quickly, they would be at their mercy.

On the day, 102 of the 112 angels turned up at the palace dressed in their best outfits. The women looked like goddesses, most in long white or rose-coloured gowns, while the men all looked as handsome as if their bodies had been carved into shape. Their excitement was immense, because most of them had never had the chance to visit the palace, especially those who had come from poor backgrounds.

The palace was decorated with the most spectacular designs, with thousands of candles scattered around the rooms. White curtains fell from the open ceilings and high walls, tables and chairs were wrapped in gold-painted ivy and surrounded by luxurious flowers and beautiful plants. Red and white rugs were spread across the floors. Lavish hors d'oeuvres were set out before their eyes on the finest crockery, and servants in long white hooded cloaks rushed around before them offering fine wines and spirits. The angels could not believe the exquisite treatment they were getting from their much-loved king.

Knowing that ten angels were missing, Petrus sent out search parties shortly after the party had started. He ordered that every one of the angels was to be found and brought before him. Nearby villages were searched, but other areas were too far for the men to travel to in such a short space of time. They would have to wait until after the party.

After an hour of mingling between themselves and the King, the angels were all asked to be seated for dinner and led to their seats. Petrus left the room after giving Fuverus a nod to go ahead with the plan. He waited out in the courtyard, pacing up and down and looking forward to hearing the news that the angels were all dead.

Some of the servants were out searching for the missing angels, but there were 102 left in the large dining hall, exactly the same number as the angels. The King's servants waited for the angels to take their seats and when they had done so they positioned themselves one behind each seat, waiting for the bell to ring so they could start preparing to serve slices of the finest meats. Excitement filled the exquisite room, and after the last few days the angels finally started to relax. The angels had tried to fold their wings away, but they were still not able to control them.

As the conversation between the angels flowed through the hall, the bell chimed for food to be served – as they thought. Little did they know that this bell meant something other than the beginning of the feast.

Each of the servants placed a hand into his cloak and took a deep breath. The angels did not notice the identical movement of each of them, as they were too busy enjoying themselves.

Slowly and carefully the servants removed short, deadly scythes from the insides of their cloaks. Then they simultaneously pulled back the heads of the angels, brought the scythes around in front of their necks and in one quick sweep sliced their throats. Screeching and gurgling noises filled the hall. The angels' wings began to appear, beautiful and bright, but it was too late. Blood splattered across the feathers and sprayed the floor as the angels drew their last breaths. Most of the angels, men, women and children, had no chance of putting up a fight. They were soon lying dead on the bloodied floor with the hooded servants standing over them.

A handful of angels attempted to get up and fight, but with blood pouring from their throats they too soon fell to the floor and expired. The servants walked over the angels that were still breathing and plunged their scythes into their bodies.

By the time the last angel had been slaughtered, the scene was something no man should ever witness. The finely-decorated room was now covered with the bodies and blood of the 102 beautiful angels, all lying lifeless with their wings spread out beside them.

Suddenly a chilling breeze blew into the room. It blew the long drapes and tablecloths, flowers flew off the tables and the candles were all blown out. Above, dark clouds veiled the late evening sunshine and a deadly silence entered the room.

CHAPTER TEN

Petrus walked from the courtyard into the dining room to find a sea of dead angels covered in fresh, bright red blood. He rubbed his hands together in satisfaction.

'Well done men, you all did a good job' he said. 'We shall celebrate after this has been cleared up and the other angels are found and returned to me, dead or alive.'

'Yes, my lord!' they all replied together. Then they set out to help the other servants who were already searching the nearby towns and villages.

'Oh, and let my brother out of the dungeons' said Petrus. He took a few deep breaths and smirked. He was so proud of what he had just achieved. Before the event he had been worried that the angels might be stronger and more intelligent that his men, or too fast, so he was delighted at the magnificent outcome. But he could not relax until the others were dead too, especially as the surviving angels would now be aware of what had happened to their brothers and sisters, and would be prepared.

After being let out of the hole he had been in for the last 48 hours, Zaid ran straight up to the dining room to see if he had time to save the angels before Petrus had got to them. As he ran through the palace he caught the scent of fresh blood, which instantly made his stomach churn, he then approached the great hall where he saw bloody footprints trailing into the kitchen and courtyard area. He peered around the corner to look at what was happening, but he knew by the silence what he was about to witness. When he saw the massacre, he fell against the wall and bent his body forward to vomit.

'Damn you Petrus! Why?' he shouted as he wept for the angels. Then a servant appeared and explained to Zaid that everyone was out searching for the other ten angels.

Now Zaid at least knew that some of the angels had taken his letter seriously and were on their way to the island of Krobir.

He knew that confronting his brother would solve nothing, so he ran back to his quarters and packed his belongings and the stone he had been given by his old friend, jumped on his horse and left the palace for good, not looking back once. He had to get to Krobir to greet the angels before it was too late.

Zaid had given them a map of the safest way to get to the island. He knew the long way round would be the safer route for them. But he himself would take a quicker route.

* * * * *

Earlier that afternoon the ten angels had set off on their journey to Krobir. They had all memorised the directions and maps in their heads. They were surprised to find that they all had clear pictures of the maps and remembered every single word from the letter. One of the angels had however rewritten the map in code, just in case there was a problem along the way.

Angels,

You must read this carefully and follow the instructions you are about to given. These are instructions from myself, Zaid, brother of the King.

This is very important. Firstly I hope you are all safe and I am so sorry that you have had to flee to save yourselves. I hope this direction in your lives is a good one and that I can lead you to somewhere which I feel is safe for you. After that the rest is up to you.

You must travel to an island called Krobir, and you must go via the southern coast of Bahrain. There is a coastal route, but I believe it will be safer to travel further down south as per the directions on the map attached. When you arrive there you will find a boat waiting for you to take you across to the island. There I hope you will find me. If I am not there, I will be making my way there.

I know of the whereabouts of a stone. This stone is no ordinary stone; if it is held by an angel it can be vital to the planet. It will change it for the better so that you will be able to return to your families and live happy lives forever.

Zaid.

The angels looked at each other confused, scared and worried. But they took note of what he had asked them and proceeded with their journey.

CHAPTER ELEVEN

The ten angels were between the ages of 14 and 50. There were six males and four females, and all were equally beautiful. They had baskets of clothes and food to keep them going on their journey to Krobir. None of them had travelled before, so this was a new and strange experience for them, especially on top of getting their heads around becoming angels.

After stopping overnight to rest, the angels were up and awake ready for the next part of their journey to the Bahrain's south coast. As they left a messenger told them the news about what had happened to the other 102 angels at the palace party. Shocked and saddened by this, they were also very relieved that they had not attended the King's banquet.

Of the females, Maya was fourteen, Clara seventeen and Anvil 27. The oldest, Viola, was 40, but she looked as young as the others. She had a rounded face with long dark hair, olive skin and green eyes, while Clara and Anvil had long flowing golden hair with piercing blue eyes and beautiful pale skin.

Maya had dark skin and dark eyes with thick black curly hair. Being the youngest, she was very scared about what was going to happen to her and she hated being an angel, as it took her away from her family and friends. She worried constantly about everything, but at the same time she was taking advantage of her new-found strength. She could demolish walls and kick down gates, rip young trees out by the roots and dig holes to plant them back into, and all with her own bare hands. She spent a lot of her time practising her levitation skills, and always floated alongside everyone instead of walking.

Anvil was very calming and looked after the group like a mother, even though she was not the eldest; she had left her husband and children behind and was not sure if it would have been better to face death with the other angels than to live a life without them.

Viola was a loner and kept herself to herself. She barely spoke to the other angels, but when she did she had the most soothing voice and pleasant mannerisms.

Clara was the loudest of the group, the most opinionated and vocal. After hearing what had happened to the other angels, all she wanted to do was go back and fight the people who had done this.

The males were sixteen-year-old Emmel, seventeen-year-old Dassius, 22-year-old Palo, 30-year-old Hamerl, Bartholomew, 32, and Zacaus, 40, who had wings which were much larger and more colourful than the rest; he was definitely different.

Emmel and Palo were cousins. Both were extremely handsome with brown skin and large brown eyes. They stood six feet tall and had well-defined muscles.

All the men felt angry and distressed after what had happened, but they managed to keep calm. They had to be strong to be able to make it to their destination and start new lives together away from their families. They had all just about got the hang of what made their wings appear and disappear, but still found them hard to control.

They headed in the direction of the north coast, hoping they would find the boat mentioned in the letter from Zaid. They walked for miles, but they never became tired and were always full of energy. During their journey they talked, laughed and got to know each other. Emmel and Maya, who had never met before, had an instant connection, and spent most of the time talking and messing about together.

After a few hours, with the sun beating down on them, they could finally smell the ocean. They came to an uninhabited village at the top of a small hill and knew the sea was just a short distance away, but still Clara, along with Bartholomew and Hamerl, just wanted to head back to land to find and kill those who had slaughtered the angels.

'Don't you even think about what happened to our people?' she asked Zacaus. 'They were all killed, and you think we should run away from it all and not even try to do something about it?'

'Look Clara, there are too many of them' Zacaus replied. 'We have no chance. You are young and naïve. You need to understand that we need to get to that island. From there we can plan something, but we need time. This is the best option. Believe me, I would get a lot of pleasure from destroying them and one day I will do that.'

'I do think we need to hurry, they could be after us now. We need to get to that boat, then they will never be able to follow our trail' Viola added.

They all agreed that they would need to hide out for a few weeks until they could learn to use their strengths and powers before they returned to the mainland and back to their families. They all carried on towards the sea.

Petrus sent the rest of his gang off to search for the angels. He sent them in two groups, fifty of them to the south and fifty to the north. They terrorised villagers along the way, as they looked for clues as to which way the angels had gone. All were well equipped with scythes, swords and other forms of weaponry.

The fifty who headed south wore long dark cloaks and hoods up over their heads, barely showing their faces. They were happy with the work they had done so far and confident that they would find the other angels and torture them before taking their lives.

The angels were only five miles ahead of them. They could now see the ocean in the distance.

'Hey, look ahead, I see water, we're almost there!' said Viola.

'Let's all fly there' said Hamerl.

'My friends, if you wish to fly then fly' said Zacaus, 'but it will take a lot out of you. There is a boat waiting to take us across to the island, but it will take ten hours to get there. We still have four miles to travel to the coastline, and they could easily catch up with us. They have probably noticed we have gone and are on our trail. By walking we can save our energy, but we must walk fast.'

Zacaus was the tallest and most powerful of the angels and had the largest wings, so they treated him as their leader.

Half an hour passed and the angels drew closer to the coast. Anvil, walking a few yards behind the rest of them, suddenly felt a strange feeling on the ground, a rumbling vibration. She knelt down to feel it with her hand and shouted to the others.

'Angels, do you feel the trembling ground?' she said. 'Something is happening. I think there must be animals, maybe a stampede coming this way!'

They all turned around and felt the ground. Zacaus jumped up and levitated himself to try and peer over the hill they had just walked over. He saw an army of around fifty men running towards them. He ducked down quickly and told the others that he believed the devils were the people making their way towards them.

'They must be only a mile behind us' Zacaus said. 'We cannot fly that fast to escape from them and even if we could it would not be worth wasting our energy. We must rush to the water's edge. By the look of this my friends, we are more than likely going have a battle.'

By now they all had their wings fully extended. 'We must run as fast as we can' he went on. 'We must get to the boat now!'

They moved as fast as they could, but the devils were catching up fast. They could now see them running after them. They had knives and other weaponry in their hands, and as there were five times more of them than the angels, Zacaus knew this was going to be hard, but they would put up a fight.

Finally they reached the coast. A beautiful stretch of golden-white sand led down to the calm blue waters of the Arabian Sea. Each side of the bay was lined with thick greenery going up the hillsides. The angels were mesmerised at the scene in front of them and wondered how they had never been here before, but there was no time to take it in.

As half of them ran forward to try and get the boat ready, the others, including Zacaus, started to try out their fighting skills, teaching each other self-defence as well as how to kill. But the thudding on the ground was getting closer and louder then suddenly stopped. The angels could not see over the hill, but they knew the devils were there, preparing and planning their moves, ready to finish off the slaughter. With their wings out, they prepared themselves for battle. They knew they needed one of them to survive to get over to Zaid and the stone, but they were unaware that it had to be the superior one, Zacaus. Zaid had left out this major detail.

Hamerl took the first step by walking slowly back up the hill they had just come from to see if he could see where the devils were and how many of them they had to do battle with. As he peered over the hill he saw fifty tall and evil-looking devils, all with scythes and swords and all looking upwards for their prey. He ran back down to the others.

'There must be fifty of them' he said. 'How will we fight them? We have never fought before.' He was looking at Zacaus for advice.

'We are stronger than them' said Zacaus. 'We have not fought before, but I feel ready. We have our natural strength, so now is our chance to test this out.'

'Well I'm ready for them!' shouted Bartholomew.

'I am ready too' said Clara.

They all walked further towards the coast to where the others were gathered, and when they reached them they huddled together and looked into each other's eyes.

'My friends, whatever happens here, we will try our hardest' said Zacaus. 'We will do whatever we can to defeat these monsters that have killed our friends, neighbours and families. You will have to kill, so do not hold back. Let's do our best!'

Out of the corner of his eye, he saw the first devils appearing over the hill, moving towards the beach where they stood. Then, without any words, the devils ran down towards the angels and the battle began.

Zacaus ran towards the largest of the devils. As they came together he struck the devil in the throat. Such was his strength that the devil's head came straight off his body. Zacaus had shocked himself, he had not realised he would be able to do such damage with his bare hands.

He turned around to see that all the other angels had also been successful in seeing off the devils. But this didn't last long. Maya was set upon by three devils and soon lay lifeless on the sand. She had been held by two of them whilst being stabbed in the throat by another.

Zacaus ran over to the three devils and one by one he took them down and killed them. Emmel ran over to Maya's young body and held her, but there was nothing he could do and no time to mourn. He jumped up and attacked the nearest devil, bringing him to the ground, stamping on his head and neck and killing him.

Viola and Bartholomew were further back, fighting a devil each. Bartholomew had by now taken three lives, but the devils now became angrier and started to use their weapons. After some minutes of fighting at least twenty devils were dead, but so were half the angels. Bartholomew, Helena, Hemerl and Dassius had put all up a good fight but like Maya they would fight no more.

Zacaus, Viola, Clara, Emmel and Palo were left to continue. With just five of them they feared the worst, for they had used up a lot of energy. But they were still strong, and after further fighting there were just 18 devils left.

The devils had now a scythe or hammer in each hand. Clara ran at the nearest one and raised herself in the air, then descended on him with such speed that the others had no time to even blink. She knocked him to the floor and stamped her foot into his neck, instantly crushing it and killing him.

Emmel and Palo ran towards another two devils and Emmel punched him, knocking him fifteen metres away. He then felt a sharp blow in his back and a harsh sensation on the skin of his neck and was pushed to the ground. Turning around and looking up he saw a devil holding a bloody nine-inch blade. The devil then jumped on Emmel and plunged the knife into Emmel's chest. He laughed as he slowly sliced down to his stomach. Emmel had gone.

Clara and Palo had killed five devils between them, but now they too lay on the sand lifeless, ripped apart by the weapons of the devils.

Now it was just Zacaus and Viola fighting for their lives and the lives of all the people. With thirteen devils surrounding them, they both levitated themselves off the ground and with sweeps of their wings they struck the devils to the ground, where they tried to crush them, but with so many devils this was a daunting task. Zacaus, with his great strength, managed to take down five of them, while Viola killed a further five by taking their heads off with her bare hands. But then two of the three remaining devils came at her with their blades and dug them into her stomach and neck. As she tried to get up one of them took her arm, digging his nails into her. He held her from behind, then grabbed her head and sliced into her neck. Viola fell to the ground.

Zacaus was left to fight the last three alone. After a few more minutes of fighting he killed two devils. It was now one on one. Kicking and punching each other, the angel and the devil rolled around the ground. Zacaus fought as hard as he could, but he was becoming weaker and weaker. His wings had been badly damaged earlier on and were causing him great pain. In the end the devil overcame him by finding a nearby scythe on the ground and slitting his neck with it.

The last devil got up. Although badly hurt himself, he grabbed the map Zacaus had written in code from one of his pockets. After studying it for a few minutes he began to walk towards the boat. When he was just a metre from the water he felt a heavy blow on his back, which almost knocked him to the floor. He looked up to see Viola, covered in blood but with her wings spread out behind her. She lifted herself up and fell on to him with great force, crushing his head with her feet. She knew this was her last chance. She threw all her strength into attacking this devil that had killed her friends. As he lay there in the sand struggling for breath, she leaned over him.

'You tried to defeat us, but you are weak!' she screamed at him. 'You might have killed the other angels, but you have not killed me, and I am about to kill you and all of the rest of your people. I will go to find the stone, and neither you nor the Iblisari will be able to stop me!' As he opened his mouth she took a large handful of sand and thrust it down his throat, forcing him to swallow it. He gasped for breath as the sand choked him, and then he was gone.

She struggled to her feet and looked at the battleground behind her and the bodies of the other angels. She wanted to go back and say goodbye to them, to make sure they lay in the right position, but she knew that wouldn't help. It was more important to get over to the island, to Zaid.

Viola jumped into the boat, but she was in great pain. She had been hurt very badly and was losing a lot of blood. Yet there was no way she was going to lie there and die slowly. She would do as much as she possibly could first.

With blood pouring over her face, Viola found it difficult to see where she was going. No human would have lasted two minutes with the injuries she was suffering. She knew she was dying, but she used her clothing to bandage her injuries to reduce the bleeding. She had to get over to the stone, but she was unaware that it had to be held by Zacaus to destroy it, as he was the superior angel.

Jumping into the boat, she managed to get it moving in the right direction, as she had memorised the map in her head. But on the crossing she kept drifting in and out of consciousness and gasping for water. It was a long trip across the clear blue waters, but she tried her hardest to stay awake and alive.

After steering the boat for hours she gave in and fell into a deep sleep. As the boat entered the mouth of a river, she awoke and managed to pull herself up.

She was amazed by what she saw and by the sheer beauty of the place. She thought for a few minutes she was in heaven. The river was clean, with bright blue water which was clear enough to see at least thirty feet down to the bottom. Trees branches gathered overhead like green velvet drapes, and the sound of birds singing was soothing and relaxing.

The river led to a lake covered in lily pads and various other plants; finally she saw a safe place where she could land, and with the greatest difficulty she dragged herself out to start the next part of her journey. Viola knew she would not be able to walk far and would not last long. She tried to take in the beauty of this stunning island, but as she became weaker and weaker she slowed down. She saw a small row of shacks ahead but couldn't move another step. Now she just wanted to lie down and close her eyes.

CHAPTER 11

Zaid was waiting there, looking out for signs of anyone coming from the direction of the coast. After waiting for three hours he heard noises in the distance. He jumped up and walked out to the garden; he could see someone in the distance struggling to walk and then falling to the floor. He ran as fast as he could to see who it was. As he got closer he saw what looked like an angel, but she was covered in blood. She could only groan at him and lift an arm. Zaid fell to his knees to help her.

'Oh my god, how did you make it here like this and where are the others?' Zaid asked. 'Do you think you can make it over to the house? It is just there look, up that hill.' He pointed to the house where he had hidden the stone. 'Do you know if you are the superior one? I assume you are as you have survived. Did you have larger wings than the rest, and greater strength?'

'No, Zacaus was the superior one.' Viola struggled to talk. 'He was taken by the devils, there were too many of them for us, we were not prepared for them. He now lies on the sands of the south coast' she said, still gasping for air. Zaid knew then that she would not be able to destroy the stone, but hoped there could still be a chance.

Zaid felt a strange connection with the angel, as if they were related in some way or had met before. She looked at him as if she recognised him as someone else other than Prince Zaid. She had never been this close to him before.

'I cannot reach the house' she said. 'I'm sorry I will not be able to help. Do you have the stone with you?'

'Oh no, I have it at the house. Please stay alive! I will run and get it' he said.

'I will not last that long' replied Viola. 'The other angels have been taken by the devils in battle, but we killed them, fifty of them. I am so sorry. Please, stay here with me, don't leave me alone!'

Zaid so badly wanted to run back for the stone, but Viola was slipping away quickly.

'You are very familiar' said Viola. 'I feel as if I know you. I can feel a connection.'

Zaid felt the same. They both felt a strange comforting feeling. She held on to him more tightly, her pain increasing.

The sun was beginning to set and the sky was the most beautiful blend of pinks and purples. The smell of flowers and sea breeze filled the air.

'I need to close my eyes now' she whispered. 'But I have one question for you'.

'Ask any question you wish' Zaid told her. He was trying to make her last few seconds as comfortable as possible, cradling her. Then Viola noticed a long, dark brown mark on his arm, which looked like a birthmark.

'What is your birth date?' she asked him, shaking with pain.

'May Ist 2038, why do you ask at such a time?' he said.

She looked into his eyes, as he did hers. 'I believe you are my son' she told him softly. 'I am sorry I gave you away, but I was young and wanted a good life for you. That was the date you were born and the mark on your arm is the one that was there when I saw you as a baby.'

Zaid knew that what Viola was saying was true, because he had felt a strong connection too, and they looked so similar. He had been told that he had been adopted from an early age, but had believed his mother had taken her life.

'I never knew you had been brought up by the Royal Family' said Viola. 'I did not know Prince Zaid was you. But now I have felt the connection. I am sorry we have met like this and I do not want you to be sad. I want you to be the best person you can and look after yourself.' She raised her arm to stroke his face.

'Mother, I am sorry I could not protect you, please forgive me' Zaid told her. 'Please stay alive! I have no one.'

'Do not worry, my son, you will have a good life here. Goodbye, my boy.' She closed her eyes and her head fell slightly back as she fell into a deep sleep.

Zaid held her tightly, tears running down his blood-stained face. He had now lost everyone he had ever loved.

CHAPTER TWELVE

After Viola's death, Zaid spent his life alone on the island. He never took the stone from the box he had kept it in, along with his parents' diaries and the stories of their lives and his life.

Petrus died twenty years later, after causing further misery and mayhem to all his people. All the devils had moved away from the palace, so Zaid decided to return there to live out the rest of his years. His cousin had become king and the land was almost back to the way it had been before his parents had died, but there was still evil lurking around every corner. He had spent his days preparing documents, writing stories and working out as much as he possibly could in preparation for the next time the angels arrived even though it might not be for another 4000 years. He also read through his parent's diaries and stories finding out how they really died.

As Zaid came to the end of his life he stored the stories in the rooms underneath the palace, in a place where no one would find them for years and years to come. In another 4000 years there would be 1112 angels, so he had to make his stories clear for whoever would be the next person to find them, to allow the angels to prepare for what was ahead of them.

Zaid helped his cousin as best he could to rule the land, and made sure serious punishment was delivered to those evil people who had anything to do with the Iblisari. When he knew his death was just around the corner, he added more stories to his collection, hoping that the day would come when evil would be eliminated forever and the world would return to the way it should be.

CHAPTER THIRTEEN

After five hours, Henrik finally finished reading. He could not believe the stories he had read and was a little confused by a note at the end of the book. It said: '*To find is to change and deeper will it be. The strength will come from superiority and love*'.

Henrik thought the stone must be somewhere nearby, even though Zaid had never mentioned exactly where he had left it. He had to keep studying the stories, for he knew that somewhere among them there was a clue to where it was.

As he closed the book, he felt a lump between the pages. He carefully pulled the pages apart and took out a bronze-coloured key. There was nothing else with the key to tell him what it was for. His torch was now starting to dim, so he quickly searched around the dusty room to see if there was anything this key might fit into, but there was nothing.

Then, after placing the last book back in its box, he remembered the small door behind the box. He placed the key into the keyhole on the door and to his surprise it opened, however it didn't open wide enough, as the box was still connected to it.

The fixings on the small door were loose on the sides. When he placed his fingers behind the box and put them through the narrow opening of the door, Henrik couldn't feel anything. He tried to get his hand deeper into the cupboard, but the opening was too narrow. He decided to investigate further.

After finding a small rock, he banged away at the door to try and get it open a little wider, without success. Time was running out. It was almost dusk and he needed to get out before the sun was up.

He struggled once more to open it further. Then he placed his hand inside the cupboard and felt around. His arm went further in and he felt a smaller hole. He could feel nothing inside, so he gave up and prepared to leave. It was time to get back to his hotel before the sun came up.

Over the next few days Henrik could not get the angels out of his head. He kept wondering how the world would react to such news if he were to tell all that might happen. He also thought that perhaps he should keep it a secret, because the stories might be just stories. He had a lot to think about, and a lot more travelling to do.

CHAPTER FOURTEEN

Amy set off on her usual journey to work. It was a beautiful sunny Friday morning in July. She was always happy on a Friday, but then she guessed everyone was, as it was the last day of the working week.

Today was definitely going to be good – she could feel it. Smiling as she walked, she thought about the fact that she hadn't seen the cute guy for a few weeks. 'Guess he works somewhere else now', she thought to herself.

Walking into Massapequa station she heard the train coming, so she ran towards her usual carriage to get her usual seat. As the train stopped and the door opened she prepared herself to step on to the train when someone pushed past her, knocking her handbag down on to the tracks.

'Sorry!' a voice shouted.

'Oh shit, my bag! Didn't you see me, idiot?' she said, looking down at the gap her bag had fallen through between the train and the platform. 'That could have been me under that train!'

'I am so sorry!' said a voice. She looked up at the guy who had pushed past her and it was him, the cute guy. They stared at each other for a few seconds. 'I can't believe it, I wasn't looking' he said. 'I really am so sorry. Wait here while I get help.' The train doors closed and the train started off on its journey. 'Well I guess I'm going to be late now' she said loudly, as he ran off for a guard to help. 'Hopefully my bag won't be crushed.' But as she waited for him to return she was glad in a way that it had happened to be him of all people. She fixed her hair and her shirt as she saw him returning with a station guard.

'I got someone, he has the equipment to get the bag back' he said, looking worried that she might shout at him again. The guard walked toward the edge of the platform with a long hooked pole. 'How the hell did you manage to drop your whole bag down there? I suppose your whole life is in that bag, huh?' he laughed.

'Well I was walking along and...' but she was interrupted by the guy. 'It was my fault, I wasn't looking where I was going' he said.

'I see why you weren't looking, she's kinda cute' the guard whispered to the guy. 'Well we will have it out in one second, lady.'

True to his word he soon had the bag off the tracks and in front of her. 'Thank you so much, I am really grateful' she said. 'Yeah thanks' the guy added.

'Do I have to wait a whole hour for the next train into Manhattan?' she asked the guard.

'Afraid so lady, in fact the next one is running late, so you will have to wait an hour twenty, but hey it's a Friday! Have a good day guys.' He turned off back to his little station office.

'Look, I am really sorry about all this' said the guy, looking worried.

'Well I have a pretty important meeting in exactly one hour, so I guess I won't be getting there in time' she replied with a cold smile. 'I'll give them a call and see if they can hold on for me, but somehow I don't think they will.'

'OK' he said. 'Look as this is my entire fault, I will get us both a taxi into town. I need to get there too, so it's the least I can do.'

Amy felt a bit nervous of the fact that she would be sitting next to him for what could be quite a long drive into town at this time of the morning.

'I guess that would be good, if you don't mind?' she replied.

'As I said before it's my fault.'

They smiled at each other and slowly walked out of the station towards the taxi stand.

'I'm Max, nice to meet you anyway, even though not in the best circumstances.' He laughed and held out his hand.

'Amy' she replied with a shy smile and shaking his hand. 'It's nice to meet you.' She had never felt shy in front of guys before, so this was very strange for her.

'I always see you on this train' said Max. 'I kinda always wanted to say hi, but…' he paused and gave her a cheeky grin.

'Really?' she replied with a surprised look.

'Yeah, you know how it is when you always see the same faces on the train, especially a pretty one', he said, wishing he hadn't in case she thought he was a little weird.

'Yeah I guess', she replied blushing.

He saw a taxi and shouted out for it.

'What the hell is wrong with me?' Amy said to herself, telling herself off quietly for blushing. Max opened the door for her, and then ran over to the other side to get in.

They started their journey through the rush hour traffic.

'So you must live nearby?' he asked.

'Oh yeah I'm from Massapequa, not far, do you know it?' she asked.

'Yeah I live just past there. I've been driving in over the last few weeks, it's so much easier by train, Manhattan's a nightmare driving.' He replied. 'That's probably why I haven't seen you for a while.'

'Oh', she said, blushing again, 'well I didn't think you noticed me.'

'Ha, now who wouldn't notice you, you're stunning!' he smiled.

'Well aren't you the charmer! If you noticed me, why didn't you come and talk to me?' Amy asked, getting her confidence back.

'I kinda presumed you'd be spoken for' he said, as if there were a question in his comment. After a long pause he came right out with it. 'Well, are you spoken for?'

'Um, no I'm not' she replied, not wanting to sound desperate.

'Cool, I mean OK. So where do you work?'

The conversation went back and forth as he explained to her that this would be the last time he would be taking this particular train, as he now had to travel to New Jersey by car to work at his new restaurant.

'I have a restaurant here too, on Bleecker Street' he said. 'But I have a good manager there, so I don't need to be there all the time and I'm rarely up at this time of day.'

'Stop!' Amy shouted. 'I work just here' she told the driver. 'Thank you so much for the lift. I forgive you for throwing my bag on to the train tracks.' They both laughed, and stared at each other.

'Hey lady I can't stop here for long' the taxi man groaned.

'OK, I'm sorry again for ruining your morning' he said, as if sad to see her go.

'Yeah, enough already guys I gotta move' moaned the taxi driver again.

Amy smiled at him as she closed the door. Max quickly wound down the window. 'So have a good day Amy,' he smiled as the taxi zoomed off.

'Goddam taxi drivers.' Amy stomped her foot on the ground, turned around and walked through the large glass doors of the building for another day at work.

★ ★ ★ ★ ★

First point of call, reception. 'Trinny, you would not believe what happened to me, the hot guy from the train I told you about? Well I spoke to him today.' She explained the story.

'And did he ask you out?' asked Trinny looking excited before Amy could get to the end of the story.

'Uh, no he didn't ask me and I won't be seeing him ever again, that was the last frigging day, I'm so pissed' she said angrily.

'How dare he not ask!' she said, joking. 'Well he knows where you work doesn't he?'

'Yeah but that doesn't mean he's going to come here. Anyway, plenty more men around here,' she said as she walked off to her office.

A few hours passed and Amy could not get Max out of her head. 'Get a grip, woman' she whispered to herself. 'You do not chase guys, they chase you!' She knew she wouldn't see him again so she got on with her work, pushing him to a tiny little corner at the side of her mind.

Amy never dwelled on men. The way she saw it, she always had more important things to think of, like her job, the kids, the house. Men always seemed to be last on the list. She only needed one when she wanted a bit of fun, and then she could get one with a click of her fingers and get rid of him before he got too close.

As it was a Friday, she decided to text her friends Millie and Harriet to see if they were around for Friday evening drinks. They both worked in the city within a short distance of each other, and usually, provided they didn't need to rush home, they would meet for a few drinks. As Jake and Scarlett were hanging out with their friends and she couldn't get Max out of her head, now was a good time to celebrate a Friday.

Amy texted: *Hey guys, I'm feeling kinda bored and annoyed today, nothing is going my way, I think a drink is in order, who's up for it?'* She waited for their replies as she started to finish off her last few bits of work.

Millie texted back: *Yo, I am so definitely up for a few. I really need something strong. How about O'Malley's bar in Meatpacking Mills?*

Harriet texted: *Babe, what's up? Tell me later but YES YES YES, tell me where and when* J.

Amy: *Cool, I need to get out of here, will be at O'Malley's at 6.*

As she sat at the bar she saw Millie and Harriet walking through the door,

'Over here you guys!' she shouted from the corner of the bar. Millie and Harriet walked over. 'Hey, how are you?' she said.

'God, do I need a drink after the day I had' said Millie.

'Same here' repeated Harriet.

'Well that means all three of us, so who's for three bottles of wine?'

The three of them started on the wine as the bar started getting more packed with the usual after-work drinkers, Amy told the girls about how down she had felt over the last few weeks and about the little adventure earlier in the day with the hot guy from the train.

'So he took your number right?' Millie asked.

'Well no he didn't, well he didn't ask, I was thrown out of the taxi. But he knows where I work, so if he wants to ask me out he knows where to find me. Anyway who gives a shit, let's get wasted.'

'Woohoo!' the three shouted out, 'Cheers, now let's party.'

And the girls drank through the night, talking and laughing.

CHAPTER FIFTEEN

The weekend passed as quickly as weekends usually do, and before she knew it Amy was on her way to work again. On her journey to Manhattan she thought about Max again and how nice it would have been to see him. She was a little annoyed that he hadn't asked her out, but there was nothing she could do now.

It was a miserable Monday in New York. The rain was coming down a hundred miles per hour and the wind was blowing everything around the place. She ran into the office from the subway, almost slipping at the front doors. 'Hey Trinny, my god this weather is annoying,' she moaned. 'How was your weekend?'

Trinny smiled and said she had had a really good weekend. Then she pointed towards a large bouquet of flowers in the corner of the reception area. 'They're for you, you lucky girl', she said. 'Go on, check who they're from.'

'What? Who the hell is buying me flowers? You're kidding me, right?' said Amy in a worried tone.

'Not kidding, check the message' Trinny told her and pushed her over to the flowers. They were large and bright, beautiful red roses and lilies, presented in the finest wrappings and kept together with a velvet bow. There was a message popping out of the top with her name on it, so she opened it up and read it. It said: 'Amy, I hope you didn't get in trouble for being late on Friday, I hope I can make it up to you with these flowers and if not maybe you will let me take you out to dinner?'

The message was followed by his number and a kiss.

'Oh my, I can't believe it, they're beautiful and he remembered where I worked!' she said with excitement. She picked them up and took them into the lift and up to her office. She was so excited that he had left his number. She had to remind herself to stop acting like a teenager but she had never been this excited or thought so much about a guy before. Why was this one so different?

All day she stared at the number, and by midday she thought it would be the right time to text him and thank him for the flowers and accept his offer. Although it took her about five takes with the text message, she finally pressed 'send' and waited for the reply.

The hours went by and Amy's day at work was coming to an end, but there was no reply. She got on her train and called the kids to see if they wanted anything from the grocery store, as she was passing it on the way home, and told Jake it was his turn to walk the dogs.

As she got off the train her phone went off with a text message alert. It was from him.

Max: *Sorry I didn't get back earlier, had so much to do at the restaurant, glad you like the flowers. Can I call you later on this evening? X*

Amy: *No worries, yes that's fine x.*

She felt a surge of excitement and found herself blushing again. 'What the hell is wrong with me?' she asked herself out loud.

Later on that evening she had the usual jobs to do, cleaning, washing up, cooking etc. When she had done all that she poured herself a large glass of merlot and she and the kids sat at the dining table for dinner.

'So who are the flowers from?' Scarlett asked.

'Just someone from work' Amy replied.

'So who is he?' Jake asked.

'A guy, that's all you need to know' she told them as she got up to clear the table.

'Ma, I hope you're going to go on a date with him, I mean we think it's time you settled down with someone, don't you'? Scarlett said, rolling her eyes.

'Yeah mom, you need a guy to hang out with.'

'Excuse me! I have plenty male friends to do that with, I don't need a man!'

'Whatever!' they both replied at the same time.

'Look I probably will meet this guy for a few drinks, OK, but nothing serious' she told them. They asked her for more details, how they had met, what he looked like etc, especially Scarlett, who loved to nose into her mother's business.

'Well he is lucky to be taking such a beautiful woman out' said Scarlett. Every man I know fancies you, and so do all Jake's friends. Why do you think they're always hanging around here?' 'Ugh' Jake cringed at the thought of his friends fancying his mother.

'OK enough already' she said. 'Help clean and then we can go watch some TV, is your homework all done?'

'Yeah yeah' they again replied at the same time.

★ ★ ★ ★ ★

The evening passed quickly, and it was almost half nine when her phone started ringing. She jumped up off the sofa and walked out to the kitchen for a bit of privacy and quiet.

'Amy speaking.'

'Hey Amy, it's Max, how are you?'

'I'm good' she replied. 'How was your day?'

Max told her he had missed the train because of the traffic going over to New Jersey and said how he had missed seeing her. Amy laughed. 'Well aren't you a smooth talker!' she told him. He told her about how stressful his day was.

'Well I can't complain, my brother and I inherited the businesses from our grandparents' he said. 'Our restaurant in Manhattan is a bit smaller, so my brother takes care of that one when he comes home to visit, he travels a lot. Anyhow, are you free tomorrow evening? I should get home around eight, so maybe if you wanna go get something to eat?' he sounded nervous.

'Uh, well, I think I'm free', she said. She checked her diary and saw she had nothing on. 'So yeah I guess so, that would be lovely.'

He asked her if he should pick her up from her house or if she wanted to meet somewhere else, and as Amy didn't know him well enough yet she decided it would be best for him to meet her at the corner of Dale Street, which was two blocks from her house.

'Ok, well it was nice talking to you again. Shall we say nine on the dot tomorrow?'

'Yes that's good for me' she replied. They said their goodbyes and hung up.

Amy stopped to think about the date and how much she fancied this guy. Then she shook her head and told herself not to go there. She didn't want to get close to any man. She wasn't ready, she just wanted a couple of dates and hopefully a few nights of passion. She laughed to herself and told herself not to worry about it, it was just a date.

CHAPTER SIXTEEN

The next day Amy got on with her everyday bits and pieces. When it came to five o' clock, she rushed home to get herself ready for the evening.

'Scarlett, I have a date this evening so I need help with something nice to wear!' she yelled from the top of the stairs.

'One minute Ma' Scarlett shouted, as she watched the last few seconds of a programme on TV. 'So who is it?' Scarlett asked, stomping up the stairs getting excited

'Just a guy I met on the train, no big deal' said Amy. They searched through the wardrobe and Amy tried on three dresses before she found the right one, a black pencil dress with off-the-shoulder sleeves.

'Perfect Mom, not too revealing and not too librarian!' said Scarlett. They laughed, and Scarlett started to help her mother do her hair and makeup. After an hour she was ready.

'You look amazing, he is going love you' Amy said. Amy had her caramel-coloured hair up in a neat bun. Her skin looked bright and shimmery, and she kept her make-up simple except for her lipstick, which was a bright red, matching her red court shoes. Her skin was a silky olive colour from head to toe.

Time went on and her phone went. It was a message from Max telling her he was outside. She got her stuff together and prepared to leave as Jake came through the door,

'Hey ma, Scarlett texted me saying you had a date, is he picking you up?' he said.

'No, I'm meeting him two blocks down' she replied.

'I'll walk you, it's kinda late' he told her firmly.

'OK, just halfway, I'll be fine' she said. 'Bye honey' she shouted to Scarlett as she and Jake left.

'I should really check him out, he could be a real weirdo' said Jake, sounding worried.

'Jake I have been on dates before' said Amy. 'I have my pepper spray, and seriously you can walk back now, he is just around this corner.'

'OK, take care and text us in half an hour' he said as he gave her a kiss goodbye. Amy fixed her hair and walked around the corner.

There he was standing by his car, leaning on the door looking at his phone.

'Hiya!' she shouted as she walked towards him.

'Hey, you look amazing, my god!' he said with a smile on his face.

'Well you look pretty good too' she replied, smiling back.

He walked closer to her and gave her a kiss on the cheek, then returned to the car to open the door for her. He looked hotter than she expected. He was tall, at least six foot three, and his shoulders were broad. He had short dark blonde hair and blue eyes with light stubble. He looked to her as if he had a good physique, and she couldn't help but wonder what kind of body he had underneath the navy T-shirt and jeans.

Holding the door open for her, she got into to the car and he ran around to his side. 'So, I know a good restaurant ten blocks away, are you cool with that?' he asked her.

'Yeah, any place is good as long as there's a wine list, my day has been kinda long' she replied.

'Well we should have a good night, even if it's only Tuesday' he reassured her.

They pulled up outside one of the most expensive restaurants in town. 'This is a pretty expensive place, you really don't need to go to this bother for me' she told him.

'Don't worry, I pulled a few strings' he told her, pulling up and getting out to open the door.

Amy had had guys treat her before, but nothing like this. They would never open car doors for her. She started to worry, thinking he was going a bit too far, when all she wanted was something simple, not a boyfriend. But perhaps she was thinking too far ahead.

They walked into the restaurant, which exuded style and elegance. The lighting was perfect, there was a piano playing classical music in the background and they were greeted straight away.

'Good evening Mr Grekov' said the head waiter, as another waiter put his hand out for their jackets.

'Wow you really do look amazing' he told her again, after seeing the dress she was wearing under her jacket.

'Thank you, you already told me that' she said politely.

'I know but I had to say it again' he replied.

They walked over to their table and took their seats, ordered some drinks and finally relaxed.

'This is a great place and I'm pretty hungry right now' she said to him, taking a sip of the complimentary champagne.

'Well you're in the right place' he replied, and they both laughed.

As the night went on they laughed and joked about the day they had first started talking. The conversation went well and they seemed to get on and have a lot in common.

'So tell me about your family. You must be Polish I'm guessing with a name like that' she asked him as they waited for their dessert.

'Russian father, American Jewish mother, but nothing much to say. My mom passed away when I was fifteen, so my dad took over. They had just gone through a divorce, and he was kinda abusive towards her. It's a long story. He was wealthy, so he fought for me and my younger brother to live with him, and as soon as I was old enough to move out I did. I do still see him, but we're not that close.'

She seemed to have hit a nerve. 'I'm sorry I didn't mean to pry', she said. She looked into his eyes and felt some kind of sadness; she wished she hadn't asked.

'Ah don't worry' he replied, and changed the subject. 'So tell me about your family.' As the waiter came over with the desserts and more wine, Amy reached over for her spoon and knocked the freshly-poured glass all over the waiter. 'Oh shit, I mean sugar, oh god, trust me!' she said. The waiter told her it was OK and not to worry.

'I'm so sorry, I can't believe I just did that' she said.

'Leave it, it's fine, it's an accident just like the one we had the other day' he said. They both laughed and carried on with their desert. They talked for hours, until they noticed they were the only ones left in the restaurant.

'I think they probably want us to leave now, don't you?' she said to him.

'I guess so; did you wanna take a stroll, burn off those calories?'

'Yeah why not' she agreed.

They got up and pushed their chairs under their tables.

'We'd better get the bill first', she told him.

'Nah, I've settled'.

'Oh OK, well thank you' she said to him gratefully.

She thought to herself that there was no way he had paid any bill. He had never left the table. She found it strange that they seemed to be treating him like royalty, but nevertheless she was enjoying herself, and whether it was the wine or not she definitely fancied him.

It was one in the morning and the night was warm. They talked about everything and Amy told Max her life story, but she felt as if he didn't want to delve too much into his life. As they crossed a busy road he took her hand, and when they reached the other side he didn't let go. Amy thought again to herself that by now she would like to have been in bed with her date.

After a further hour of walking and talking they reached the car.

'Jump in, I'll take you home' he said.

'Well thank *yew*, kind sir' she replied in a mock southern accent.

He searched for his keys, standing just a foot away from her, struggling to find them in his six-pocket jacket. When he found them he looked at Amy and she gazed back at him. It was five seconds, but it felt like forever. They each wanted to kiss the other, but instead they both turned away and got into the car.

'So am I dropping you two blocks from your house or outside your gate?' he asked her.

'Well I think you seem pretty sane, so you can drop me all the way home' she told him.

On the short journey home it felt a little awkward after what had just happened. Why hadn't they kissed? Would they kiss when they said goodbye to each other? Both of them were thinking the same, by the looks of it.

As he pulled up outside her house, she told him what a lovely evening she had had and he said the same. He leaned forward and gave her a kiss on the cheek. 'I'll text you tomorrow', he said, as if both asking and telling her.

'Yes that would be nice' she replied as she walked up the path of her house. 'See ya!' she shouted.

Max waited until she reached the door and was in the house safely, then he drove off. She ran straight upstairs, wondering to herself that she had never had a date where a man was not all over her, and he hadn't even kissed her properly. Maybe he wasn't interested. She shrugged her shoulders and carried on preparing for bed. She washed her teeth and face, threw herself into bed and dozed off.

CHAPTER SEVENTEEN

As Max drove home he couldn't stop thinking about Amy. He was used to women throwing themselves at him, beautiful women, but he had never once had the feelings for them he had for Amy. He was in a happy place, especially after the last few years of his life. He thought of his mother and knew she would be happy and proud of him right now.

Max thought back to how he had wasted his years and why he had been put on this planet with an evil father like his. His father Vladimir had grown up in the slums of a Russian town and as a teenage boy he had started living on the streets, where he had fallen in with the wrong people, selling drugs and weapons. Not long after that he became involved in a ring of evil mobsters who would terrorise the people of the town, demanding money to protect businesses, buying and selling drugs and torturing innocent people who got in their way.

He gradually made his way to the top and became one of Russia's most notorious gangsters. With his money and power he decided to move across the water to New York, where he carried on with his business and made millions of pounds. He opened restaurants and hotels to disguise his underground businesses of drugs, dealing in weapons and forcing local businesses to use his company for protection whether they wanted it or not. Vladimir was a dark soul who had no regard for any other human.

In his early thirties he had met a woman whom he had married and had two sons with. Madeline was a pretty American Jewish woman who was kind and sweet and had innocence about her. She got on with everyone and was a breath of fresh air to Vladimir. Madeline had a perfect body and face to match, with long thick blonde wavy hair and piercing blue eyes. When she met Vladimir she was unhappy with her life at home, where she lived with her parents and younger sisters under strict Jewish family rules. She had always been well behaved for her parents and never got herself into trouble even as a teenager, but after her father set up an arranged marriage for her, she disagreed. Her father told her she had to go along with it or they would send her off to Israel to live with her grandparents. Madeline did not want to move out of New York. The day after her father told her that, she met Vladimir, and within days she ran away from home and into his arms. Two weeks down the line, they were married.

Of course Vladimir kept his dark secret from her. He just wanted a wife to look after him and bear his children. More importantly, this would give him full rights to live in America.

Madeline was showered with luxurious gifts, a mansion and money to do whatever she wanted. Her new life seemed like a fairy tale to her.

A few years later, after she gave birth to their second son, she noticed a change in Vladimir. Not only was he having affairs and didn't care much if she found out, but he was obviously up to something illegal. She would find weapons hidden around the house. There were late night calls when Vladimir had to leave to go and sort things out. She found blood-stained clothing in bins and he would always have his bodyguards following him around. When she questioned him he would shout at her and tell her she was imagining everything, but she knew she was not.

Over the years it became worse, Vladimir would even bring women into their home, and on two occasions the house was shot at.

A few years later, after the boys were born, Madeline had made up with her parents; she needed them in her life especially as she didn't have any close friends. After years of worrying for her two sons just after they turned five and ten, Madeline decided one morning that she should attempt to take them from the family home to stay with her sister in the peaceful town of Sayville on Long Island. But two days after they had moved out, Vladimir located her and dragged her and the boys home. He begged her to stay and swore he would change, and for two years he did, except that he still kept his underground business, hiding it from them. The boys spent more time with him and he became the father he should have been, but by then Madeline had fallen out of love with him and just wanted the boys to have a family life. Even though she too thought Vladimir had changed his ways, she felt happy to go along with it.

One evening Vladimir held a gathering at their house to celebrate his birthday. The boys were spending the weekend with their grandparents. Madeline hated every single one of Vladimir's friends and business associates, so she decided to drink the night away to get through it.

As the party was coming to an end she saw Vladimir showing a young woman towards his office at the back of the house. She followed him until she was stopped by two of his henchmen.

'I want to see my husband, get your hands off me!' she screamed at them.

'Mr Grekov is very busy and does not want disturbance' one said in his deep Russian accent.

'I don't care, let me through, this is my house, get the fuck out of my way!' she yelled.

'Mr Grekov has given us orders that you are not to disturb him' the other man said.

Then a minute later the woman walked out of the office looking angry and annoyed, and Vladimir shouted at his wife to come in. Madeline turned after the woman. 'You, what have you been doing in there with my husband?' she shouted at her. The woman turned around to Madeline. 'I'm done with him, you can have him' she replied.

Madeline grabbed the woman's hair and dragged her to the ground, which led to a violent fight. Vladimir ran out of the office while the two men were trying to drag the women apart.

Suddenly the woman took a gun from her pocket and pointed it at Madeline and the three men towering over her. 'Do you want to know what your husband does?' she shouted.

'Get her out of here now!' Vladimir shouted.

Madeline couldn't speak with fear that she would be shot. She had never been involved in anything like this.

The woman pointed the gun towards Vladimir. 'Be quiet or I will shoot you all!' she screamed. 'Your husband runs an underground illegal business and an evil cult. Did you know that, ever heard of the Iblisari? Did you know he is involved in drugs and weapons, and now he takes innocent girls from their countries and sells their bodies to old perverts over here?' she screamed out.

All of a sudden there was a noise from behind, followed by three loud bangs. Blood splattered the walls and the faces of everyone around. The woman fell to the ground. She had been shot in the head by another of Vladimir's men.

Watching her bloodied head and body fall to the floor in what felt like slow motion, Madeline sobered up, but still she couldn't speak. She ran through the large marble-floored hall to her room and locked herself in it. 'I need to get out of here' she whispered to herself still shaking, her heart pounding. She stayed in her room all night, not sleeping at all, thinking of the dead woman downstairs and fearing she might end up the same way.

She didn't speak to Vladimir until the next day, when she told him she was leaving. The boys were fourteen and nine at this stage, and there was no way she was going to let them anywhere near this.

Vladimir accepted this, to her surprise, but gave her a warning. He held her tightly and whispered in her ear,

'Madeline, I will let you go, but I want to be able to see those boys once a week, and if you mention to anyone what is going on here I will see to it that you will be taken care of just like the woman downstairs. You know those boys will be well protected. I am a feared man so rest assured on that.'

Madeline knew this was a serious threat. She agreed to it so that she could leave the house with her belongings and the boys as soon as possible.

Madeline spent the next year in Sayville near where her sister and parents lived, in a new house, happy with the boys and enjoying a normal life. However she still had the worry that the boys had to spend one day a week with their father, and she never looked forward to seeing him. The boys knew nothing, as she kept everything about Vladimir away from them and if she wanted to stay alive she knew she would have to abide by his rules. Although Vladimir offered her money regularly she didn't want any of it, it was dirty money to her, so she got herself a job managing her parents' restaurant.

CHAPTER EIGHTEEN

At fifteen Maximus, the elder son, knew his father was up to something, but he never let his mother know about it. He did well at school and was looking forward to becoming a doctor when he was older. At ten Andre was just a normal happy kid, into the usual kid things. They were all happy, and for the first time in many years Max noticed his mother smiling more, so there was no way he wanted to tell her the things he had seen his father get up to behind closed doors, and especially that he had already involved his son in some of his dirty work.

One evening driving home after collecting the boys from their father's, she heard them talking about guns.

'Boys, I have told you before not to talk about dangerous things like that' she shouted at them. She was worried they would get influenced by their father.

'Dad, let us play with real guns today' said Andre.

'Shut up man!' Max whispered.

'Hey I heard that!' shouted Madeline pulling over in the car.

'Don't you ever keep things like that from me, that is wrong, I have not brought you up to lie like that. Is there anything else you're hiding from me?'

'No ma, just that, nothing else', the boys said, sounding a little scared at their mother's tone.

'Look I'm sorry, I shouldn't shout at you like that, but you must understand guns are dangerous, they kill thousands of kids every day in America. Promise me you won't touch them ever again. I will speak to your father about this.' She said calmly and carried on driving

Ten minutes later pulling up outside their house, Madeline screwed her face up with anger, then took a few deep breaths,

'Right boys, we will talk more about this when I get back. I need to pop out to the grocery store for some bits, so you go on in and I won't be long.' She watched the boys go inside the house and then turned the car around. She was making her way back to her ex-husband's house to have a go at him for involving her children in his dark world.

When she arrived at the house, she put the code into the gate and skidded up the drive. No one was around, and she found this strange as there were always bodyguards hanging around somewhere. She pulled up to the front door and knocked on it, but there was no answer. After waiting for three minutes she walked around the back of the house, as she could smell something like a bonfire, but she still could not see life anywhere. Then as she prepared to return to her car she heard some kind of strange noise coming from somewhere. It was a kind of chanting sound and it was definitely going on at the end of the garden behind the outhouse as she could see smoke. It was starting to get a little dark and Madeline felt a little worried sneaking around the house of a mafia boss, but she was so angry she wanted to find Vladimir and tell him how annoyed she was about allowing the children to play with weaponry.

Slowly she crept around to see what the weird noise was. When she put her head slowly around the corner she saw Vladimir and his men, along with a group of people, chanting in a circle and uttering what sounded like praises to Satan.

She stared at them for twenty minutes, watching them walk around the bonfire like zombies shouting weird words she did not recognise. 'The Iblisari live on' was one of the only things they shouted out that she kind of understood. She knew that Iblisari was something to do with the devil.

Scared, she ran around the corner and back through the garden towards the side of the house and her car. But as she ran, one of Vladimir's men called out, shouting that there was someone watching them. The entire group stopped what they were doing, and a few more men ran back towards the garden.

'Find out who it is and kill them' Vladimir shouted. Seconds later three gunshots went off. Vladimir and all the other men ran over to see who this person spying on them had been, and there was Madeline, the mother of his children, lying dead on the grass.

'What the fuck have you done, you idiot!' he shouted to the man holding the gun. 'This is my ex-wife!' But all Vladimir really cared about was how he was going to get away with this. How was he going to disguise her death without getting caught? After thinking further he knew he would have had to ask his men to kill her anyway.

'OK you' he told the man with the gun in his hand. 'Put her back in her car and drive her to the woods, then crash the car. Put her in the driving seat and set it alight and make sure you do it properly, go now! You killed her so you will clean up this mess.'

'I'm so sorry, but boss, you told me to take out whoever it was', the man said.

'Well just sort out the mess. I don't want any trace of this anywhere in my house' Vladimir said, walking back towards his house. 'And everyone else, this meeting is over, we will rearrange it for a week tomorrow'.

To Vladimir this meant he would get sole custody of the boys, so there would be two more to add to his collection of underworld mobsters.

CHAPTER NINETEEN

At nine o' clock Max started to worry about how long his mother had been at the grocery store. He had a strange feeling she might have gone to see their father after hearing about the guns. Max worried about her being anywhere near him, as he knew his father was no angel.

When the clock struck ten he knew there was definitely something wrong. His younger brother Andre was fast asleep on the sofa and she should have been back at least two hours ago. She was not answering her phone, so Max called his father. After trying five times to get through to him he heard a knock on the door.

'Max, open up, it's your father' Vladimir shouted at the door. Max ran down the stairs and to the front door and opened it quickly, worried as to why his father was at the door and not his mother.

'What is it Dad?' Max asked as the door swung open.

'Max, there has been an accident, you better let me in, it's your mother' Vladimir said. He looked at the ground, knowing he couldn't look his son in the eyes and lie to him about having his mother murdered.

'What's happened, where is she, is she OK?' he cried.

'I'm sorry Max, she was in her car and the accident was very bad, they couldn't save her, your mother is gone' he said. 'I'm so sorry son, you two will have to come with me now, you will have to live with me.'

Max went into shock straight away, screaming at his father, 'what did you do to her?'

'Max, calm down, she had a car accident' he said calmly. 'It was nothing to do with me. You're in shock, now wake your brother up and grab your things, I will be in the car.'

A week later the boys laid their mother to rest. Max had to take care of his younger brother and especially had to protect him from their father. He was so close to his mother and now she had gone. He was unable to talk or communicate with anyone except Andre over the following few weeks, and he didn't realise much of what was going on around him. He vaguely remembered telling his younger brother his mother had gone to heaven. Max found it hard to deal with and locked himself in his room for weeks.

As the years passed he found himself picking up traits from his father, mainly the bad ones. He began to care less for life, and as he felt himself slowly slipping into his father's way of life he suggested his brother should go off to boarding school. He knew he would be safe there away from his father.

Max had never got on with his father and was very scared of him. Vladimir would beat Max regularly and punish him for the smallest things. But before Max knew it he found himself working with his father in the Russian mafia. Although Max didn't care much for his own life he felt he had to make sure his younger brother was happy, so when Andre decided to go off to college after boarding school and then travel the world Max was happy. At least he knew his brother was safe away from them.

A few more years down the line Max had been forced into a world of evil by his father. Since his mother had died he felt as if there was no need to do anything good with his life. But this wasn't Max. He had been brought up well by his mother.

Vladimir started him on guns and women by the age of sixteen, and when he received his first batch of money he became addicted to the lifestyle. By 20 he had been heavily sucked into his father's way of life.

Max always remembered the first time his father made him kill a man. He had just returned home one evening and Vladimir called him to the basement of their house where he had a man tied up. The man had been tortured badly and Vladimir asked Max to finish him off. Max turned around and attempted to leave the room, but Vladimir shot at the wall to scare him.

The man sitting in the chair was barely recognisable from the blood all over his face. He was a shop owner who was behind with payments. He had started using another company and attempted to hire someone to kill Vladimir after failing to get help from the police about the bullying he had endured over the last few years.

Max couldn't bear to see the man like this. He told his father to let him go back to his family and said he had been punished enough, but Vladimir wouldn't accept this.

'Max you are to take his life now, if you don't I will have to deal with you myself and it will not be a very nice experience' he said.

'I won't do it' said Max. 'I don't know him, he has done nothing to me, why don't you just let him go home?' Max replied, shaking with fear.

Vladimir walked closer to Max with the gun in his hand. 'Here you go, take it and kill him' he said, but Max said no for the second time and attempted to walk out again. Vladimir ran over to him, pulled him around, raising his hand and striking him on the head with the gun. Max fell to the floor crying.

'You have one more chance boy! You kill him or I'll put a bullet through your kneecaps!' shouted Vladimir.

Max knew he was serious. He had never been given such a difficult job to do, but the man shouted out 'Kill me now please, I cannot take this pain'. His eyes were hanging out of their sockets and his chest had been ripped apart by numerous slashes of a sharp knife. His trousers had been taken down and all Max could see was blood. He could only imagine what they had done to him. Max then thought the man would be better off dead, so with his hands shaking he closed his eyes and pulled the trigger.

That messed with Max's head over the next years, but a few years after that Max, like his father, had become one of the most feared men in his circle. He was thought of as one of the most powerful men in Manhattan and on most of Long Island.

When Max turned 30 he had time to think about what he was really doing. The more mature he became the more he understood that he needed to get out of this way of living. He wasn't like his father, he had feelings towards people. After he hit 30 he started to care more about people when he hurt them, and more often than not when his father wasn't around he would let his enemies off the hook by keeping them alive and advising them to get away from New York. He could no longer do as his father had told him to do. He would try to get out of working as part of his father's team, and many times he tried moving away, but his father never accepted this. Max had unfinished work to do and would never be left alone as his father warned him.

It was only when Max turned 33 that he decided enough was enough. He had been shot in the arm, neck and chest by some enemies and spent four weeks in hospital, where he thought a lot about his life and his mother and what she would have wanted for him. He stopped and realised that he had been lying to himself over the years about what had happened to his mother. He knew deep down inside she had tried her best to keep him and his brother away from their father, and now he knew why. She hadn't stood a chance against him, and he probably had something to do with her death.

Max there and then decided this life was not for him. He was not this person his father had forced him to be. He was sick of the killings, the tortures of enemies, the abuse of women. He could no longer carry on with this worthless life.

While he was in hospital he thought long and hard about whether his mother had died in the way his father had told him.

He started to think that his father might have had something to do with her death and how he could easily have disguised it as a crash. Max hoped his father had had nothing to do with it, so whilst lying in bed day in day out he made calls to some of his colleagues to check the records of the crash eighteen years before. Then after he left hospital he spoke to the people he knew who had dealt with the crash on that day to find out exactly what happened to his mother.

The people on the inside did not want to get on the wrong side of Vladimir, so Max was given information that could only mean it wasn't an accident. He was told her body had been dead for at least an hour before the crash from the way she was positioned in the car when it was found.

Max became more and more angry every day, but he needed to get his strength back before he could confront his father. It was time to tear himself away from this evil and start a new life, and if his father didn't accept it he would tell him he would investigate his mother's death. He did not think his father would be able to kill him, but he prepared himself just in case.

A week passed and Max paid a visit to his father's house to discuss leaving the mob and his mother's murder.

'Max, it's good to see you are up and well' Vladimir said smiling at the front door.

'Well you would have known if you had visited me in hospital' Max grunted barging through the door.

'You know how I am with hospitals ever since your mother died' he said as he looked down.

'Oh yeah and about that, I know you killed her so don't act the innocent, I know you or your mob killed her. I've been investigating' said Max.

'Max, you have no idea what you are talking about, you must not be feeling right since the accident' Vladimir said slyly.

'Are you seriously going to deny it? I have looked into it and she was dead before the crash and before the car was set alight. You sicken me. I know she came to see you on that evening. Oh and just to let you know, I am leaving this shit, leaving you all and I want nothing more to do with any of you. If you come after me I will make sure you are found out, found out for killing my mother. And the worst thing is that I am not shocked you did it. I know you are the most evil and despicable man and you deserve to rot in hell. Do not come after me!'

Max walked towards the front door.

'You really are a foolish boy' retorted Vladimir. 'You won't be able to keep away from this life, it's in your blood. You are no different to me, in fact I see myself in you every day. You will be back! And your mother deserved it, she interfered and sneaked around me like a parasite. She tried to tell me what to do with you boys, she was a very silly woman. But they will never be able to prove how she died. She was never a good driver!' He snarled at Max and gave him a wink.

Max was infuriated by the fact his father had no remorse, no feeling, no disappointment in himself after admitting to his mother's murder. He ran at his father and punched him in the face. Vladimir fell to the floor and laughed as he lay there. His men came out from around the corner in case he needed protection, but Max turned around and walked out of the door planning on never seeing his father again.

Driving off in his car, he felt mixed emotions; sadness that he had not been there to protect his mother whilst she was being murdered by those animals, and anger that his father could get away with this and there was nothing he could do about it. But he also felt relieved that he was finally able to stand up to him and walk away and start a new life, start a new company somewhere other than this town. His mother had left him and his brother $200,000 in her will and $300,000 from the life insurance she had taken out, which made Max think she must have been worried for her life.

Max and his brother were also in line to own the family's Jewish restaurant passed down from his grandparents.

There was no way he was going to use the blood money he had earned over the years. He needed to get rid of it, and the next day he gave the money to a charity. That confirmed it for Max, it was now over.

CHAPTER TWENTY

The morning after her first date with Max, Amy woke up with a slight hangover and noticed her phone light was flashing to tell her there was a message. She slowly picked it up and saw that Max had texted her to say he had enjoyed the night and wish her sweet dreams. This made her smile and she perked up a little as she dragged herself out of bed and turned the shower on.

'Kids, I hope you're up, I'm leaving early today so make sure you don't sleep in' she shouted. Then she went downstairs to put the coffee machine on. After her shower she took the dogs out. The morning air was crisp but still mild, and Amy felt good. She didn't want to think that it was a guy making her feel this good, because that was not her style.

On her way to work she replied to his text, saying she had also had a fun evening, and thanked him again for treating her. Over the next few days they talked on the phone every night. They always had so much to talk about and had interesting conversations and debates. Amy had never communicated with a guy like this unless it was one of her friends or family.

They planned the next date for the Saturday evening and Amy couldn't wait. Saturday came around quickly and their date went well. She had never felt so comfortable with a guy before, yet still at the end of the date he just gave her a kiss on the cheek and dropped her at her front door.

They met again a few days later and Max collected Amy from her house. Jake opened the door to him and Scarlett ran downstairs to check out this new friend of her mothers.

'Come on in, nice to finally meet you, I'm Jake' Jake greeted him, and led him to the front room where Scarlett was. Jake thought the best way of sussing him out was to invite him in to see if he was OK or not for his mother.

'I'm Scarlett, nice to meet you, can I get you a drink?'

'Yes please, and I'm Max' he replied.

'Beer OK?' asked Jake,

'Yeah cool.'

'Who was at the door, guys?' Amy shouted out.

'It's Max, he's cool, he's having a beer while you get ready.'

'Hey Max, I won't be long, be nice to him kids!' she told them, laughing.

When Amy was finally ready she joined them in the sitting room and carried on with the conversation that they had started. Two hours passed and they were having so much fun that they decided to all hang out together and get a takeaway. Amy felt safe with Max and was happy for him to spend time with her and the children.

Midnight came along and Jake and Scarlett went off to their bedrooms. Amy and Max stayed up talking and before long it was 4 am. 'My god look at the time, I need to get to some sleep I need to be up in two hours, how am I going to do that?' she groaned.

'Well I'll get myself home and leave you to rest' Max replied.

'I hope you had fun and my kids didn't embarrass you with all those questions?'

'No they're great kids, I really enjoyed their company, and you've done a great job with them.'

Max held Amy's hand in his and stared into her eyes. Then he pulled her slowly closer to him and put his lips carefully to hers and kissed her. Amy kissed him back and put her hands around the back of his neck and caressed him, and he put his hands on her cheeks, still kissing her.

'I have waited so long for that' he said. 'I didn't want to push you, you're different, I don't think I have ever met someone like you. I can't believe the amount of times I saw you on the train and I never spoke to you. I'm really glad I knocked your bag on to the tracks that day.'

Amy smiled 'I'm glad too' and they kissed again before he left.

The next date they had, Max took Amy to the zoo, which she found kind of strange, but they ended up having the best time. Then a few days later he took her and the kids out for a meal and on to the cinema. Amy was still holding back from Max. She didn't want to fall in love and she didn't want the problems that came with relationships, but it was hard. They got on so well and the kids loved him. At least she knew that if it didn't work out they would definitely always be friends.

CHAPTER TWENTY ONE

The next date went just as well as all the others. They spent the evening talking and laughing over a meal in Brooklyn's Park Slope and again when they walked into the venue they were treated like royalty. On the way home Amy asked him why everyone looked as if they were afraid of him.

'Are you some sort of Russian prince or something?' she said.

Max replied with a laugh. 'No, I think it's just working in the restaurant industry we all gotta impress each other.'

'Oh OK' she replied. But Max knew it was because of who his father was. He needed to start keeping away from these places, or he needed to tell Amy about his dark past.

'Amy, I need to tell you something, I… I really like you' Max told her. But Amy felt there was something else he wanted to say instead.

'Oh, well that's nice, I like you too' she said. 'I have never really got on with a guy as well as this. I'm really enjoying your company.'

After the meal Max grabbed her arm as they approached the car and held her tightly next to him. Amy felt the blood rush to her head and her stomach did somersaults. They looked into each other's eyes and slowly came together. His lips softly caressed hers until they opened and passionately, as they kissed, Max put his arms around her and she put hers tightly around him. Slowing down, she whispered to him, asking if he wanted to come back to hers for a drink as the kids were away.

'If you're sure then I would love to' he whispered back in her ear.

They kissed for a little longer, then stopped and smiled at each other. 'Wow, that was pretty nice', he said to her as they separated to get into the car. Amy laughed at him and jumped into her side. Half an hour later they arrived back in Massapequa and Amy got out a bottle of wine and they plonked themselves on the sofa. Another two hours passed quickly as they were talking and talking, then Amy stopped, stood up and held out her hand to Max. Max stood up keeping his eyes on her and they pushed their bodies close together.

'Come upstairs' she whispered into his ear, and she led him up to her bedroom, guiding him to the bed and pushing him down softly on to it. In front of him she undressed herself, slowly unbuttoning her shirt and staring at him, never losing eye contact. Then she leaned towards him, pushing him back on to the bed and slowly unbuttoned his shirt, pushing it back off his shoulders. As she felt his warm soft skin against hers, she unzipped his jeans and pulled them down.

Max leaned up slightly and put his arms around her. Amy softly kissed his smooth firm chest and neck, and then he pushed her over and on to her back. He kissed all over her body and down to her lower stomach, teasing her.

Max felt the blood pumping in all the right areas of his body. He placed his hand down past her stomach, ending up on her knee. He grabbed it and lifted her leg up, kissing it, before positioning himself in between her. She held him tighter and with her hand firmly on his bum Max pushed himself inside her, gently to start with. When he felt her wanting more and breathing heavier, he pressed himself harder and faster into her.

Amy grabbed his buttocks again, pushing him down, ensuring he hit every spot. He was giving her more pleasure than she had felt for a long time, keeping eye contact with her, kissing her, both of them breathing heavier and heavier until they held their breaths and experienced something neither of them had experienced before.

He carried on kissing her softly, and then lay back on the bed, both of them out of breath. He lifted up her hand, kissed it and turned to her.

'Are you OK?' he asked. She was still a little out of breath.

'Yeah, never better' she said, holding his hand tighter and turning to lie on his chest. Amy had never felt anything like this and it felt so good to actually have sex with someone and have strong feelings for them at the same time.

They lay in bed holding each other for the next two hours and talked some more.

'Max, at dinner earlier you mentioned you liked me but it felt like you had something else you wanted to say, did you?' Amy asked him.

'Oh, oh no I just wanted to say that' he stammered.

'Max if there is ever anything you want to talk to me about I hope you feel you can' she said. 'I have never spoken in depth about my life and feelings like this to anyone before. I trust you and I feel comfortable with you and I know you do too, but it feels like there is something more you want to say but can't. I don't know what it is, but please trust me.' She stroked his face. 'And if you ever want to talk about your Mom I am always here.'

He kissed her again. 'Amy, there's nothing more than what I have already told you', he said, and he looked away from her and raised himself up on the bed and placed his head down with his hand rubbing the back of his neck.

'Max,' Amy said knowing there was something he was about to say, 'What's wrong? What is it?'

'Amy, I do need to tell you something. I tried before and I just couldn't get it out' he said to her with his head still down.

'Max what is going on, are you married?' she asked jumping up and sitting in front of him.

'No no no, I'm not married, you're the only one I promise, I would never do that to you' he told her, looking into her eyes.

'Max, I promise I will understand whatever it is you have to tell me. Please be honest with me as I have been with you.'

Max turned away from her and put his feet on to the floor at the side of the bed.

'Amy, I have something to tell you about my past, but you need to understand that I am no longer that person nor am I involved in any of it anymore.'

Amy's eyes closed together slightly and she had a confused expression on her face. 'Max what is it?' she asked again.

Max took a deep breath. 'After my Mom died when I was just 15, my dad took us and had sole custody of my brother and me. My father is not a good man, Amy. He runs a ring of gangsters in Manhattan and West Queens and a few other towns. We were brought up into that. I managed to get my brother out. I had no choice at such a young age and he forced me into this dark underground world of it all. Amy, I only managed to get away from it all three years ago, and for those last three years I have been trying to forget it all. I tried to leave so many times before that, to get far away from them all, but my father and his mob were always there and because I had been part of this group there were people after me, and my father threatened to kill me. He said he would kill me if I left. He is one of the most feared Mafia bosses out there.'

He took another deep breath.

'So what are you saying?' she asked him. 'Are you trying to tell me you're a gangster or mobster or whatever and you have killed people? Do you have people after you?'

Amy couldn't believe what she was hearing. She started shaking. She was in her house with the son of one of the most powerful gangsters in the world.

'Amy please it's all over for me now, I have got out of it and I have nothing to do with those people including my father' he reassured her.

'Have you killed people?' she asked, still shaking.

'Amy, that was in the past.'

'So you have killed people?' she asked again.

Max couldn't reply. He held his head down.

'You have killed people! I can't believe this. How could you not tell me, you are part of the most notorious group of evil people in America! I need you to go!' she shouted at him with tears running down her face.

'Used to be, not anymore and I regret everything I have done, I had no choice having him as a father, I was forced into it and grew up around it. I hated every minute of that life and it's now so far behind me I promise you, you have to believe me!' he shouted back at her.

Amy chucked a T-shirt on and moved to the corner of her room. Max got up to walk towards her, pulling his jeans up.

'Stay back, don't come near me!' she cried.

'Amy please, you don't need to be scared of me, I won't hurt you, come on'.

'Get out!' she told him. 'So you thought you would sleep with me before you tell me this? Well that's really nice of you!'

'No Amy, it wasn't like that, I love you'.

She stared into his eyes as he did hers.

'I can't deal with this, I can't have someone from the Mafia, a murderer, around my children and I cannot believe you let me introduce them to you knowing this. There could be people after you and they could be watching right now. Please leave, I don't want to see you ever again.'

'OK Amy, I'll go' he said. He walked back to collect his clothes to prepare to leave. 'But I beg you, I need you to understand that when my Mom died my dad took over our lives and me being 15 at the time he forced me into the business, he had control over us. I tried to get out so many times, but then with the anger I had over the years after my mother had died I just felt there was nothing to live for and with the pressure from my father, I didn't want that life. Three years ago when I found out my father had caused my mother's death I went mad. I haven't been working with them or involved with them since then and it's the best fucking thing I have ever done. I am free from my past and I can guarantee no harm will ever come to me or anyone I am with. I can't believe you are going to let me walk out of here, I need you in my life, for the first time I finally meet someone that I actually care about. I love you and I'm sorry, so please don't forget that.' He turned his back and walked out of the bedroom and out of the front door.

Amy ran crying to the window to watch him walking down the front path and into his car. He stared back up at her, then jumped into his car and sped off.

In her room she fell to the floor crying. She couldn't believe what had just happened. After being with men over the last 15 years without feeling anything for them, the one man she had fallen in love with had to be a criminal who had actually taken the lives of people.

But sitting there, she didn't feel any less love for him. She had just realised that he had told her he loved her, and if anything her feelings seemed to be getting stronger for him. The sick feeling in her stomach knowing she wouldn't see him again felt horrible. Should she have let him explain further? Was it really his fault he ended up like that? And had he really left them and started a new life, or was he still with them?

With all these questions in her head, Amy spent the next five hours trying to sleep, but it wasn't working.

The next day, after just an hour's sleep, Amy called in sick to work. She couldn't bear to see anyone, and she needed to be alone to think about what happened last night. She felt as if she had been too hard on Max. She felt sad that he had grown up into this life but angry after all of the time they had spent together he couldn't tell her.

Max tried to call twice over the next couple of hours but she ignored her phone.

She didn't know what to do. She wanted to be with him so badly, but she feared that something would happen or would he end up being a monster months or years down the line, like the last relationship she had.

The kids were back the next morning, so at least she had a day to sort herself out, but all she could think about was Max. After a few more days she realised she couldn't be without him. She had to believe he had changed and that he was the right man for her regardless of his past. She had ignored him enough. He had struggled to get over his past for the last three years and by the sounds of what he had told her, he was happy to be separated from his father and was happy with his new life. Amy just felt she needed the time to think about this and whether it was the right thing to do, as there were children involved. She kept picturing the sadness on his face when she told him to leave and the pain he must have felt as he walked out of the house after what he had been through in his life.

When they returned home from their trip Jake and Scarlett kept on asking Amy how Max was and why they hadn't seen him over the last couple of days. They really liked Max and it was nice for them to have a young man in their lives; he was the only man she had ever introduced to them. She felt that as they were both in their mid-teens they would now understand relationships, and it was about time they saw their mother with someone she liked. But Amy couldn't tell them what had happened between her and Max. It was too soon, and she had to talk to him first.

Her friends all told her she should believe that he had changed. They had met him and they really liked him, and thought he was good for her regardless of his past.

Amy decided she would give him a call tomorrow. She missed him so badly and it was affecting her everyday life. Picturing her life without him was unbearable, even though they had only known each other for two months. She just hoped he would want to speak to her after she had ignored him over the last few days.

Later that evening she picked up the phone to dial his number, but it was as if he picked up the phone then put it down again. She tried again, but the call was forwarded to his voicemail as if he was deliberately ignoring her calls.

A few minutes later the doorbell went. As she was expecting the kids back she ran to the door to answer it, and to her surprise Max was standing there.

'Max, what are you doing here? I just tried to call you!' Amy asked, shocked.

'I cut you off because I wanted to speak to you face to face. Are the kids out?' he asked.

'Yeah they're out, but Max, listen, I need to tell you something, I need to tell you I am so sorry for how I have treated you over the last few days. I was shocked to hear of your past and was annoyed you didn't tell me before, but it scared me, I was worried. But after having a long think about it I knew I was out of order.'

'Amy please…' he interrupted.

'Max wait, I need to say this. I know what I said was wrong and it was just that you told me this after we slept together and I just felt as if you waited until then, but I know now you wouldn't do that to me now, and I understand how scary that must have been for you to have the courage to tell me about your past and how much I must mean to you for telling me that. I know now that your past was not your fault and that you've turned your life around and maybe if we talk a little more about it, it will become clearer to me why and how you went through that.'

Max just stepped forward and grabbed her tightly and kissed her. Amy didn't move, she was just glad he had her in his arms. She slowly put her arms around him too and closed the front door.

'Amy, I'm sorry I told you so late and believe me I tried to tell you before, but it was so hard, and I promise you I am free from that life, I have been for years now. You will never be in danger and I would never ever let anyone hurt you, ever. My life is as normal and regular and yours. I missed you so badly.' He grabbed her tighter and kissed her.

'Same here' she said as she stopped for a breath. 'Let's never let this happen again.'

Amy now knew that he was the one. Their love for each other was so intense, so passionate and loving. It was a feeling she had never thought existed, and even though she tried to avoid the feeling for as long as possible she was overcome by it and there was nothing she could do about it now. Max also felt the same, he had never in a million years thought the woman he would fall for would have two children, but he didn't care. He wasn't bothered about having children himself, so he was pretty glad hers were older and that he got on with them so well. In fact after meeting them a few times he felt he had known them and Amy a lot longer.

For the next hour Max explained further about his childhood with his mother and losing her. Then he told her everything else, not missing a thing, and explained the things his father had made him do and how scared of him he was.

After this Amy knew she needed to look after Max emotionally after what he had been through. He needed a good woman in his life and she was there to do the job.

CHAPTER TWENTY TWO

Weeks went by and their relationship grew stronger and stronger. They went on holiday to Paris together and took a trip to Florida with the kids.

After a few months Amy spoke to Jake and Scarlett about how they would feel if she was to ask Max if he wanted to move in with them in the new year, maybe around April or May. She had not mentioned it to Max before because she thought it only right to discuss it with the kids first. Jake and Scarlett expressed their happiness about the idea, especially Jake who really wanted another male in the house.

A few weeks later, after having her friends around for thanksgiving dinner and the kids had gone to bed, Amy was about to bring it up when Max turned to her and asked her first. 'How would you feel about us moving in together maybe next year sometime?' he said. 'I'm always at your place, I live in a three bedroom house that I hardly ever use.'

Amy replied by saying that was the best idea she had heard for a while, and to do it in another four or five months seemed perfect. It would give Max time to put his house on the market and it would give them more time in their relationship to prepare for it. It had been a long time since Amy lived with a man, so it was a lot to get her head around, but every day their relationship grew and Jake and Scarlett became more and more attached to him. They loved to see their mother happy and loved the friendship they had with Max.

CHAPTER TWENTY THREE

With his travels over, Henrik arrived back into JFK. After the length of time he had travelling he was still shocked at the history he had read about in that old book. He knew there was truth to the stories and believed that should a similar date come up in the future, as the stories stated, their prediction would come true.

He stopped to think about when the next date would arrive. 'The 12th day of the 12th month of the year ending 12 after four millennia' he thought aloud. 'Oh my god – that's just less than three weeks away! Why did I not realise that before?'

His heart started to race. He had two weeks and six days to prepare the world for what was about to happen. For all he knew he too could be an angel. How would anyone believe this? They would think he was a mad old fool. Even if he managed to go back and get the papers and the books, show everyone the stories, they still wouldn't believe him. And how was he going to warn everyone that there might also be devils among us, ready and waiting for the angels to appear? They might have grown in numbers, and the Iblisari were more than likely still out there. One thousand one hundred and twelve angels would appear on this planet in a matter of weeks, and if no one acknowledged his plea for preparation, they would end up being slaughtered again.

They would need to find a safe place to work on their powers before they came in contact with the devils. Then they might have the abilities to overcome the danger that the other angels didn't have the chance to.

'What to do, what to do?' he asked himself. Even his wife Barbell probably wouldn't believe him.

Finally Henrik arrived at the front door of his house. Barbell answered the door with open arms and a hot meal ready and waiting for him. They cuddled for a minute, but she knew something was up.

'What is wrong dear?' she asked softly.

'I have so much to tell you about my findings' he replied. He took a seat at the dining table and started his story from start to finish.

'Darling, that's a wonderful story but it is just that, a story' she said, looking sorry for him. 'There are many magical and mystical stories out there from many years ago, and even though some of the stories may have been just a little bit true, they just wouldn't happen in this day and age.'

'But they could, they must have happened and especially this story. The last one happened in 2012 BC and will happen again in 2012 AD, I can feel it' he said abruptly.

'It is going to happen, and it will happen, 20 days from now. The chosen ones will appear as angels, so when the 12th day of the 12th month of the 12th year is here, the 12th December, that's when the world will change forever.'

Barbell just stared at him, worried about how he might start turning a little crazy with this. She just hoped it wouldn't take over his life.

The next day Henrik got up at 5 am after a sleepless night. He went downstairs to his computer and started to search 'angelology', hoping to find a group of teachers who would know a bit more about this. He needed to spread the word and get the information out about what was going to happen.

Looking through various web pages, he stumbled across a professor he had known many years before who was now teaching history at Harvard. Henrik knew he was very much into the history of angels and devils and if he could find his old address book with Dr Luciano Konte's own personal numbers in it, that would be a good start. He couldn't go out and preach to the world about what was going to happen until he had received a little help and advice first.

Rooting through cupboards and desks searching for the book he had misplaced months ago, he became stressed. He couldn't find it anywhere, and he knew Dr Konte's details were in there.

'Henrik', Barbell called, 'what in God's name are you doing down there at this time?'

'Nothing dear' he shouted out, 'go back to sleep, I will be up in a minute.'

He finally found the book and Luciano's number. He researched a bit more. Then he waited for the sun to come up before he dialled the number he had in his book. After two rings the phone was answered by a man's voice.

'Dr Konte speaking?'

'Ah Luciano, it's Henrik from New York, Henrik Orsson' he said.

'Henrik, how good to hear from you, how have you been and for what do I owe this pleasure so early in the morning?' Dr Konte replied.

Henrik was relieved his friend had recognised him. After finding out what each other had been up to over the years, Henrik advised him of what he had seen and read on his travels. Dr Konte knew exactly what he was talking about and explained that he had heard vague stories of certain things that had happened back then. He had known a man a few years ago who attempted to go down into the lost underworld temples over 40 years ago and was able to write of some of the things he had seen, but he had not come out alive.

'Henrik, you are lucky to be here' he said. 'This information is vital. Luckily you found this out so we can prepare, should this actually happen.'

Henrik told him he had left all of the books in their original places and only taken out the memory of the stories. He also explained about the stone and that it was nowhere to be found. 'OK, we must meet soon and discuss this and work out what to do' said Dr Konte. 'We must discuss what will happen if angels appear, or if the devils also appear. We have a hell of a lot to talk about. I have some other people we should also meet with who have great interest and knowledge about this.'

The men then arranged to meet two days later. When the day of the meeting came they discussed what information they had and prepared for what they should do when it happened. Over the next few days Henrik attempted to advise the world about what could happen by writing to newspapers, contacting the government, and even preaching on radio shows if he was allowed, but no one believed him. The public all thought he was just another crazy old man. Even Amy had to have words with him about what he was doing. Henrik ended up handing out leaflets and pinning up posters, but no one took any notice, and Amy and Barbell started to worry about him.

CHAPTER TWENTY FOUR

Meanwhile across the globe, all the most evil people in the world who had decided to take their dark secrets further came together into little groups and cults to see what they could do should the angels appear, and how they would get this stone and hold on to it before they were wiped out. The devils knew everything about the historical stories of the angels the stone. They had spent the last 4000 years searching for it, but it was nowhere to be found. Over the last few years they believed they had come closer to finding it, but they had now realised that the angels would know no more than them as to its whereabouts. They had to prepare themselves in case the angels got their hands on the stone, and the only way of doing this was to kill each and every one of them.

All the devils involved in the Iblisari knew of the history and what the stone was about and what they needed to do to take over the world, or at least keep evil on Earth.

Each of the Iblisari sister groups had a leader, someone who was evil and with no heart. There was also a main leader in each country, one who was far evil than anyone else, and in New York it was Vladimir, the Russian Mafia boss. He and his men ran the top Iblisari cult in the world. Vladimir called on as many of these people as he could find. He had word from other leaders from around the country and they were all set and prepared. They held no bars when it came to destroying these angels, though of course it would not be as easy to do it as it had been four millennia earlier.

They would have to be careful, and of course there would be protection and security all over the place. Vladimir was given the duty of being the Iblisari leader, as he seemed the most powerful.

There was nothing they could do for now. They would have to wait until 12/12/12 to see if the information from this old man and the history they all knew about would come to life or not, but from what they knew about their history they were confident it would happen.

CHAPTER TWENTY FIVE

Two weeks on, Amy was realising how happy she was with her life. She had wanted something interesting to happen, and it had. She just hadn't thought it would involve her falling in love, but she was happy for now and that was just how she liked it.

On Wednesday 12th December, she arrived at work early. 'Hey guys', she shouted across the office as she sat at her desk and noticed the large pile of paperwork she had to get through. 'Ah man, I forgot about this shit', she muttered to herself. Amy had planned to get off work early to do a bit of Christmas shopping with the kids.

'Hey Amy, did you have a good evening?' Steve asked her as he passed her desk.

'Yeah it was OK, Max took me out for a meal, then went home and relaxed, nothing too exciting' she replied. 'You?'

'It was all right. Oh well, another Wednesday in the office. But don't forget the date today.'

'What's up with the date?' she asked.

'Well it's the twelfth of the twelfth of the twelfth.'

Amy looked confused.

'You know, the day the angels come out.'

'Ha' she replied, 'you don't really believe that crap, do you?' She squinted at him and nodded her head in disagreement.

'Aw man, course not, but you gotta take the piss, right?' he said, laughing. 'I mean come on, does anyone believe there are actual angels on this planet? People with big wings who are stronger than normal humans? I don't think so!'

'I know, it's ridiculous' she said, 'but I know the guy that went public about it, he's a good friend and neighbour. I just don't know what the hell got into him but I do know he is pretty sane and a real good guy. I mean I spoke to him a few times about it and he is so adamant it's going to happen, I worry he must be kinda losing it at times. I guess after today he will realise it's a load of crap.' She felt sorry for Henrik.

As they were talking, Sam and Paul, the office comedians, walked in with fake wings stuck onto their backs. The whole office laughed.

'How did I know you guys would do something like that?' Steve said. Sam and Paul also laughed.

'Well hey I'm a good person, I have the qualities to see through people and I have the ability to be highly intelligent, so I must be an angel', Sam shouted across the office as he walked up to his desk.

Everyone then sat at their desks after hearing the boss come out of his office telling everyone to get on with their work. They all made a few wisecracks about the whole angel scenario, and even though they knew it wouldn't happen they still waited. It was on the news, on the radio and online, from people who believed it would happen to people making practical jokes about it.

'Hey Tinny, how are you?' Amy asked as she walked by reception to get a coffee from across the street.

'I'm good, looking forward to see if I know any angels today' she said, knowing she looked stupid.

'Oh god, come on, not you too?' Amy sighed at her. Amy always knew Trinny was a little bit of a daydreamer, a nice girl but simple never the less.

'Don't you believe?' Trinny asked her.

'No sorry but I don't, it's not possible.' Trinny put on a sad face, Amy felt sorry for. 'Well Trinny you could be right, we'll see by midnight right?' she told her, as if she were interested.

'Yes midnight it is' replied Trinny, smiling again.

'OK cool, did you want a coffee?'

'Uh, no thank you babes'.

'All right, see you in a bit.'

Amy went for her much-needed three-shot latte. She had felt a bit queasy since this morning and her body ached a bit, as if she were about to get the flu.

Halfway through the pile of paperwork on her desk, Amy lay back in her chair and put her feet up on the desk, something she only ever did when the boss was away. 'Man, I cannot be bothered to do any more work today' she said to Suzy and James, who were sitting opposite her.

'Hear hear' they both replied.

'Oh well it's brunch, what do you guys wanna do?' Suzy asked. 'I kinda just want to get this done so I can go early; I'm meeting the kids at Bloomingdales to do a bit of shopping. Is it eleven yet?'

'Two minutes to' James said, as he prepared to leave his desk. 'See you guys in a bit, I'm going over.' He walked out of the office after telling Suzy to meet him at the café in ten minutes.

Amy got up from her desk to go to the kitchen for a glass of water, but as she rose from her chair she felt a sudden overwhelming feeling of warmth all over her body. It was a strange relaxing feeling, but as she stood up she suddenly she fell back in to her chair. She felt strange as she tried to get back up. She couldn't lift herself out of it, and now she had started to feel a niggling pain in her back.

'What's wrong hon?' Suzy asked, preparing herself to go over to meet James in the café.

'My back feels weird, I don't know what the hell it is' she replied in an uncomfortable voice. She tried again to get up. 'Ahh!' she screamed as she bent backwards. Now an excruciating pain was running through her shoulders, and she heard a crunching around her shoulder blades.

'Shit Amy you're freaking me out!' shouted Suzy, looking terrified.

Amy screamed again and now the whole office was staring at her. Julia ran over asking if she needed help, as she was a first aider. Amy carried on crying and screaming, constantly moving her shoulders, the pain getting worse and worse.

'Should we call an ambulance?' a worker called out.

'No, no, I think I have just hurt my back' she shouted to everyone. And then she blacked out, slumping back on her chair.

The workers in the office all crowded around her, thinking she was either having a seizure or a heart attack. Then Julie gave her a light shake and she regained consciousness. Five seconds later, with another painful scream, she rose a little from her chair and her back made another loud cracking noise.

'Go away everyone, leave me!' she screamed. Suzy and Julia shooed everyone back to their desks.

A few seconds went by and then suddenly Amy felt another loud crunch and this time a spasm followed in her shoulder blades and she felt her clothes rip. She put her arms round to feel her back, but she couldn't reach the spot where the pain was. She heard a ripping noise as if razors were scraping her shoulders. Then she felt warm liquid ooze out of her, dripping down her back as she tried to get up again.

'Am I bleeding?' she moaned.

'Oh Jesus you are!' Suzy cried. 'Oh my god, there is something coming out of your back!' She ran to the corner to vomit.

'What, what is it? What the hell is coming out of my back? Why am I bleeding?' Amy cried out loud. She felt and heard tears in her back like someone ripping a cotton sheet in two halves. Then she screamed louder than ever and threw her head down again on to her desk, numbed by the pain.

For a few seconds there was quiet throughout the entire office. Then there were gasps, and cries of shock and horror.

Amy raised herself up. The pain had now stopped, but she felt heavy and strange. She could see everyone looking at her with shocked and surprised faces, and as she stood up she could see at the corner of her eye something hovering over her. She twisted her neck around to see two large, brightly-coloured objects that seemed to be stuck on her back.

'What the fuck?' she said. She thought it was a joke and tried to grab the things behind her to rip them off, but then realised they were not moving and that they were feathers, thick, soft, large feathers coming out of her back.

She needed a mirror. She took a few steps over to the office mirror to see what her reflection was like. She looked away until she was standing directly in front of it. Then she looked up, and gasped in shock.

A pair of large, sparkling wings were coming out of her back.

'Ahh!' she gasped, placing her hand over her mouth. 'Oh my god what happened, what's happening?' she shouted across the office.

Everyone in the office was still very quiet, shocked at what they had just witnessed. Again Amy turned around to try and grab these strange things that were sticking out of back. She tried to rip them off again, but they were stuck firmly to her body.

She fell to the floor crying. Suzy walked over to her, a little scared

'Amy, Amy, are you OK?' Amy slowly looked up at her with pain in her eyes. 'You look absolutely stunning Amy, I'm sorry but that's all I can say, it's a miracle, I cannot believe this has happened.' She smiled and held out her hand to help her up. Amy pushed herself up with Suzy's help.

'This can't be real Suzy, what the fuck is happening here? I can't believe this' she said. She turned around to the mirror again to look at the wings. Now she saw other changes. Her hair was shinier and thicker and two inches longer. Her skin was clear and glowing. She didn't understand what it was but she could see that she looked very different.

She turned back to see everyone looking at her in the office and stared at them. They were all quiet until James walked through the door with his leftover breakfast roll and a coffee in his hands ready to sit at his desk.

'Suzy, you took way too long, making me sit there alone like I'd been stood up by a date, you didn't answer your phone, what the hell?' he asked as he looked directly at his desk and walked towards it without noticing the angel standing at the mirror. 'Hey, have you heard the news? Goddam it, there are angels in the world. Apparently there have been a handful of people already online that have turned into angels. A guy in South Africa, two people in England and a few in Australia so far anyway, and I know that old guy said there would be over a thousand angels, but I won't believe it until I see it.'

Now he was logging on to his computer, still not looking up at everyone standing around Amy. But as he reached his for his pen, he could see at the corner of his eye that everyone was standing over at one side. He finally looked up and saw Amy standing there, with wings sticking out of her back.

'Wow, that looks real convincing Amy' he said, laughing slightly and looking nervous, not knowing whether it was a joke or not. 'How did you get that done?' He walked towards her to see if he could touch the wings. Amy stood still and as he walked towards her, the closer he got the more real they looked.

'It's real!' one of the workers shouted out. 'You just missed some serious shit man.' He turned back to her. 'Amy, you're an angel, for real, so the old man was right?' he said, starting to get excited. 'This is unreal man, what the fuck!' he said again and again.

He touched her wings. 'Wow, they are real' he said, looking under every feather and inspecting exactly how and where the wings were connected to her body. Then everyone else came forward and circled around her. No one really knew what to say. Before long the other floors of the office had come to the glass doors to see the angel.

Amy was now a fully-fledged angel. She walked back to her desk, still saying very little. Sam and Steve asked if she could try to fly and other workers asked if she could punch a hole in the stone wall to check her strength. Suzy and Julia shouted at everyone to go take a break or get back to work; they didn't want Amy to feel too abnormal, because they knew she was still the same person.

Amy sat at her desk and took a few deep breaths. 'Right I need to compose myself' she said to herself. 'I need to speak to Henrik and to the kids and my family. What the hell am I going to tell everyone?' she moaned. 'Right, Henrik first' she whispered to herself.

'Amy, we will be in the kitchen, so give us a shout if you need us, go make the call' Suzy told her, and everyone then gave her some privacy. Amy called Henrik, but his phone was busy. She then tried his landline and that was busy too, so she left a message for him to call her ASAP. She couldn't wait, so she attempted to call the two numbers again and again and again until she got through to Barbell.

'Barbell, hi it's Amy, is Henrik there?'

'Amy, have you heard the news? Have you seen that there are angels, real angels out there?' Barbell excitedly asked her,

'Yes I have seen it' Amy replied. 'I really need to speak with Henrik right now.'

'He is speaking to someone important right now, I think it's the government', Barbell said.

'Well please get him off the phone, it's really important. I'm scared Barbell, I have turned into an angel myself.' She couldn't believe she was actually saying this.

'What? You *have*?'

'Yes Barbell, I'm a friggin' angel, please get Henrik to the phone! I never took too much notice of what he said before and I'm kinda panicking right now!'

Barbell shouted to Henrik, 'Henrik, its Amy on the phone, she says she's an angel, she needs to speak with you right now!' Amy heard Henrik slamming down the phone and running over to pick the phone up from Barbell.

'Amy, what is it?' he said sounding worried, Barbell told me...'

Amy butted in before he could finish. 'I have wings Henrik, wings, big ugly ones, and my body has changed, I look different, what's happening to me?' she cried as she spoke to him. 'This can't be happening, there are wings coming out of my back, damn it!'

'Amy, calm down' Henrik said in a soothing voice. 'You need to listen to me. You are one of the chosen humans. This means you are one of the most precious people on this planet, and there are more like you, the reports are coming in thick and fast from all over the world. I told you this would happen, but so many people did not believe me.'

'But what's going to happen to me? What about the kids, will they be like this too?' she cried.

'Highly unlikely my dear,' he told her. 'There is next to no chance you would have a child with the qualities that lead to becoming an angel. It is not hereditary, there are traits angels need to have, and only the lord above or whoever is in charge of this can decide.'

Amy hoped to God the children would not be like this.

'You will be required to go to a meeting with Dr Luciano Konte' said Henrik. 'He teaches history at Harvard and studies angelology with a group in his spare time. He is an old and good friend of mine. There you and all of the other angels will congregate and find out more information as to how you go forward, how this has happened and all the other information about this. I can assure you your life will be able to go on and you will be able to lead a normal life'.

'What, are you serious, lead a normal life with wings stuck on my back like a freak show? I just can't believe this is happening. Is there any way this can be reversed?' she asked, still trembling with shock.

'I really don't know what will come of this, but I do know the wings won't be visible all the time, they will appear and disappear regularly' he told her in a reassuring voice. 'I know you will be able to control them in time and this will be something that you will have to get used to. You will be taught many different things by Dr Konte and his people when you meet. However you must keep him and his team a secret for now, as it may jeopardise their careers'.

Amy took some deep breaths. 'Are you at home? I'm meant to be meeting the kids at four to go shopping, how am I going to tell them this?'

'Amy, I don't know what to say, I will be at home all day so call me after you speak with Jake and Scarlett and I will pop over. I will be able to take you through the history in full so you have some understanding of what you need to do.'

'OK' she replied, and hung up.

Her wings were still there as she put the phone down. They were a meter wide each side and at least two meters tall. They sparkled brightly in shades of grey, white and gold with spots of light pink. They were thick and strong and swayed softly as she moved.

Sitting back down at her desk, she rested her chin on both of her hands with her elbows on the table. Everyone asked her if there was anything they could do. 'No, no thank you guys, I just need a few minutes to take this all in' she said. She sighed and closed her eyes.

They all returned to their desks and within seconds she felt weightless again. She opened her eyes and looked behind her. Her wings had disappeared.

She jumped up. 'They've gone!' she shouted, and the guys in the office turned around to see the normal Amy standing there. She grabbed all of her bits and her bag and ran out of the office, hoping to get home before the wings reappeared. As she passed Trinny she kept her head down, but although Trinny was talking to someone else she jumped up. 'Amy, did you hear?' she shouted, but Amy walked quickly out of the building ignoring her altogether. When she was out of the building she called Jake.

'Hi Jake, have you finished school yet?'

'Yeah, we had a half day remember? We're on our way home, then we're coming to meet you, we're going shopping right?'

'Jake, something has come up. I want you guys to wait at home, I am on my way there' she said to him quickly.

'What's happened?' he asked.

'Just be there!' She raised her voice. 'No one has died so don't worry about things like that.'

'OK man' he replied. 'Mom, have you heard there are actual angels? How freaking cool is that!'

'Jake, I'll see you in an hour' she said as she pressed the end call button and threw her phone into her bag.

CHAPTER TWENTY SIX

Amy walked up the path to her house. Then she suddenly stopped before she reached the front door and thought about how she was going to do this, how she was going to tell two teenagers, the two people that knew her most in the world, that she was an angel. Would they freak out? Would they be excited? Would they think it was a silly joke? She had no idea how she was going to tell them and whether they would even believe her. All she knew was that she could not keep this from them. She wanted it out in the open straight away.

She stood at the front door and started looking for her keys. The door opened straight away.

'Hey mom', Scarlett greeted her, 'Jake said you needed to talk to us about something important? Oh man, does that mean we're not going shopping?'

'Yes I have something to tell you, and no, we are not going shopping, not today anyway, but let me get through the door first will you?'

'Come into the kitchen when you're ready guys' she shouted loudly so Jake could hear her from his room over his loud music. He strolled down to the kitchen from his room and gave her a kiss on the cheek.

'So what's up?' they both said at the same time.

'Guys enough, calm down, take a seat, I have something really important to tell you' she said.

'Hey, did you hear about the angels Mom, it's all over the news, Henrik next door has had people knocking on his door for the last hour, I think they're journalists and people from the government like men in black. He was right!' Scarlett sounded excited.

'Arron from school reckons his grandma turned into one, but he's probably talking crap' said Jake.

'Guys, be quiet!' Amy raised her voice over them. 'Something happened to me today, something very serious.'

'What Ma?' they both said, looking worried.

She took a deep breath and swallowed. 'Guys, what happened to those people today, the angels, well… well… ' she took a long pause and looked down. 'Well, it happened to me.'

'Mom, be serious man' Jake responded.

'Mom come on', Scarlett added.

'I am serious. I was at work and it happened. I don't know how to explain further, but I am freaking out right now and I don't know what the hell to do, everyone in the office saw it.'

'Well, where are your wings now then?' Jake asked, still thinking it was a joke.

'Jake, the wings are not constantly out, they come and go apparently. I spoke to Henrik and he will be coming over shortly to explain a bit more about what the hell is happening to me. Kids, this is no joke. I don't know what the hell happened today but I can assure you I had wings the size of a small car stuck to my friggin back.'

'Mom, if this is right and you are an angel, then that's so cool, I hope you're not joking!' Scarlett asked her.

'Scarlett honey, this happened to me today and it's not friggin cool and it really hurt, I was in serious pain' she said sternly.

'This is so cool Mom! Can I put it on Facebook?' Jake asked.

'No!' she shouted at him. 'Guys, for the second time, this is serious!'

Just then they heard a knock on the door. Jake ran out of the kitchen to answer it. It was Henrik. They all greeted Henrik as he entered the kitchen area.

'Afternoon all' Henrik said and smiled. He looked at Amy as if to ask if she had told the kids. 'I've told them about what happened, I don't think they actually understand though' she told him.

'Yes we do understand Mom, you're an angel!' Scarlett said excitedly.

Henrik joined them around the table to explain a bit more of what he knew. 'Amy, kids, I am still in shock to find I was right, a part of me thought this wouldn't happen' he said. 'I thought I was going mad myself. It all started on the trip I went on to Iraq's ancient cities'.

He sat back and explained to them his findings, along with the letters, diaries and stories he had read. The first thing he mentioned was that the stories did not end well, because the angels had not had enough practice and did not know anything about their new lives. He said it had happened long ago and times were different now.

Two hours passed and Amy and the kids were the quietest they had ever been, engrossed by the stories Henrik was telling them. They started to worry when they heard the story about the slaughter of the angels. Henrik reassured them again that they were different times and things like that were not likely to happen as they did thousands of years ago, and should the devils also appear we would now have the powers to be able to control them.

'There will be obstacles to pass, but at the moment your mother will need to meet up with a group of angelologists over the next few days and weeks. I will also attend along with all the angels to go through what has happened and to delve deeper into the story. The more we know about the situation, the more they will be able to protect themselves and others. Barbell can watch over you guys while your mother goes on these trips, if there is no one else. I know you are old enough to look after yourselves but she will be able to keep an eye on you. Is that OK Amy? You will need to go to these meeting. They will be very, very important.'

'But you have just told us what happened at one of these

meetings four thousand years ago' said Amy. 'The angels were slaughtered! What if it happens again?'

'Listen, that was many years ago. I can guarantee the meetings will be safe. They will be with my friends and security will be high all over the place. What happened years ago will hopefully never happen again. I'm not saying there won't be devils out there, but that is what the meetings are for, to prepare for such things. Many years ago the angels were tricked by an evil man.'

'OK, I understand, and yes, I'm fine with Barbell watching over the kids, but they will be off to stay with my brother from Saturday for a couple of days, so they will be OK for the first meeting. Kids, are you OK with that?'

'Yeah we'll be fine, but we're going to be worried about you Ma', Scarlett said.

'Scarlett will be very safe' Henrik assured them. 'There will be plenty of security, not that it's needed. They will be fine. Let's not forget you have great strengths now. These angels are stronger and more intelligent that the angels from years ago.'

'Kids, I don't want you telling the whole world about this' said Amy. 'I need to speak to your grandparents and everyone else and especially Max. He has no idea. Obviously my wings can come out at any time and when this happens there will be no way I can hide them. That's another reason I have to go to on this trip, to meet the other angels and teachers. We will all be able to find out how to control when our wings come out and when we can get them to disappear, how to control our strengths, how to levitate and how to ensure we come out on top. There is just so much to find out and learn.'

'Well, I just want to see your wings, I want to see you fly and beat someone up!' Jake said, getting excited.

'Jake, for God's sake, I won't be beating anyone up, even if my strengths are now here permanently! Look, I think we should get on and do things as normal, we won't be able to go out shopping because I will probably have to stay indoors for the next 24 hours at least, so the most important question is what do you guys want for dinner? Will you stay for dinner Henrik?'

'Oh no, thank you but Barbell has something on, I will get back and update her with what's going on, she'll be dying to know' he smiled. 'Kids, everything will be OK. You are truly blessed to have an angel for a mother, because she really is something special.

'Well I must get back now, I've had everyone knocking on my door today from newspapers to government officials. It's been a long day and I'm sure it's been a hell of a lot worse for you Amy.'

Amy smiled at him and walked him to the front door.

'Thank you for explaining everything and reassuring the kids. I really don't think they are aware of what this may turn into, but then again nor am I, so we will have to just wait and see. I'll speak to you tomorrow.' She closed the front door, took a long deep sigh and pressed her back against it with her head back, then closed her eyes. There was another bang at the door.

'It's me again, Henrik, sorry' he said as she opened the door. 'I just wanted to let you know that the pain you felt today would be the last of it. When your wings appear again there should be no or very little pain. Goodnight.'

'Well thank God for that' she said to him as she closed the door for a second time.

As she tried to compose herself she thought of one person. 'Oh shit!' she whispered. 'Max!' She worried about telling him. She couldn't involve him in this. How was she going to tell him- or should she tell him at all? He might think she was a freak and run away. She couldn't tell him, no way.

She pulled herself together and walked back into the kitchen where the kids were preparing dinner. 'Mexican? Just what I fancy' she said picking herself up and smiling. 'Kids, one more thing, I don't want Max knowing about this, it's embarrassing enough for me and I need time to work out how to tell him, so please keep it to yourselves until I'm ready. Oh, and don't forget your other trip too, you guys are going to have to go to your grandparents alone next Thursday until the 23rd, you know I have to sort this mess out, I hope you understand. I'll drop you to the station that day. You're looking forward to seeing them I hope?'

'Yeah, but are you really going to be OK on your own?' Jake asked, looking worried.

'Yes, I'll be fine. I have a lot to do so I'll be well occupied, and I have to go on that trip so don't you worry about me. In fact it will be better you guys have these trips booked, because I could do with a bit of time to sort this out. And you want to collect Christmas presents, don't you?' she reminded them. They looked at each other raising their eyebrows.

'Oh yes, of course' said Scarlett.

She gave them both a kiss and left them to cook while she took a shower.

CHAPTER TWENTY SEVEN

When Amy undressed in front of the mirror, she looked at her back through the other mirrors on her walls. It still hurt after what it had gone through earlier, but she was surprised to see that there were no scars at all, considering the wings had ripped through her skin and bone. Her back felt like it had been broken in five different places and she hoped the next time it happened it would be a lot less painful, as Henrik promised.

Before she stepped in to the shower her phone rang. It was Max. She couldn't answer it so she left it ringing. Two minutes later a text message appeared.

MAX: *Hey babe, how was yr day? I am so tired but I want to see you. How about I cook you dinner later?*

She didn't reply. She just turned her phone off, got into the shower and wept as she let the warm water run down her face and body.

Amy had difficulty sleeping during the night. If she wasn't tossing and turning she was having nightmares and thinking about how she would break the news to other people about what had happened and what she had become. At 3 am she got up and walked over to the window to look outside. She felt as if she was overheating, so she opened up the window. The cool breeze that came through the small opening felt good on her skin and she started to relax, taking deep breaths.

Amy walked over to pick up her phone and turned it on. Max had texted three more times.

MAX: *Hey, is everything OK?*
MAX: *I just remembered yr out shopping with Jake and Scarlett so call me when yr back. X*
MAX: *I'm kinda worried now, are you OK?*

She hated ignoring him, but she didn't know what to say to him. She thought back to a few months ago and wished she had ended the relationship when she had found out about his past, as she wouldn't have had to do it now. Even though she didn't want to, it sure as hell would have been easier. But either way, she had to end their relationship.

She felt a tear run down her face as she sat on the chair looking out at the stars and the street lights. Then she felt a sudden thud on her back. She could see out of the corner of her eye that the wings were back. At least there was a lot less pain this time.

She stood up and closed the curtains but kept the window open and walked over to the light to turn it on. She turned to the mirror to have a good look at the monstrosities on her back. As she stared longer and longer she noticed for the first time, looking at her face and body, that she was prettier than usual. Her teeth, skin and hair looked so much brighter and her body more toned and curvy. The wings were indeed very beautiful, such lovely colours and so soft. She couldn't believe how big they were.

Amy started to try and move them, which was difficult at first, but once she got the hang of it, it became easier and easier. However, they were so large that every time she moved them they caused everything in her bedroom, including items on her dressing table, to blow all over the room, as if there was a gale force wind. She still hated them, no matter how beautiful they looked, and wished this had not happened to her, but it had, and there was nothing she could do about it.

Amy tried to raise herself from the ground, but she knew the ceiling in her room was too low, so she crept downstairs and past the dogs; they didn't bat an eyelid. Then she went into the kitchen, picked up the back door key and went out into the garden.

Taking a few deep breaths, she fluttered her wings, trying hard to go faster and faster, but nothing was happening. She tried again, and suddenly she rose up in the air about a metre high. She panicked and her wings stopped beating, leaving her falling to the floor with a large thud. Picking herself up, she tried again. A light sprinkling of snow was falling from the dark skies and even though she only had a pair of shorts and a vest on she felt warm and relaxed.

Flapping her wings again to pick up more speed, she pushed herself from the ground with a small jump and slowly she started to levitate. Now she was two metres from the ground. Her wings still flapping, she managed to go higher until she was four metres up.

It felt wonderful. She had never felt so free. She started to laugh; it felt so extraordinary, an inexplicable feeling of exhilaration. However she could only stay up there for a few minutes with her fear of heights, so she lowered herself to a couple of metres from the ground and practised a little more at that height.

'Oh my god', Amy heard Scarlett shout from the upstairs hall window. 'Shit!' she shouted. Her wings stopped and she fell to the ground again. She looked up, but the kids had left the hall and she could hear them thudding down the stairs.

'Oh my god Mom, that was amazing, your wings are awesome!' Scarlett shouted as they both ran outside to get a closer look, 'I can't believe it, you really are an angel, you look so beautiful!' She reached out to touch her mother's wings.

'Mom, this is freaking heavy' Jake added. 'I can't believe you can fly.'

'Jake, I am just levitating, not flying' she corrected him.

'Whatever man, do it again, please?'

'Guys, it's hard work you know' she said, but she stood up straight and told them to move back.

'Right, you ready?' She flapped her wings again and was able to get her feet off the ground within seconds. Levitating in front of them seemed so weird; their faces were shocked and mesmerized at the same time.

'Mom you look amazing, really, really amazing', Scarlett shouted. 'You have got to tell Max Mom, he won't care, he will love it!'

Amy lowered herself back down. 'Jake, Max and I are going to need a break for a bit while I sort myself out.

'But…'. Jake moaned.

'But nothing keep out of it young man' she replied.

They all walked back into the house.

'So what do you think now guys?' She was hoping for approval.

'We think it's cool, you're still the same person, and nothing is going to change now you're a superhero' Scarlett joked. Amy nodded her head and they all walked inside laughing, without noticing her wings had disappeared.

'Well I guess that's all the excitement done for the day, so off to bed. You guys need to be up for school and I'll be needing a lie in, so please don't get me up before ten.'

'Ok, night Ma, love ya' they both said tiredly as they walked back up the stairs.

'Love you too guys'.

CHAPTER TWENTY EIGHT

Amy felt a little better than she had earlier, but she would still rather be normal. The next step was to tell her family first thing in the morning and then get the girls to come around for dinner tomorrow evening to explain to them, but right now it was time for some sleep, and she hoped to god she would be able to get some.

As she lay in bed she looked at her phone and read over the messages from Max. She thought the best thing to do would be to speak to him tomorrow and tell him she needed some space, but all she could think of was that she just wanted to be with him right now, cuddling him as she fell asleep. She really didn't want to do this, but she knew he would run a mile if he found out she was an angel. She would be too different for him, it just wouldn't work, so the best thing to do was not to tell him.

She lay awake for another two hours, working out what lies she could tell him, if and when she saw him.

* * * * *

After spending the next day explaining to her family and friends that she was one of the angels, it actually made her feel better. They were understanding and made her feel like it was a good thing and that no matter what came of it, they loved her all the same.

Her two best friends popped over, and over a few glasses of wine and a take-away they ended up making jokes about it. Her wings appeared twice during the day, and when Millie and Harriet saw them they were amazed at their beauty and how stunning she looked.

The day passed and she still couldn't bring herself to speak to Max or even send him a message, even though he tried to call her twice and sent numerous messages asking if she was OK. She felt bad and guilty.

As Millie and Harriet left they both told her she needed to speak to Max before she did anything else and that she would be making a mistake ending things with him, but she thought otherwise. She was glad the kids were going away so that she could sort things out. She thought that maybe when they had gone she could speak to Max.

'Why has this happened to me' she sobbed. 'The moment I find the person I want to spend the rest of my life with, this happens!'

★ ★ ★ ★ ★

After taking the kids to the bus station for their uncle's house in Chicago she hurried home in case her wings broke out whilst she was driving, because she was afraid they would rip holes in the roof of her car. When she got home she ran to the computer to look on line at angels and their history to see if any others had come forward in New York. After she had made a coffee and settled down at the computer, the doorbell rang. Amy thought it might be Henrik, so she ran to the door and opened it quickly. There was Max, standing behind a bouquet of roses and lilies.

'Max!' she said. 'What are you doing here?'

'What do you mean, why are you so shocked to see me?' he said.

'Look I am really busy right now, I can't talk' she said as she went to close the door.

'Amy, what the hell is going on? You ignore me all day yesterday and the day before, I surprise you with flowers and you wanna slam the door in my face?' He pushed against the door with his foot so she couldn't close it. 'Amy come on, why are you ignoring me?' He followed her into the hall and placed the flowers on the stairs. He looked confused and worried. He knew there was something serious she was hiding.

'Max, I told you, I can't talk right now, I am going through a hard time at the moment and I need some space' she said, without looking at him.

'But why? What's happening? If you're going through a hard time why can't you talk to me about it? Is it because of my past? Because I thought we got over that ages ago. I told you it's over with and done with. It won't ever bother us. I'm sorry I was brought up like that but I can't change it'.

'Max, it's not that. I just really don't think I am ready for this, so please stop asking questions' she replied,

'But you said you loved me and wanted to spend the rest of your life with me. I don't understand, have you met someone else?'

'Are you serious? Of course not!'

'Well, why can't you look me in the eyes then? I love you Amy, I at least need a proper explanation, you can't just turn off like this.'

'Look Max, please leave, this is hard enough for me. I don't love you any more and I just need to be back to how I was' she said, still not looking at him. She felt a tear running down her face.

'Amy look at me, please!' He grabbed her arm to try and look at her face. 'Look me in the eyes and tell me you don't love me and that you never want to see me again.'

Amy turned around to him weeping and looked into his sad eyes, struggling to say the words. She closed her eyes for three long seconds, then opened them. 'Max, I don't love you anymore and I don't want to be with you' she said.

She carried on looking at him; he stared back at her, finding it hard to believe what she was saying. She shrugged her arm to loosen his grip.

'Amy, I can't believe you are doing this, we're good together, we've opened ourselves up to each other, we can slow things down if you want, but please don't do this. I know you don't mean it. You told me you loved me a few days ago and that we should move in together next year.'

He tried to get closer to her.

'Max please go', she whispered sadly. She walked to the front door and opened it for him.

'I'm sorry Max, I need you to go and please don't come back', she said without even looking at him.

'Amy, I thought you were the one, but obviously not. I can't believe I fell for all the crap you have been telling over the last few months. I guess I will be better off without you' he said. Then he walked out and Amy slammed the door behind him.

As she heard his car pulling off she leant on the wall and slowly sank to the floor crying. She couldn't believe she had done it. She felt sick for doing that to him, knowing she might never see him again. It was the first time she had ever lied to him like that, and she wished she could have told him the truth, because it was a horrible empty feeling she now had. Amy once again was back to square one, her life in a big mess.

Two days passed and Amy was still not able to sleep properly. She still moped about the house feeling the pain of being without Max. She wanted him to knock at the door, and every time the doorbell went she jumped, but it was never him. She spent a lot of time with Henrik discussing things and arranging dates for the meetings. She practised her levitation skills and worked out her strengths. Her wings still appeared and disappeared when they wanted to, but she was getting more and more used to them.

All the angels had been told to attend the big first meeting in Rome on the 20th and a further meeting for those who couldn't make it would follow, but the angels were advised it was imperative they all attend to find out why this has happened, what would be likely to happen next and how to use their wings, powers and strengths. Amy was glad it was booked for this date as the kids would be back home on the 18th for just one day before she would have to drop them to the station the next day for their grandparents. Much as she missed them when she was away from them, she needed to sort things out.

CHAPTER TWENTY NINE

Wednesday 19th December came along, the kids were now safe in San Diego and Amy was getting ready for her trip to Rome the next day. She still couldn't get Max out of her head and was constantly thinking about calling him, just to hear his voice. Her stomach felt as if there was a large knot in it and she couldn't eat or sleep, and knowing she had been so horrible to him made it even worse. She wanted him back so badly, but the only thing she could do was wait. She just had to get through it, then she would be over him.

Having not left the house for a walk since discovering she was an angel, Amy thought it was about time. She was sick of rushing out in her car and rushing home from places in case her wings appeared. She needed some bits for her trip, so now was as good a time as any. She just hoped her wings didn't pop out of her back while she was out.

As she got to the front gate she took a deep breath and stepped out on to the pavement. She felt weird, as if everyone knew what she was. But when she passed people they didn't bat an eyelid at her; the odd guy stared, but guys always had stared at Amy. Having walked a mile to the town, she felt better, and had forgotten about her fear of people knowing what she was.

Finishing her shopping, Amy decided to walk back through the park. Although the day was cold, the sun was shining and it felt like a summer's day in winter. There was a light dusting of snow on the grass and trees and the park was empty.

As she walked over the bridge, halfway across she saw a man walking towards her, and as he got closer she realised it was Max. 'Of all the people I have to see, I bump into him' she said to herself.

There was nowhere she could turn. She didn't want to see him as it would only make things worse, but there was nothing she could do as they slowly walked towards each other. Amy could feel her heart thudding loudly inside her chest. She felt so nervous.

'Hello' she said.

'Hey, how are you?' he asked her awkwardly.

'Yeah I'm good.'

'You look amazing' he told her.

'Thank you.'

There was a long uncomfortable silence.

'Well, take care' she said quickly. She wanted to get home before her wings came out. She walked past him, but just then she heard him say, 'I miss you'. She stood still and closed her eyes, then turned around.

'I'm sorry Max about everything, I didn't mean to hurt you and for the record I miss you too.' Then she carried on walking. She didn't hear him walking after her, so she presumed that would be it and it was officially over between them. But as she headed towards the end of the bridge, she heard footsteps.

'Amy!' Max shouted. He was running after her. 'Can we talk? I just don't believe you want to end this. At least if we talk I can understand what is going on and I can move on, you can't expect me to accept this!' He was breathless from running. 'Surely I meant a little more than that? Don't I deserve an explanation?'

Amy felt tears starting to fall from her eyes. 'Max I can't explain, but I really am sorry. I just can't tell you, but all you need to know is something has come up in my life and...' before she could finish he grabbed her and held her close to him. She didn't pull away. She looked into his eyes and felt the pain he was feeling, just like hers.

Max moved closer to her and kissed her softly. She closed her eyes and kissed him back, then abruptly pulled herself away and ran off. Max ran after her, grabbing her arm.

'Get off me Max!' she screamed.

'No Amy, I won't let you go, why are you doing this?' he asked, shouting back at her, still holding tightly on to her arm.

'Max, please let go of my arm you're hurting me!'

'Not until you tell me what the hell is going on!'

She grabbed his arm and pushed it away, but she had forgotten the new strength she had. He had been thrown fifteen feet away from her. She stared at her hands. She was shocked at how she had been able to push him like that.

'I'm sorry, I have to go!' she cried. Max sat on the ground wondering how she had thrown him to the floor like that. As she ran off into the distance towards her house she could feel her wings about to explode out of her back. 'Oh no, please not now!' she sobbed to herself as she approached the park gates. There were people everywhere, and she didn't want anyone to see her if she turned.

Two blocks from home, her wings came out. They stood so high and flowed out as she power-walked home. Everyone stopped and stared at her, some took photos and others filmed her, while some stared in amazement. Amy freaked out and started crying. She stopped in the nearest alley, which was between two shops, then ran around the back and crouched down out of sight so she could wait until everyone who had seen her had gone out of sight.

There at the back of the shop, she wept. She was sick and tired of crying. She needed to start embracing this, because she was going to have it for the rest of her life.

After a few minutes of thinking she stood tall, took a deep breath, got up and went back through the alley. 'I have had enough of this, goddamn it, I'm not the only one', she mumbled to herself. 'I can do this, I no longer need to hide away.'

Her wings were still out and she thought to herself, 'this is my life now and I will have to face it.' She walked through to the next street, and as she entered she took another deep breath. Turning into the street she walked back towards her house. She kept her head down and with her eyes looking forward, she embraced her wings, walking through the people on the street as they dodged out of her way. She didn't care who was looking, who was taking photos and who stepped out of the way to stare. She just walked and walked, and felt in control.

After a while she realised it wasn't so bad; in fact she found it quite exhilarating to just walk and not notice anything around her. She knew she would have to get used to it.

By the time she arrived home, her wings had disappeared. Walking through her front door and feeling as if she had achieved a new step in her life, she heard her phone bleep and knew exactly who it was texting her.

Max: *What the hell happened? I'm sorry I grabbed you but you didn't need to throw me to the ground like that.*

Amy: *Yeah I'm sorry about that and I'm sorry about everything I have done to hurt you. I don't want this but there is nothing I can do x*

Max didn't reply. Amy was about to relax on the sofa when she heard the door.

'Who is it?' she shouted out.

'It's me' Max shouted back.

She opened the door.

'What do you want? I thought I told…'

'I want to talk, come on Amy, we need to talk about this, you can't just tell me you love me then do this! If you don't want to be with me then I will accept it, but it's kinda hard to do that when I don't know what the hell is going on. Can I come in?'

'Max, I don't think that's a good idea' she told him. But he ignored her and barged his way into the sitting room.

'Amy, I need you in my life' he said. 'If you can't give me a good reason for this then I will keep on at you. I don't believe you don't love me.'

'Max I don't love you, what can't you believe about that?'

'That's not enough and you know it. It's about my past, isn't it? All I need is the truth and I'm gone.'

Amy walked away from him to look out of the window so that he couldn't see the tears in her eyes. 'I love you', she muttered softly under her breath.

'What? You love me?' Max asked. 'You said you didn't. What the fuck Amy, why are you doing this?' He grabbed her shoulders tightly and then wrapped his arms around her,

'Whatever you're scared of, I'm here for you, I will look after you, please talk to me.' He turned her around.

'Max go away, I can't speak to you right now' she sobbed.

'I am not going anywhere' he told her sternly.

She tried to push him off, but his grip was too tight. 'Max get off me' she cried, and pushed him away.

'Look here is your explanation!' she shouted. She could feel her shoulders starting to get heavy. 'I'm not human any more, how's that for an explanation? I am an angel! I have big ugly wings that come out of my body when they feel like it, and I can fly!'

They both stood staring at each other for a few seconds.

'I don't believe you' he laughed.

'Well you'd better, because this is why I ended our relationship. I am a freak, an angel, why would you want anything to do with me? I'm not normal and never will be, so please get out and leave me alone.'

Amy could feel the wings coming out. 'Get out!' she screamed. Max's face suddenly had a serious expression on it.

Then suddenly, right there in the sitting room, he saw the wings. They were brightly coloured and beautiful. Amy fell to the floor on to her knees and held her head down, then slowly looked up at him, not saying a word, just looking scared and lost. Max stared at her wings, then looked into her tear-filled eyes. He couldn't believe what he was seeing. He took a few steps back, still gazing at her, then turned around and ran out of the house.

Amy stayed on her knees. She held her head in her hands, sobbing uncontrollably. This was it, exactly what she had predicted. He had run off and left her for good, and she would never see him again.

CHAPTER THIRTY

Max walked out of the house without closing the front door and headed straight for his car, parked at the end of her drive. He fired up the engine and raced off down the road. He couldn't believe what he had just seen. He had heard of the angels, but he couldn't believe that Amy, the only woman he had ever fallen in love with, was one of them.

Halfway down the road he suddenly stopped the car and put his head on the steering wheel between his hands. There was no way he could be with someone who changed into a creature every five minutes, but then he stopped and thought of the time they had together, how amazing a woman she was, how much he loved every single little thing about her – and not only her, he loved her kids too. An angel? A superhuman mythical creature? How could he have a normal relationship with her?

Max knew now he needed to be with Amy to look after her and love her for the rest of her life. There was no way on Earth he could be without her. She had forgiven and forgotten his past. How could he leave it like this?

Max spent the next few minutes contemplating on whether he should go back or give her some time. Then he sat up, took a deep breath, spun around in the middle of the road, almost causing a crash, and raced back towards Amy's house. He quickly jumped out of his car and saw that her door was still wide open. Without knocking he walked straight through the door, slamming it shut, then past the hall into the sitting room, where Amy was still on her knees in the middle of the floor crying. Her wings had now disappeared.

Max stopped in the doorway and stared at her. He felt as if he couldn't breathe. His stomach was tied up in a knot and his heart was racing faster than he had ever felt it before. Now he saw how truly beautiful she was.

She slowly looked up at him with glistening eyes. Max walked towards her in small, careful steps, worried she might think he would harm her. He held his hand out to help her up from the floor, still saying nothing. The room was filled with the sound of breathing and of their two beating hearts as she raised herself up.

Max carefully pulled her tighter towards him. Amy felt her heart racing, knowing he was about to kiss her, but she didn't care, because she wanted him to. He felt her trembling as he held her hard with his arms tightly around her, showing her he would be there for her to protect and look after her. As they gazed into each other's eyes, slowly they brought their lips together, kissing each other softly.

He whispered in her ear, 'Amy, I'm sorry, I'm so sorry, I didn't mean to react like that. I just got a little freaked out when I saw the wings, and well I don't know, I just…'

'Shhh' Amy whispered in his ear as she kissed his face and neck.

'Amy, I hated every minute I spent without you, I love you and I'm going to be right here for you if you let me' he told her. He kissed her harder and put his arms around her back.

'No, I'm sorry. I should have talked to you and not made you feel like that. I tried so hard, it killed me to do that to you. I really needed you but I just thought you would think I was a freak.'

He kissed her again and slowly moved his hands towards her buttocks. Then he picked her up and with her legs wrapped around him, they kissed again as he walked over to the doorway to carry her upstairs.

Twenty minutes later as they lay in bed together, Amy thought she would never have this moment again. Here he was holding her and kissing her after having the most passionate sex they had ever had. She explained to Max everything that Henrik had told her and how the angels had appeared before, and the fact that none of them knew anything about the dangers they were walking into.

Max asked her many questions about how it felt and how strong she was.

'Oh, so that's why you were able to throw me across the park' he said. 'That was pretty impressive!'

'Hey, this really is not a laughing matter', she said with a smile on her face. 'But to be honest I have had the worst few days, finding this out and not having you around. It was pretty unbearable, but the kids have been great. They're very excited about the whole thing, but they don't understand the seriousness of it, it could get bad. We just don't know yet. Something like this would normally really scare me, but I'm not scared at all, I feel ready to take on anyone that gets in my way. The scariest part was having to tell the people I love. Oh that reminds me, I have to get ready, I have a meeting in Rome and we leave first thing in the morning. It's with the angelologists and all the other angels along with some other guys. We all have to get together and check each other out. They will give us advice and everything about what is going on.' She jumped up from the bed. 'They'll let us know how to control our powers and when our wings will appear and so on. I need to leave in a few hours, Henrik and I will be having a small meeting with the other experts at a hotel near the airport before our flight in the early hours.'

'All the way to Rome? What if the Iblisari are there?' he replied.

'They won't be. We will have constant security there and they chose Rome because I guess they had to choose somewhere holy, not that I have a holy bone in my body! But I'll be back on the 23rd. The kids will also arrive back then so hopefully Christmas will go to plan. Which reminds me, would you like to spend it here with us?'

Max grinned. 'I would love to, I can't wait. Let me know if there's anything you want me to sort out for you while you're away.' Amy shook her head and told him all was fine.

He got up and gave her a hug, telling her not to worry about anything. 'I need to go to the restaurant now but I'll be here waiting for you when you get home, call me if you need anything.' He kissed her again. 'I really am going to miss you, I've been away from you for days and miserable ones at that! And now you're off,' he complained to her.

'I wish I didn't have to go, but I really have no choice.'

They said their goodbyes and Amy finished her packing and waited for her ride to the airport later that evening.

CHAPTER THIRTY ONE

Amy felt nervous as she sat on the private aeroplane bound for Rome. She also felt alone, as if she were the only one in the world this had happened to. She couldn't imagine there being any others like her, but now she was about to meet all 1111 of them, all congregated in the gardens of the Vatican.

She turned to Henrik and Dr Konte, wondering when the other angels were likely to arrive in Rome, along with the members of the AAG, the Association of Angelologists and History.

'How do you know for sure all of them have come forward or have even been found?'

'Amy, Dr Konte and his team have found all of the angels from around the world, even the ones that did not come forward' he said. 'Some were very afraid when we met them, but we have reassured them that it would be in their best interests, and that if they did not attend this meeting they would have troubles controlling their strengths and powers, and they would know nothing about being an angel or the reasons and the history behind it' Henrik told her. 'They all seemed a bit keener after that was explained that to them. As you know there are also young children among them, so we have had to get their parents to accompany them. Though we do ask that the angels try to keep the information they are given as quiet as possible. If any information is leaked, especially regarding the stone, it could be dangerous. However we know that in this day and age it is not possible to keep things quiet so we have prepared for this. We will be heavily protected from when we get off the aircraft. My team and I have a lot of information to give you all.'

'But what if the devils appear as they did many years ago? They will want to kill us, surely? I mean you are going to have to explain again the dangers of what could happen and what they did to us all at the last gathering. I know I keep saying it, but what if they try it again? Will we have more strength than them? Will they try to kill us all?'

'Amy you must not worry, we will prepare and train you for the worst. But there are more pros than cons. You are more gifted and much more aware and stronger than the last angels. I can see you all changing history for the better, but we will explain more when we all meet tomorrow at noon in the gardens of the Vatican. Then a few of you will be summoned to see the Pope' the doctor replied.

'The Pope? Are you serious?' Amy asked.

'Well yes you are angels, the most holy beings of all! He will bow down to you no doubt' said Henrik. 'Anyway, let's get some rest. This will be carried on tomorrow when you are all together.'

Henrik turned away and reclined his chair to go to sleep. Amy turned to her window and stared out at the clouds, thinking of Max and the children and how life would carry on from here. She slowly closed her eyes and fell asleep.

★ ★ ★ ★ ★

Walking out of the airport and making their way towards the private black taxi, Amy noticed men wearing black suits scattered around. She felt as if she was being watched, and it felt creepy and weird.

An hour later they all arrived at the hotel, one of two large hotels next to each other which had been reserved solely for the angels for the next three days. At reception they were advised that

500 people had already checked in. Amy got excited over this. She really couldn't wait to meet them and see if there were any the same age as her.

Having arranged to meet in the morning, Henrik and Dr Konte walked off to their rooms and Amy walked headed for hers. She entered her room to find it was the most lavish and elegant place she had ever seen in her life. It was as if she was walking into the French Renaissance. The bed was a four-poster draped in dark red velvet and lace, there were large finely-decorated mirrors in every corner and the marble floor was warm. Sheepskin rugs lay dotted around the floor and the voile curtains softly swayed in the breeze through the slightly-opened French windows.

She walked over to the balcony doors and pulled back the curtains to see the most beautiful sight. The bright lights of the city of were revealed by the trees rustling in the breeze, along with countless stars that lit up the sky.

Amy walked out onto a beautifully-decorated stone balcony wrapped in ivy. It was like a scene from *Romeo and Juliet*. She took a deep breath as she felt her wings about to come out; this was the first time she had a warning feeling. She stayed out on the balcony and embraced her wings for once. Her hair was flowing in the wind and her body became brighter, as if she were lit up like an angel on a Christmas tree. Her wings were swaying slowly back and forth, sounding like the leaves of a palm tree on a Caribbean island.

She stood with her eyes closed for a few minutes until she heard a soft giggle from somewhere nearby. She looked around and on the balcony to her left she saw a young girl who also had her wings out and was doing the same thing.

'Yes I am an angel too' said the girl. 'My name is Maria. I am from Morocco.' Your wings are beautiful, what's your name?'

'My name is Amy, I'm from New York, and your wings are very beautiful too.'

Maria was about 10 years old, with olive skin and long dark

curly hair. She had stunning beauty and looked so innocent and elegant with her wings.

'Can you fly yet? I have tried but it's so hard' the girl said.

'Well I have tried and I managed it, but it didn't last for long, I guess they will teach us that tomorrow,' Amy replied.

'Well I hope so because I'm having difficulty too!' shouted a voice from above. The girls looked up, and in the middle two floors above them was a man with wings out smiling down at them.

'My god, are there any more of us here?' Amy shouted up to him

'By the morning I should think all one thousand, one hundred and twelve of us will be here, all very close together' he told her in a very posh accent. 'I'm Charles Weston from London, England. So pleased to meet you both.' He stood up proudly.

Charles was very tall and slim with silver hair and a silver moustache. He looked around 65 years old and in very good shape. His wings were large, but nowhere near the size of Amy's.

'Well nice to meet you too Charles' both Amy and Maria said at the same time.

'I guess we should all get some sleep for the big day, goodnight ladies!' he called. He took a deep breath and waited for his wings to disappear.

'Goodnight Charles' shouted Amy. The three of them stood on their balconies with their eyes closed, breathing in the cool night air until their wings had disappeared.

An hour before the midday meeting, Amy made her way to the Vatican. She walked through the grounds to find the whole place empty except for the security guards everywhere and some of the other angels they were there to protect. Amy had already bumped into other angels in the hotel and en route to the Vatican. They all seemed so normal, just everyday people going through the same experience as her.

Finally she entered the courtyard outside the Grand Hall, after having seen a large group of people congregating and talking to each other.

'Hello, is this where all of the angels are having the meeting?' she asked a middle-aged woman.

'Yes it is, and after the rain has stopped the sun is due to come out so we'll be meeting in the garden' said the woman.

As she walked forward into the Grand Hall, Amy had never seen so many beautiful people in her life in one room. Every single person had exquisite beauty and there was a glow in the room, like a bright haze. It gave her an overwhelming feeling, but it was a little eerie at times.

The Grand Hall was large, with ceilings so high you could hardly see the designs on them. Candles surrounded the place, on walls, on tables and standing in the corners. The cool marble floors were a grey colour and the walls white and gold with pictures and statues of saints, angels and biblical life. Amy had never been to Europe before, but what she had seen so far was very impressive.

The room was filled with people from all around the world, young and old, from the islands of the Caribbean to Siberia. All these people had endured the same thing as Amy over a week before, and they were all the chosen ones. She wondered why the people in this room had been chosen to be angels and wondered if they all had the same personality and traits as her, the same thoughts and the same nature. She wanted to find out a little more, so she walked over to a woman who looked around the same age and style as herself.

'Hi, I'm Amy from New York' she said as she held out her hand to shake the woman's hand.

'Hola, I am Christina from Madrid', the woman replied.

'My god, can you believe this is happening?' Amy asked Christina.

'This is so weird, don't you think?' replied the woman. 'I can't believe last week I was a normal person getting on with my normal life and now I have all these strengths and abilities to do things I never thought possible.'

Christina was gorgeous, with long black hair and big dark eyes. She was a little taller than Amy and had the most amazing body she had ever seen.

'Yeah, I just can't wait for them to tell us a little more about what we can and can't do and how we control things' Amy replied.

The two women carried on talking about their experiences and soon they were joined by two women, Heidi from Norway was a six-foot blonde with bright blue eyes, and Emilia from Scotland had a large mop of beautiful red curly hair and emerald green eyes.

'Well it's good that we are all now bilingual, that has to be about the best part of this so far' Amy said to the three women.

'I agree' replied Heidi.

'And the fact that we are the most stunning creatures on the planet, that's kinda fun too!' added Emilia.

The four women laughed and joked about the situation and told each other their life stories, or as much as they could in an hour.

* * * * *

Half an hour later, an hour behind schedule, the grand doors opened and six men walked in with boxes of books. They all looked very serious and important. Two of them were Henrik and Dr Konte.

Dr Konte appeared to be the lead man. He started by asking for everyone to be quiet and then asked the angels to remain where they were standing but ensure they had at least a metre gap between themselves and the angel standing next to them. He had no need for the use of a microphone, as the angels' hearing was exceptional.

'Welcome everyone' he shouted as loudly and clearly as he could. 'I would like to start by saying how grateful we are that each and every one of you made it here today. The next two days will be full of vital information, advice and guidance for you to go out there and get on in the world as angels. We will be giving you a history of how we believe you have been chosen and why, a history of what happened to angels in the past and some stories from thousands of years ago about those who had connections with the past angels.

'You must be warned that some of these stories are evil and upsetting, but you must hear them. You will understand that we are not the only beings with great powers and strengths. There are creatures on this planet that can cause great damage to us. Fortunately we are stronger than them, but there are more of them than us, a lot more! And they also carry weapons, especially scythes, the deadly weapon of all.

'However, we will be here to teach you how to control and use your strengths, how to use your wings and how to levitate, and much more' Dr Konte said firmly. 'There is one more thing we must advise you of. Among you there will one leader, one of you who will understand the history and stories of the angels better than the others, one of you who will be the strongest angel of all. We will know this by the size of your wings.

'There will also be a second angel who will also have very large wings, though not as large as the superior one. He or she will have powers just as great, but it will be clear who the leader is. The only way we will be able to find this out is by seeing you all with your wings out. You will start seeing your wings appear, and the angel with the largest and brightest wings will be the one with the greatest strength and wisdom.

'Well that is definitely not me' Amy joked. 'There is no way I could lead five people down the road, let alone over a thousand angels.'

'Well I think I would be pretty good at that' said Emilia, giggling. 'I lead people all day long at work, but I think it would be kind of different leading this lot. I mean where the hell would you even start? Oops, shouldn't have said hell!'

Dr Konte continued. 'I must advise you that after we go through these stories and all the information we have, we have Mr Peter Wilson here from the British Government, who will give you information about how life should go on as normal and how the Iblisari, the devils, are being closely watched, which of course we will explain to you shortly. You will be able to stay in your normal jobs and have a normal family life, but if evil does come upon you, you must be prepared.'

The rest of the team introduced themselves. They included Mary Suarez, who was there as a counsellor and medic, and two men, Mustafa Abwali and Michael Brady, who were there to help with fighting and self-defence skills. Henrik then came forward to read out the stories he had found, and explain how the last angels had disappeared off the planet. He also gave them other historical information. This was something Amy had already heard about, but she was eager to hear more.

Henrik held nothing back from the angels. They needed to be advised of everything that had gone on to prepare them for the future.

Three hours passed as he recounted the history of the angels. Those present all looked horrified at his account of how they had died. Some, like Amy had already heard parts of this story, but it still became more and more scary when they thought that these devils were after them and were likely to try and kill them, or at least attempt to.

Then it was time for questions. Many were asked, including 'What will happen when we die?' 'Will our children be angels?' and 'How will we know when a Devil is following us or watching us?' The team reassured them and Henrik told them that they would be taught over the next two days how to protect themselves and others, how to fight the devils if necessary and how to spot them in a crowd. They were advised they could not just go and kill the devils; the devils could be very different from the way they had been years before and the angels should only use their powers in self-defence unless they were attacked and overpowered. If that happened they were to go in for the kill. They would also be able to sense when there was danger nearby to give them at least a few minutes to prepare, but they always needed to be aware that the devils would more than likely be carrying weapons and that there would be double or triple the number of them.

'After this, when you go home, I guarantee you will have no fear of them and no fear of anyone' said Henrik. 'Even better, if any of you find the stone, you must hold on to it and keep it safe. If the right angel gets hold of it, we will be able to change the world for the better.'

CHAPTER THIRTY TWO

After the talks had finished, Henrik and Dr Konte allowed the angels to mingle again to discuss what they had just heard. They also mentioned that within the next 10-15 minutes their wings would start to appear, and then they would find out who would be the superior angel. They advised them that over the next three weeks they would feel more control over their wings, becoming more able to extract them by thinking long and hard about them. In any case they needed to be out twice daily.

One by one, the room filled with beautiful, bright, glowing wings. Some were smaller than others and some brighter and wider. Most of the male angels had white, silver, blue or grey wings, while the females had every colour under the sun.

Everyone looked at each other with amazement and admiration at how spectacular they looked. They now realised that they really had become these creatures, beautiful, strong, intelligent, endearing and compassionate and all with the same amazing gift. The sound of the wings swaying as the angels moved was entrancing, and the room lit up as if there was a layer of fresh snow on the ground. Dr Konte and his team were witnessed a miracle in front of their eyes. Henrik almost collapsed at the beauty of it all; it was the most exhilarating thing he had ever seen. He had known since he was a boy that something like this would happen, and here it was. A tear ran down his cheek and he embraced what was before him, then he smiled.

'This is it, this could make the world a safe place, a place free from evil', said Dr Konte.

'I think you're right' said Peter Wilson. 'But we cannot get too excited. There is probably a hundred times more evil out there and it will be hard to overcome, especially if they are looking for us and have destruction in mind. These angels could get wiped out if the devils come for them. We do not know how many groups are out there preparing for this. The Iblisari must be huge now. They will all know the stories of how the last angels were slaughtered and taken off the Earth, and they will be worried that the angels will fight harder this time.'

'Well then, we need to teach these angels the best we can' said Dr Konte. 'They have their powers and strengths already, but we will teach them control, self-defence and of course how to kill. They will have no choice.'

Serj, an Armenian American Musician from California, so far had the largest wings, but there was one more person to go.

'Come on Amy, think', Amy said to herself, trying hard to make her wings appear. 'I can't wait to be able to control these damn things.' The other women's wings were all out. Looking around the room she noticed that none of the wings were as big as hers. She started to worry.

'No way am I going to be the superior one. It must be that guy over there' she mumbled to herself, 'I can't be, I'm Amy from New York, mother of two kids, works for an insurance company, boring life, no way!'

Finally she felt her wings softly emerge from her back, she bowed her head and closed her eyes, not wanting to look. Everyone close by had turned their heads to see her. She hated having everyone's eyes on her, watching her to see if her wings were twice as big.

Seconds later she heard gasps from around the room. She slowly lifted up her head and opened one eye, turning her head back

162

slightly. And there it was, exactly what she didn't want to see. Every single person in the room was staring at her with their eyes opened as wide as full moons. She had the biggest wings in the room.

'Jesus Christ!' she shouted as she looked over at one of the mirrors on the wall. 'Sorry, I mean – oh my… I can't believe this, it can't be me.'

Amy's wings stood higher and wider and were more beautifully coloured than any other angel in the room. She stood out clearly and everyone could see that. Looking over at Henrik, she could see that he was shocked and excited at the same time.

'I'm not the last, am I?' she said desperately. 'Who else has not got their wings out yet?'

'Amy, all of the wings are out, you are the superior one, the leader!' shouted Dr Konte.

'But I cannot lead, I don't understand, I can't do this' she said, looking worried.

Henrik called her to the front, and as she made her way forward the crowd made a path for her, so they could have a good look. They had all been used to seeing their own wings and they had all thought theirs were big – until they saw Amy's. Serj was also called forward, as he had the second largest wings. The team spoke quietly to the two of them.

'Amy, you have been chosen as superior angel and Serj, you have been chosen as the second' said Henrik. 'We have not chosen this for you, someone up there has and they have done it for a reason.' He put his hand softly on her arm. 'I have known you for many years and I knew from that first day I met you that there was something special about you.'

'But I don't know what I'm supposed to do, Henrik!' she cried.

'You will oversee the angels. When there are serious problems you will be the one they communicate with. You are more powerful than the others and you will be the one who will be able to change the world. The main reason you have been given this role is your nature, your inner strengths and qualities. And you Serj will be the same, but Amy will always be that little bit stronger than you. She is the only one who will ever be able to physically hold the stone and destroy it.'

'Guys, this won't make you look any different from the rest when you are in human form, the only difference will be your strengths and abilities, they will be greater' said Dr Konte. 'And as I said before, your life will go on as normal. We will be taking you through everything over the next few days and in a few minutes we will be heading out to the gardens to take you through some other things.'

'OK everyone!' Henrik shouted out to the room. 'This is Amy and Serj. As you can from her wings, Amy is the superior angel. But they are to be treated no differently from the angel beside you. They are merely a little stronger, more intelligent and have more able minds, to see more things than the rest of you. Should danger come to you throughout your lives, she will be there to advise and comfort you.'

He ushered them all out to the gardens for the next step. After chatting with Serj, Amy re-joined the women she had been with earlier as they all walked out into the lush gardens of the Vatican. The day was a little chilly, but now the sun had appeared and the sky was crystal blue. The angels looked impeccable as they fluttered their wings in the cool air. The gardens were immaculate, with beautiful plants and shrubs surrounded by freshly-cut lawns and cobble-stoned paths.

Over the next few hours the angels were taught how to defend themselves, with Mustafa and Michael helping them to understand how to fight and use their bodies. In the days that followed they were given more details about the Iblisari and how the devils worked. In time they would be sent out to search for the stone, but for now they had to learn about themselves and get comfortable with the changes they had just gone through. In a few weeks' time they would all be ready.

★ ★ ★ ★ ★

Later that evening Amy was taken over to meet the Pope, who was waiting for her and Serj at the altar of the Church of Saint Anne. As they walked into the church they were mesmerised by its beauty, the ceilings went so high up and were covered in the most amazing art they had ever seen, encrusted with gold and finely decorated, painted with every colour under the sun, it was hard to look ahead there was so much to see.

The aisle had candles at each side of it leading up to where the Pope stood. There were statues of angels dotted around and Amy felt as if they were watching her every move. A choir sang out loudly as the two of them glided up the aisle. Their wings came out, matching the colours of the church.

As they reached the Pope, he and his men all bowed down to them, their eyes fixed on Amy's enormous wings.

'Welcome, my children, my angels' The Pope said as he raised his head up to them. 'You are the ultimate of God's children and a true miracle and we are very honoured to meet you at last. Come forth and I will bless you with the holy waters of the Vatican.'

Amy and Serj walked closer to the Pope and he blessed them, holding his hands out and touching their faces, shoulders and wings. Even he looked shocked that there truly were two angels standing in front of him.

'I am not worthy of this post as Pope of the world when there are angels now living on Earth' he said. 'This changes everything. I hope there is an angel to take my place when I depart from this world, but for now we need to celebrate this moment and pray to the Lord above and thank him for bringing you here.'

Amy and Serj did not know what to say to the most holy man in the world. They were scared that they would say something out of place, so they just thanked him for taking the time to meet them.

'We are so very privileged to meet you, it is a true honour and if there is anything you need us to do for you we would be happy to do so' Amy said as she and Serj bowed their heads.

'I advise you to keep a low profile. You know there is danger out there and should you or any other angels come across it we will pray for you. Please enjoy your stay here and enjoy the grounds. We will welcome you in our home whenever you need us.'

'Thank you so kindly' said Amy. 'We appreciate you inviting us here and we do believe you are worthy of this post. Your people love and idolise you.'

'Thank you my angels. I wish you a pleasant stay for the duration of your trip' the Pope said as he walked back up further to his altar with his men at each side helping him. Amy and Serj turned back towards the church entrance and walked slowly and quietly out of the church, both feeling a little dazed.

CHAPTER THIRTY THREE

Now that the angels had appeared on the planet, the devils had called forward all the most evil people around the world to join the Iblisari. Their headquarters were in a Russian warehouse, where they would hold meetings and teach each other extreme fighting skills. They wished to be able to take on the angels and bring to life the evil that was needed to rule the world.

As a good majority of devils were behind bars, it was left to the rest. These were usually the cleverer ones, those who knew how to avoid conflict with the law. They ranged from murderers, rapists and paedophiles to ordinary people who kept out of trouble, but had evil minds and thoughts. All of them joined sister cults to the Iblisari, and all had waited long enough for the moment the angels appeared. After years of studying, they all now knew about the history of the angels and were determined to make sure that this time, like the last, they would be removed from the Earth. They all praised Ibli, Sari, Prince Tobias and King Petrus, and spoke of them as the Kings and Queens of the Iblisari after the good work they had done thousands of years before. To them they were heroes and role models.

Not knowing the whereabouts of the stone concerned the Iblisari, and as the angels were more intelligent than them, they worried that they had the ability to hide or secretly to get to the stone before they themselves could. If they retrieved the stone somehow, they could secure it forever and they would never be wiped off the Earth; they would be able go on forever by introducing more evil into the Iblisari and into the world. Like the angels, they too had a series of meetings to discuss further what they needed to do and how they would go about getting rid of these creatures.

The Iblisari believed that a human who was able to fly was neither normal nor worthy of a place on this planet. Winged humans were too strong and powerful, and the Iblisari needed to be the most powerful creatures on Earth. The only way to make sure of this was to kill them. They understood that the angels they had killed before were not ready because they had no information, no help and no time to prepare for the danger. They knew that this time around they would have to work a lot harder, but regardless of that, they were confident with their numbers that they would beat the angels and find the stone.

The devils knew that the angels from years before had never had the information about the stone and its benefits. It was only in the last few hours of the angels' time that it became known - but by then it was too late.

Devilishness was hereditary, but only 40 per cent of the time. Some took the genes from their parents, but most humans skipped many generations down the line. Some were just born evil, and although brought up by decent parents and guardians, would take the path of evil later in life. Some devils knew of their evil but had chosen to fight it to lead a normal and good life. Sometimes this worked out, but most of the time it didn't. Those who had controlled it and ignored it lived happy normal lives, but those who proceeded into darkness took as many steps forward as possible. They had been around at all times, noticed by some and not others. It was the Iblisari where the hardcore devils resided, and there they could end up taking over the world.

The Iblisari knew that once all the angels were slaughtered they would have enough time to grow in numbers and power before the next date in 4000 years' time, and by then they would be too strong and wealthy to allow the angels to stay.

CHAPTER THIRTY FOUR

As he stepped out of his private aeroplane and on to the Russian soil of his childhood, Vladimir Grekov felt stronger than ever, and ready to take over the world. Greeted by his mob of twenty tall, darkly-clothed men in dark glasses, he made his way to the Iblisari headquarters.

Everyone feared Vladimir, not only because he was one of the world's most notorious mobsters but because he was also the Iblisari leader of the devils. He had been placed on this planet to do evil as discreetly as possible, but now he had reason to get even more evil and he did not want to hide it. As one of the most feared men in the world to both humans and devils, he felt he was only steps away from making a difference, and he would not be defeated.

Vladimir had one thing on his mind, and that was to find the whereabouts of the stone and get his hands on it. From what he had heard about Henrik, there was a good chance he knew a little more about the stone, possibly even its whereabouts, so his first job was to find out where the old man was. Details of the meeting had spread fast around the devil world, and as soon as they heard about the angels appearing they got to work. Leaders from around the world congregated at the headquarters in the big Russian warehouse, which was large enough for over 100,000 evil souls.

Soon after they had all arrived, their great leader, Vladimir Grekov, stood in front of them wearing his long grey cape. Most of the men and women wore dark clothes, and many of them also had their capes draped around their bodies, not showing any flesh except for their faces, and even they were obscured.

Vladimir and the other leaders began.

'People, welcome to the beginning of a new era, where we will be able to conquer the world without being punished, where we will be able to do as we please and where most importantly we will wipe out these winged creatures from the entire planet!'

Vladimir felt an explosion of blood quickly running through his veins and he shouted from the top of his lungs, 'We have had enough of people telling us how we can live and controlling our lives! If we wish to steal we shall. If we wish to rape and torture, we shall. And if we wish to murder, we shall!' Chants of support filled the enormous warehouse.

"We have one thing to do, and to do it we must get rid of each and every one of those angels. Then and only then will we be able to take the stone and hide it where no man will ever look. We will become the Kings and Queens of the world!' Vladimir shouted out.

'As you know we succeeded many years ago. We must always remember our faithful Petrus, who so bravely and cleverly did as any true believer should have by taking out all the angels.

'Now you all have the finest fighting powers, but we must always work harder and keep practising, because as you know these creatures have powers, and they will be greater than they were all those millennia ago. They will have knowledge of their history and of what happened to the previous angels, and as I told you before they will most definitely be prepared for us. We are here to advise and help with any questions you have. We must all work together to succeed!' He paced up and down in front of the devils.

'You will hear about where these angels are. Some of you may even pass by them in the street, so you must be prepared. You must follow them, find out where they are going and when the coast is clear, you must not hesitate to destroy them. But you must remember that we live in a world surrounded by humans who are constantly watching everything, so we must tread carefully. We are not to kill humans unless it is necessary, because as you know we cannot afford to be found out. There are so many of us already in prisons and mental asylums all over the world. We must stick to destroying the angels discreetly and retrieving the stone.

'I will now introduce you to the other leaders of our underground world.'

After three hours of talks they went on to some training in fighting skills. Then they discussed the best ways to defeat the angels and Vladimir also spoke to them about the stone and its history.

'My people, I must explain the history of the stone,' he said. He explained as far back as the time when Ibli and Sari had lived, told how they had created evil and why the Iblisari had been dedicated to them. He also told them of the story of Tobias, along with other stories. After the meeting Vladimir felt energised and confident about what was going to happen. The devils went away very excited and full of ideas on how to kill the angels. They all understood how careful they needed to be with humans. But if any stood in their way, they would not think twice about killing them too.

CHAPTER THIRTY FIVE

Over on the west coast of Africa, Augustine Muballa made her way home from church on a Sunday afternoon. She had led the service after having been given the honour since the village people had found out she was an angel. Augustine had short dark hair and a dark complexion, almost jet black. Her skin was smooth and clear and she had perfect bone structure. She took her usual route home, walking through her local village and into a country lane after saying goodbye to her friends and the church pastor.

As she walked she felt as if someone was following her, but there was no one in sight when she looked around. She had always been vigilant since the meeting with the angelologists in Rome a few days before, so she always looked over her shoulder. In fact this was the first time she had ever walked alone, but as it was the middle of the day she thought there was no chance of danger in the town she had grown up in, especially as there were cars passing every so often.

Augustine turned up the smaller lane which was a short cut to the home where she lived with her husband and four children. As she walked along humming a song to herself with her fan waving in her face in the 90 degree heat she saw in the distance the figure of an elderly woman. This didn't disturb her, so she carried on walking towards the woman. However she had a strange feeling, as if danger was nearby, so she discreetly prepared herself.

Then, ten metres from her, she heard a rustle in the bushes that lined each side of the road. She thought it might be wild dogs or maybe even a wild cat, so as she passed the woman she walked faster and faster to her house.

Augustine knew she should always be ready for danger and she began to feel stranger and stranger as she walked further along the road. Then she started having feelings of worry, and her wings began to emerge from her back. This made her start forgetting about how she felt, and the urge to fight came to her.

Taking a look behind her, she saw that there were twenty darkly-clothed men and women slowly walking towards her. She knew these were not the village people, so she threw her books and bag to the ground and made a run for it.

As she ran she looked behind her to see that the people were catching up to her very fast. She didn't want to get any closer to her house in case her husband and children were hurt, she now knew these people were the Iblisari.

She stopped still suddenly and turned around to face them, looking at them with her piercing eyes. Her neck bent slightly forward and her wings stood high as she clenched her fists, knowing this would be a tough fight. She didn't even have to ask them what they wanted, and they didn't need to tell her. It was clear that they were about to attack her with scythes, knives, hammers and swords, but she still felt no fear towards them. She was ready, ready to use every power she had and ready to take them down.

'Ahh, we can have fun here' the first devil said, as he walked over to her. 'Where is the stone?' he asked.

'I have no idea what you are talking about' Augustine replied to him, loudly so that they could all hear.

'Well then, you should prepare to die!' he shouted out at her. The devil took a swipe at her, thinking she would be knocked to the ground, but she only moved a couple of centimetres to the side. Then she took a swipe back at him, and he flew over the road and almost into the bushes.

The other devils gasped at this, and then one by one they came forward. The first five were thrown over to the kerb and killed instantly by the impact. The next two walked over to her while a third grabbed her wings from behind. She struck him so hard he fell on a rock and split his head down the middle. But the others now had their arms around her neck, and within seconds there were more surrounding her and holding her down, punching her and trying to rip off her wings, like crows picking on a dead carcass.

Underneath them all she struggled to get up. She took a deep breath and with one jump she managed to flick all six of them off her. Once they were on the ground she kicked and stamped on them with such force her foot went straight through them, tearing skin and cracking their facial bones. Augustine was surprised how strong she was when she really put her powers to work.

Now four more devils walked towards her. When they got up close, she made a single swipe of her arm and took off the head of the next victim. Then one by one she sliced the other devils' heads off with her bare hands.

Now that she had killed or injured more than half of them, the devils decided it was time to turn to their weapons. Out of their cloaks they took scythes with nine-inch blades.

'So you think you can beat us? Well that won't happen! You remember the angels we slaughtered many years ago?' he asked her, walking closer.

'We are not scared of you' she replied. 'We will find the stone and you will be gone from this world for good. We are stronger than ever.'

'Ah, but you have no idea. We are very close to getting that stone and we will keep it far, far away so that we can live on forever and take over this planet' he responded. 'So prepare to die!'

He swung the knife at her and missed. She jumped high in the air and levitated over them, landing on the devil furthest away and managing to knock him to the ground. When he tried to get up she kneeled behind him and ripped his head from his neck. She threw it at the remaining devils.

'I think you should leave before I kill you all', Augustine said as she returned to them.

But just then one of the injured devils rose from the ground. He quietly crept up behind her and drove his scythe into her shoulder, dragging it along to the top of her wing. Augustine quickly turned around and punched him in the face, instantly finishing him off, but he had left her with a damaged wing and in great pain.

The other devils surrounded her. Her wings had been weakened by the stab wound to her shoulder, and she knew she was in trouble. She tried to kick and punch her way out, but with their weapons she had no chance.

As the remaining devils slowly walked closer to her, tightening the surrounding circle and bringing their weapons closer, she tried to jump, but then she felt the knives being driven into her sides. She was weakening. She fell to the ground. Blood was spraying everywhere from her body and, she knew she could not survive.

As Augustine lay dying on the ground, the devils thrust their knives into her head and neck to finish her off. Then they walked away from her, laughing at her helpless form. Augustine did not want to die, but she knew it was her time to go, and she took some satisfaction in her last moments for having taken the lives of some of those evil creatures. She hoped to God that there would be others stronger and better prepared than her to take on the rest of them. Then she looked up at the sky and took her last breath as she lay on the dusty, blood-stained road.

CHAPTER THIRTY SIX

News had spread quickly about the death of the first angel, but she was praised greatly for the fight she had put up and for the devils she had destroyed.

The news had got worse as the days and weeks went on. There was word of other deaths. Two male angels in Germany were tortured after being set upon by an army of forty, and although they managed to kill all but three of the devils they too became fatally weakened after their wings were injured during the fight. There were also three female angels in Australia who had been slaughtered after putting up a good fight and managing to kill many devils in the process. The same happened in India, Europe and New Zealand. In a short space of time too many angels had died. Far more of the devils had died, but not enough. The remaining angels needed to take more precautions and have more lessons on how to avoid such danger. They never went out to kill the devils, as they had been told not to do so unless it was necessary, but things now had to change if the planet was to be saved.

Before the deaths the AAG had arranged another private meeting for all the angels in Arguineguin, a small town on the island of Gran Canaria. This was a place where they were unlikely to be found, which was vital as they could not chance the Iblisari knowing they would all be under one roof.

All the angels except the unfortunate ones who had lost their lives over the last few days made their way to their airports to start their journeys to Las Palmas. Over the next 24 hours, they would be meeting in a church hall up in the mountains two miles west of Arguineguin.

As the sun beat down hard from clear blue skies, Amy and Serj stood in the old church hall on the edge of the small town as the AAG welcomed the angels.

Once they had all arrived, Henrik was first to speak.

'You all know of the deaths of our precious angels, but I have further sad news' he said. 'We have just been informed that 300 angels have now died. The problem we have here is not your strength but the large number of Iblisari devils. Their weapons are so dangerous, and we need to find ways of fighting back. We know we were not as prepared as we should have been. This is a bad situation, and we must think of ways to fight harder and protect you. Of course we prepared you for danger, but we did not know they would attack so hard and so soon. We need to be prepared for the next few days. We are going to have to go after them if we want this planet to remain a safe place, we cannot stand back.'

'The angels who perished put up a good fight and were able to wipe out thousands of the devils, but this is not enough; there are still, at a guess, seventy to eighty thousand left. I think with preparation we can succeed in this. I know we are not evil creatures and to go out and kill is not in our nature, but we need to think about the future. They will wipe you out if we don't do something about it.'

Serj then stepped forward. 'I was approached by twelve men in dark cloaks' he said. 'They came at me, we fought and I succeeded.' Then a woman shouted from the back of the hall 'I too was attacked by eight devils and I killed them all!' A further ten angels told them of their fights and how they had survived.

Amy stood up. 'We will be able to do this, but we will have to teach you all some more fighting techniques and how you can spot a devil from afar' she said. 'Two of you have survived them, and knowing we will be able to find them and kill them is a step nearer to a different world.'

'But what more can we do?' called out one of the angels. 'How can we get more strength to fight when it's one against twenty? Especially when they have weapons.'

'With the scythes we have no hope' shouted another.

'There is nothing we can do about their weapons, but their knives are no different to our bodies. We can slice off the head of a man with our bare hands. We can do so much, but you will all need further training and that is what we are here for. Serj will show you all the techniques you will need to know' Amy told him. 'You who fought and survived, we need you to step forward and make yourselves known. You can also assist your fellow angels with your fighting skills.'

'My name is Meredith', came a soft voice from the back of the room. The angels all looked across to see a petite and very slim woman walk forward. She was extremely beautiful. She spoke with a cultured London accent and had long dark hair and rosy cheeks. The other angels wondered how such a small woman had fought off eight devils and killed each and every one of them.

'Meredith, you too must help Serj teach the angels how to fight and be aware of their surroundings' said Amy. 'We will need all those of you who have succeeded in battle out there to come forward and help.'

Dr Konte then stood up. 'I know some of you may be scared, and yes we were foolish to think no harm would come to you, and for that I apologise' he said. 'With those evil creatures on this planet there will be times we will need to go for them, even find them ourselves and go in for the kill. We cannot wait around for them to kill us. The Government is on our side and it will be kept quiet when we do kill them. However they cannot get involved in the war between us and them, and that's what it will be - a war!' He lifted his fist up to the crowd.

'We must also try to work out where this stone is and get to it as soon as possible. That will be a job the AAG will take care of and we will keep you updated.'

'But how will you find out where it is? It could be anywhere in the world' shouted an angel in the crowd. 'Where do you start?' said another.

'We will have to look deeper into the possibilities of its whereabouts' said Konte. 'We need to investigate the stories further. They should give us some kind of indication. We will have to travel far. There are at least twelve places where we think it could be. Of course it will be an extremely hard and tedious task to find it, but we will get it and secure it for Amy.'

'Or of course whoever has her heart', added Henrik.

'Amy, do you have someone in your life, family, a partner or anyone?' asked the doctor. Amy looked straight at Henrik. 'No Dr Konte, I am not in love and have no one special in my life' she said. 'My children are too young to take this on.' She looked back at Henrik and shrugged her shoulders.

'Well maybe you will find love amongst these beautiful creatures, you never know', the doctor replied and walked off.

'Amy, what about Max?' Henrik murmured to her.

'I don't want him involved in any of this. If he finds out some of us have been killed and that we are in danger, that will be it,' she whispered to him. 'And mostly because I do not want him in any danger, they would kill him so quickly if they knew. Sorry Henrik, but I am serious, he is not to know a thing.'

Henrik gave a look of concern as she walked off. Amy really felt the pressure after hearing this, but she had a job to do and there was no time for thinking about it.

For the rest of the afternoon and evening the angels went through strict training and learned more about the history of the angels and the devils. They took it in turns to practise, and by midnight they were all exhausted. A large banquet was laid on for them out in the gardens, which had views of a black ocean under dark skies in the distance. There was enough food and wine for at least five thousand. This was a chance for the angels to get to know each other even better and to discuss their lives with each other, as well as having some fun.

Amy enjoyed the evening, watching all the angels having fun and dancing the night away as if they did not have a care in the world, but she just wanted to be home with the kids and Max. She longed to be normal again.

CHAPTER THIRTY SEVEN

'Hey are you OK?' asked Serj. 'You seem a bit quiet.'

'Oh I'm fine, I just have so much to think about' she replied.

'Wanna take a walk?' he asked, holding out his elbow. She slipped her arm through it and they took a walk around the grounds. The night was warm with a nice breeze from the sea. They talked about their lives and loves and tried to make sense of what had happened in the last few weeks.

'How do your family feel about it?' Amy asked him.

'Well my wife was kinda freaked out, but then she found it kinda sexy.' Serj laughed. 'The kids found it pretty cool, but they are young.'

'Well my kids found it cool too and they are older!' she replied, laughing. 'Just where do we go from here though? It all seems so much hard work, so much looking over our shoulders. I still can't believe I am an angel, let alone a superior one, can you?'

'I am seriously freaked out about this I can tell you that. I mean I am a musician, my music is doing really well out there and I have to keep this so quiet. And there's my family, I can't even look after them properly with all this going on, I've never had to lie so much.' He looked at the ground.

'I know Serj, I feel your pain. I just want my life back to how it was, get up, go to work, get home and go to bed day in day out. It all sounds so boring now, but so much safer' Amy replied.

'The only thing I can think of is getting these devils, killing them, getting that stone and going back to my normal life, but to be honest with you, with so many of them to one of us, how the hell are we going to do it? Especially with the weapons they have' Serj asked.

'I don't know, but we have taken a lot of them down already so that's a start' she reassured him.

'I know Amy, but it's hard to think about leading a normal life when we have this hanging over us and sometimes, sometimes, I just wanna go and hide on a desert island away from everyone, just my wife, me and the kids. But then other times I get the urge to be out there fighting for this world.'

'I feel the same. I worry for my family, and the fact that my partner Max also has a chance of saving us is even more worrying for me. I would just freak out if he got involved, he wouldn't last a minute against them. Oh and you mustn't say anything about Max to the AAG, because I don't want him knowing there is danger around me. I don't want him to be involved in any of this.'

'Amy, I won't say a word. I would do the exact same. We will get through this, we will survive it all and then we will make this world a different place and for the better. Someone up there has given us this job to do and we have no choice but to do it.' He was softly holding her shoulders. 'Everything will be fine'. He leant forward and gave her a hug and they both walked back to the party, deciding life could be too short and they needed to have a little fun.

CHAPTER THIRTY EIGHT

Henrik walked back to his room to try and get at least six hours' sleep. They all had to be up early the next morning to continue with the next day's work and training. As he walked back, all he thought about was the last few words written in Zaid's stories: 'To find is to change and deeper will be the key, the strength will come from superiority or the heart of it'.

He screwed his eyes up and came to a halt in the corridor, moving his eyes around and repeating the message over and over again.

Suddenly it clicked.

'Oh my God that's it!' he said. 'The temple, the stone is the thing I couldn't remove from that little cupboard!' He spoke in a voice a little louder than he should have and looked around to make sure no one had heard him, even though the hotel was highly secured and only boarding the angels.

He thought it might be best to keep quiet about his realisation of where the stone could be. He would only tell Dr Konte, Amy and Serj. He decided that until he actually knew the stone was the object, he could not remove it from the cupboard. Only then would he tell the others about it. The main thing was to get it and return to New York with it. He would do this in secret, so there could be no one watching him or following him.

All through the night Henrik couldn't sleep. He lay on his bed with his eyes wide open staring up at the ceiling, constantly thinking about the stone and wondering whether it was there or whether it was somewhere else. If it actually was the stone, he thought about what this could mean for the world. He would then pace up and down the floor of the apartment and out onto the balcony, worrying about whether the devils would get to Iraq before him and find the stone first. Surely they knew the stories of the history of the angels.

Three hours had passed and Henrik had still not slept. He decided he needed to work fast. He had to sneak out of the hotel and find the quickest flight off the island and towards Iraq.

He started to pack his belongings in an attempt to get out before sunrise. He thought he should say something to Amy about what he was up to, so he quickly wrote a letter to her stating he had an idea of where the stone might be and also that he had to leave straight away to retrieve it. He also asked her not to mention it to anyone just in case the Iblisari were watching them.

Henrik added that he would explain more in full in a few days, and that should he find the stone he would bring it back to New York. At the end of the letter he stated that she was not to say a word to anyone. He would leave a small note at reception for Dr Konte saying he had had to pop home for a family matter.

Henrik crept out of his room carefully before sunrise, looking around every turning in case someone saw him. He passed Amy's hotel room and carefully slipped the letter under the door. Then he carried on walking fast towards the main entrance and reception. The security man was fast asleep, so Henrik left the note for Dr Konte and walked until he saw the first taxi to start his journey to Las Palmas Airport.

After four hours of waiting for flight cancellations, Henrik finally boarded the plane to Algiers, where he would pick up his connecting flight to Iraq. Five hours later he finally reached the little hotel not far from the ancient ruins and temples of Vuoil.

As last time, Henrik had to wait until the last admission at the tourist entrance of the main temple, so he waited in his room for the time to go by. He had memorised the steps he had taken the last time he had got in. He had also remembered to take equipment which would allow him to get further into the small cupboard; to reach what he hoped would be the stone.

★ ★ ★ ★ ★

Back in Arguineguin, Dr Konte made his way to Amy's apartment at 7 am after being given the note by the receptionist as he had his morning cigarette.

He knocked on the door with three loud bangs,

'Amy, Amy, can you hear me? Wake up, I need to speak to you immediately' he loudly whispered at the door. Amy was lying in bed fast asleep when she heard the knock. 'Hold on' she shouted as she searched for something to cover herself up with.

'Amy, it's Dr Konte, I need to speak with you' he said again.

'OK, give me a second' she shouted back in her croaky voice. As she walked over to the door she saw the letter on the floor. She picked it up before she opened the door, quickly opening it and scanning through what Henrik had written.

'Jesus Christ, what is he doing?' she said to herself. She stuffed the letter into her pocket and opened the door.

'Hey, what's up?' she said.

'Amy, Henrik has gone and I know it is because of something to do with the stone' he said. 'Do you know anything?'

'No, I have no idea, did he not say anything else?' she asked.

'No, he just left this note. I am worried he is returning to try and find the stone. I believe he thought of an idea of where it might be and decided it would be safer for him to go alone.' Dr Konte looked very worried.

'The devils know who we are, this is not safe for him' he said. 'He must not return there to find the stone! The devils know he is the one who found the ancient stories and they will more than likely be watching him more than anyone else. We need to know where he is. He could be in grave danger. He does not understand that if he finds the stone they will be only metres away from him, ready to pounce, and they will not hold back from killing him'.

'Doctor, I really don't think he would be that stupid' replied Amy. 'If I know Henrik, I know him as a genius. He will get out of anything and survive anything. I think you have nothing to worry about'.

'I'm really not sure about this, I fear the worst. The stupid man, what has he done?' He sat on the edge of the sofa and placed his head in his hands. 'Amy, will you please find out where he is and go after him and knock some sense into the old fool?'

Amy looked a little shocked at this request, but she thought he knew deep down that Henrik had gone to Vuoil.

'Please sort this out, maybe Serj can accompany you, they both knew Henrik would never survive out there on his own', he said. He stood up and put his hands on her shoulders.

'Yes, OK I will search for him, but I have no idea where to start', she groaned.

'You should start in Iraq' he said. 'I will give you a map of how to get to Vuoil. I will book the flights right now and get you there as soon as possible. If he is not there, which I think is highly unlikely, I will have the next flights booked and ready for your return to New York.'

'Ok, I'll do it, but I will need to make sure Serj can come along, I don't want to travel alone.'

'Amy, that's fine, I will arrange the flights for you both as soon as possible. Just to let you know that once you enter the temples you will feel the presence of the spirits of the angels and they will guide you. Trust me Amy, you will be safe. You will find it difficult to go into the temples as the corridors may be too narrow and the ceilings too low if your wings are out, so please be careful. I will meet you in reception in thirty minutes.'

Amy stepped out on to her balcony and read Henrik's letter again. She thought he wouldn't be so stupid as to try and get the stone, but as the letter said, he was definitely on his way. Yet Henrik was old and wise. Surely he knew what he was doing, and he would be fine.

Amy was down in reception waiting for Dr Konte when Serj walked towards her with his weekend bag in his arm. 'What the hell is going on?' he asked. 'Doc asked me to be here, packed up and ready to go.'

'Oh god, I will explain on the way' she told him as the doctor approached them.

'Here are your e-tickets for the flights and here is a map' he said. 'I hope you can stop the old fool before it's too late. Now go. Keep me posted on whatever happens and I will see you back in New York in a few days to get the update.'

Amy and Serj stepped into the taxi for the airport, where she explained what the doctor knew and what she knew. Although Henrik had told her not to tell a soul, she could trust Serj and knew he would never tell anyone.

'This really is crazy Amy. I can't believe we are going to these temples, the place where the angels were slaughtered all those years ago and the palace of King Gabir and Queen Amira. I know I shouldn't worry but I feel kinda scared' he told her.

'Serj, come on, remember we are the superior ones, we will not be defeated!' she said and laughed. Serj laughed with her and the two of them embarked on their journey.

CHAPTER THIRTY NINE

A couple of hours passed and Henrik was ready to make his way into the temples. He dressed up as a poor tourist with an unclean top saying 'I Love Gran Canaria', even though he was nowhere near there now. He also wore broken sunglasses just in case he was recognised. He carried his rucksack with his hammer, small saw and crowbar all wrapped up in a towel inside it and set off on his journey.

The sun was still shining brightly, but it was starting to slowly sink towards the horizon.

Henrik arrived at the temples with an hour left of admission. He paid and walked into the ruins, after spending half an hour in the main area where he walked towards the locked up and prohibited areas at the entrance of the underground temples. He hung around there until security came to check the place was empty, when he hid between two large tombs behind a pile of rubble.

Finally the guards had come and gone and dimmed the outdoor lighting for the evening. Henrik rose up from between the small tombs and slowly crept around to the locked gates. He forced his way through the gate as before and walked into the open area of the old city.

Once again the atmosphere was something words could not explain. It had a deep mystery to it and felt a little scary, but Henrik felt safe. He felt again as if he were being watched, but he knew it was the spirits of the angels. He felt them brush up against him, as if pushing him in the right direction.

It was now starting to get dark, but the ruins were lit up with small spot lights in shades of green and blue. He stood for a few minutes with his eyes closed, breathing in the air of this spectacular place and taking time before he went down into the dark, just in case he never returned.

★ ★ ★ ★ ★

On the other side of town Amy and Serj landed at the airport. They ran from the plane and jumped into a waiting private transfer which took them to their hotel.

'Let's just drop our bags at the hotel and get to the temples straight away' said Amy. 'I hope we're not too late to see them.' She was disguising the fact that they were actually going to look for someone, in case the driver wondered what they meant.

Serj looked through the tourist leaflets he had picked up in the airport. 'Amy, it says here that the temples and ruins close at dusk and that was an hour ago' he said.

'Oh no no no, you will not get in palace ruins now' the taxi driver said as he looked back at them in his mirror. 'You must wait until 8 am tomorrow morning.'

'Well if I know Henrik he will have made his way in there and is probably still in there now' whispered Amy to Serj. 'He would have waited for closing time. Hopefully he will not have been followed.'

'Well, we will have to get there and wait around at the front gates until he comes out so we can get him and the stone back safely, if he has it that is' Serj replied.

'He probably doesn't even have it, and this trip is a complete waste of time' she replied.

They soon arrived at the hotel, where they dropped their luggage off and jumped straight back into the waiting taxi to take them to the ruins.

* * * * *

Henrik pulled himself together after his ten minutes of meditating. He took another deep breath before heading towards the opening of the old palace. Again he had to use his tools to break through the large gate with the angels on it. He managed to do so without damaging it. Having got through safely, he made his way past the halls and corridors and directed his torch towards the small temples that led to the small rooms. As last time, he felt he was being guided. He didn't feel scared, because he now knew that he was in the presence of the angels. After having read the stories, he could now see the actual places and rooms Zaid had mentioned.

He continued deep into the darkness, past all the lights and through the doors that were signed 'Access Strictly Forbidden'. This time he knew what to expect and which rooms and doors to head for. Finally he had reached the area where he last found the book. The room was as it had been the last time he had been there, which meant the tiny cupboard should still be untouched. He went further into the darkness until he reached the room with the hidden cupboard.

Henrik sat down in the corner of the room and searched through his tool bag for the equipment he had brought to unscrew the door carefully and open the cupboard. He managed to get all the way in, then he placed his screwdriver and crowbar down on the dusty floor and cracked his knuckles. The room was completely empty, but Henrik could feel again a hundred spirits staring at him, watching over him. He wished he could just see their faces.

Suddenly he heard a creaking noise; it was followed by a rumble under his feet. Henrik kept still, wondering if it was an Earthquake. Ten seconds later an almighty rumbling sound echoed around him and the room began to drop, as if it were sinking into the ground. Henrik fought to stay calm, although he had never been more scared in his life. Bricks fell from the ceilings and walls, filling the room with dust. He guessed that the room had dropped five inches. He thought he should get out of there straight away if he wanted to survive, but as he prepared to leave, he remembered what he was there for; he had to retrieve the stone. There was no way he was letting it sink underground with the rest of the building.

He rushed to get his utensils and hurried to open up the cupboard. He only managed to open it a couple of inches more than he had the last time, and it was still slightly too small for Henrik to look directly into, but he was able to squeeze his arm in further and feel around with his hands.

Carefully he reached in deeper, flicking through the thick dust. There it was - the object he had felt before. He curled his fingers around it and pulled, but it refused to move.

Henrik turned to his screwdriver to see if it could help him lever it out. He still couldn't tell if it was the stone or not. Whatever it was, it was covered in rags and rattled when it was shaken. It seemed to have been placed in some sort of cloth protection wrapped around the outside, but it felt as if it was padlocked down. He decided to use his wire cutters and cut until it became free, so he could finally see what this thing was.

After struggling for fifteen minutes cutting the chains and wires, Henrik finally felt it come loose. He put his wire cutters on the floor, picked his torch up and carefully took the object from the cupboard.

It was indeed a box, and it was thickly covered in dust. Henrik wiped the dust off and saw the cloth covering it, tied with an ancient piece of fine cord. He unpicked the cord and placed the box on his lap, slowly unwrapping it. Finally he came to the last piece of wrapping.

Inside the box was a small, ancient pot. He recognised it as a pyxis, a circular pot with a separate lid. He stopped in shock, his heart beating so fast that he could hear it pounding. He held up the little pot and knew by the slight rattling inside it that it contained a solid object of some kind. Pulling the lid off the pyxis, he looked inside.

There it was glowing in the dark, a beautiful, shiny stone. He couldn't believe his eyes. Even in the dark he could clearly see the colour. The stone was beautiful.

Henrik knew from previous descriptions that this was *the* stone, the stone that held the key to the fate of the world. He placed the lid back on the pyxis and carefully wrapped it back up as he had found it, making sure he did not damage it. Then he tied the cord back around it, took a container out of his bag and placed the wrapped-up pyxis containing the stone into it.

He felt exuberant that he had been proved right. But his mission was not over yet. Now that this vital stone was in his hands, he would have to be very, very careful when it came to taking it over to the States.

Thirty minutes later, having got himself out through the dark corridors, Henrik sneaked back around past the securely locked numbered temple where he believed the stone had originally been lying because of the numbers printed on it. He knew Zaid hadn't mentioned this in his stories in case the Iblisari had got hold of the information. He thought about placing a fake stone in it to fool anyone who might attempt to take it.

After forcing open the locks with his equipment he stopped. He had heard faint voices coming from the other side of the wall in the distance. Henrik started to panic. The devils must be there watching; he had to place the stone in the temple. If he kept it with him there was a terrible danger that it would be captured with him.

Leaving the stone on an altar inside the tomb, he placed new heavy-duty locks on the gate and doors, then slowly stumbled towards the entrance. He thought that if he pretended to be a drunken down-and-out he might get away with it.

The ruse worked. The guards ran over to him, and as they got closer they started shouting at him in Iraqi. They grabbed him and searched him thoroughly to see if he had taken anything from the grounds, then escorted him out of the premises and across the street.

Henrik knew the voices he had heard earlier were not guards. They must be the devils. He had to get out of the area and back home as soon as possible, before they caught up with him.

Once he was safely on his way back to the airport, Henrik felt glad to be alive and relieved the stone was safe. The guards would be guarding the temple with their rifles, and there was no way the devils would be able to reach the stone.

★ ★ ★ ★ ★

Not knowing they had missed Henrik by seconds, Amy and Serj walked around the high walls of the temples.

'If Henrik is in there, how the hell he is going to get back out?" Amy asked Serj. "The security guards are in there, did you hear them shouting?'

'Maybe they were shouting at an animal or something, I have no idea. More to the point, security seems pretty tight, how are we going to get in? There must be a way somewhere around the side or back. It says here there are four entrances.'

He led the way further around to the side of the temples. They waited there until they could no longer hear the footsteps of the security guards.

'I'm worried about Henrik' said Amy. 'He may be a smart guy but he is also very foolish at times.'

'Listen' said Serj, 'Henrik isn't stupid. He will be disguised and he will be vigilant. He will sneak his way out of anywhere. No one knows about this, it will be fine'.

Little did they know that Henrik had heard them and thought they were devils.

'This place must be forty acres. How the hell are we going to find somewhere to sneak in?' said Serj.

'We'll just have to keep looking' Amy replied.

Luckily there was no one around to see their wings emerge from their backs. It was almost midnight and the area was deserted. The walls were 25 feet high, but there were small windows every few feet. They raised themselves up to see if the coast was clear on the other side. Then they attempted to levitate over the wall, but it was higher than they thought.

'Right, do you want me to go first, boss?' Serj asked Amy.

'Very funny, please don't call me that again', she replied sharply. 'Go on, you try and see if you can get up there. We need to get him out of there safely with the stone. If he gets caught he will end up going to the local jail and you don't know who or what he could bump into in there. The Iblisari could be there.'

Serj took a big jump, rising two feet from the ground, and then flapped his wings and started to levitate. His wings made the dry mud and sand blow around the place like a small cyclone. Amy watched as he tried to raise himself higher and higher. At last he reached the top. He looked over the stone wall in amazement.

'Get up here', he called softly to Amy standing below. He placed his hands between the small pieces of shattered glass which had been stuck there to prevent trespassers.

'We can make it over, come on, there's no one about'.

Amy prepared herself to levitate from the ground, but just before she jumped up she felt a push and she was up and away. She looked back down, thinking there was someone under her, but could see no one. As she reached the top where Serj was waiting he took her hand and they got themselves over the wall. As they gently landed, they both felt a force going through their bodies.

'What the hell was that? Did you feel it?' Serj asked Amy.

'Yes, I swear I felt something push me up from the other side.'

'This place is awesome' Serj said as he walked a few footsteps in front of Amy.

'It is definitely something else,' she replied. 'I can't believe I had never heard of it.'

They both stood still and closed their eyes. They felt as if hundreds of people were watching them in an empty room. It made the hairs stand up on the backs of their necks.

'Can you feel that?' Amy said. But just then they both heard a voice. 'Welcome, angels' it said; a soft female voice. Both Amy and Serj opened their eyes in shock.

'Who are you? Where are you?' said Amy. But there was only silence. They walked further into the temple gardens.

'I can't believe the beauty of this place' said Amy. She could feel the strange but comforting presence again. It felt like heaven to her. Every now and then they could feel something brush past them. The air was warmer and more fragrant the deeper they went into the old palace.

'Let's walk on and head for the gates into the underground temples, I have no idea how to follow this map, do you?' Serj asked.

But within seconds they felt a pulling on their hands. They did not fear this. They just closed their eyes and let the spirit lead the way, not reading the map at all. They ended up in front of what looked like a doorway with two metal gates protecting it.

Just then they heard another soft voice in the air, a man's.

'You do not need to proceed further' the voice said. 'The man has gone, the stone has been moved, and you must go now and help him.'

'But where has he gone? Will he be safe?' Amy asked.

'You must find him' the voice carried on. They then felt a soft force drawing them back over to the place where they had entered the site.

'OK, so I guess we have to get to the airport and hope he has not got on the plane yet' said Serj.

'But Serj, the next flight out of there is at 2 am, and it's ten past midnight. There's no way we will get back to catch that flight, and the one after that is 48 hours from now. How are we going to get back to him in time?'

'Look, I think we should try for the two am flight, we need to try'.

They jumped off the ground, levitating their way to the top of the wall. Then they both turned back to look down at the area they had left, and there, to their shock and amazement, they saw a crowd of ghostly figures; angels. They were standing in a great circle with their hands together, looking up at them. Amy and Serj floated in mid-air, staring down at the terrifying but beautiful sight in front of them. These beings could only be the angels who had been slaughtered all those years ago.

They felt such emotion that it almost brought tears to their eyes. The angels looked so perfect, yet so sad. The angel in the centre with the largest wings, almost same size as Amy's, raised his hand and spoke.

'We trust you will overcome evil and we pray for you' he said. 'You are very much aware of the dangers around you, unlike us. We will do our best to guide you in this fight.'

Amy and Serj looked at each other and then looked back at the angels, but they had disappeared.

Now they were both even more determined to fight for the evil to be removed from the planet and to win justice for these beautiful and good creatures.

Safely on the other side, they took a deep breath. 'Wow that was insane', Serj said to Amy. 'I mean seriously, I think that was the weirdest and most amazing thing I have ever seen'.

'It was mad, but beautiful' Amy said.

They both walked slowly back to find a taxi, still stunned by what they had just seen.

'Right, you heard them, we need to get to Henrik, but he must be almost at the airport to get that flight to New York. We really need to hurry. If we don't make it, it will end in disaster.'

'Well we can only try. We need to get back to the hotel and straight to the airport. At this time of night we can do it in an hour and a half and we can stop that plane', Serj replied. 'It's tight but it's worth a try. If not we'll just have to get the next flight out and hope for the best. Come on, we need to run.'

Amy and Serj ran to the nearby town hoping they would see a taxi, but there were none to be found.

'Dammit, I knew this would happen' Amy said, worried.

After ten minutes of walking through the derelict streets they finally saw a taxi approaching with its lights out. The driver was probably making his way home, but Amy stood on the road so he could not go past. He beeped his horn several times, but finally stopped when Serj flashed $300 at him.

'I feenish for the night, but I make one more treep' said the driver in his best English.

'Oh that's great, thank you so much, we need the Hotel Amari and then the airport as soon as possible and we really need to hurry. We only have dollars but we'll pay three times the price.'

The driver seemed happy after receiving the first instalment and sped off down the hill towards their hotel. From the taxi to the hotel they had never run so fast in their lives. They got in and out within seconds and were now on their way to the airport.

CHAPTER FORTY

In the meantime Henrik had started to proceed to the departure lounge to board his flight. He was annoyed with himself for making the journey, but glad he had found the stone and placed it somewhere safe.

Speeding down the motorway, the driver asked Amy and Serj what they thought about the Pope stepping down from his position. 'Oh, dear, I never knew that, do you know why?' she asked the driver.

'Everyone talk, no one know. Maybe ees the angels' he said, shrugging his shoulders.

As they carried on driving towards the airport, the street lights suddenly went out. 'What the hell?' the driver shouted out as he slowed down. When they were close to stopping they all felt a loud bang as if a rock had hit the car. The rear window was shattered. The driver cursed in Iraqi and pulled over. The motorway suddenly seemed to be empty.

'Jesus, we are not going to get there!' shouted Amy. 'Driver, please I will pay you double again if you just get us to the airport and I will pay to get the car fixed!'

'Please, this is very important' added Serj.

'OK, OK, you have money?' asked the driver. Amy got out another large wad of notes and handed them over to him. 'OK I take you' the driver said, excited at the amount of money he was being offered.

'Come on then!' Amy shouted as he walked towards his door. But as the driver went to open his door, they heard a loud bang. The driver staggered against Amy's window. Serj jumped out to see what was happening and saw blood on the car. Their driver had slumped to the ground, clearly dead.

'Amy, get out of the car now!' he shouted. Amy jumped out and ran around to see the driver dead on the floor in a pool of blood. They both looked up, knowing what was about to happen. Before they knew it, their wings were up in full array.

Looking around as best they could in the pitch black, they could see nothing. Yet they both knew there was something evil close by and they were going to confront it.

A few seconds later they heard rustling in a nearby tree, then faint laughter. A street light came back on, then another.

'Well I knew it would happen sometime soon', Serj whispered to her. 'They're here. Are you ready for this Amy?' He put a reassuring hand on her shoulder,

'I thought I wouldn't be, but I feel so ready' she whispered back.

Then, out of the darkness, they saw the figures of at least thirty men and women slowly walking towards them. Amy and Serj stood up straight and waited for them to get closer, their fists clenched, their heads down and eyes up.

The leading devil spoke. 'Your poor driver, did you know him?' he asked in a smug tone. But the two angels had no time for silly chat. Amy wanted to get her first fight over and done with.

'So you think you can kill an innocent and get away with it?' Amy asked. But she did not wait for the reply. Remembering what she had been taught, she ran forward and struck the leading devil terrible blows with her wings and fists. Eight devils fell to the ground, but they were soon back up again.

'Please, we have our strongest fighters here, for you are the superior one are you not? We find out many things' said the leading devil. 'You have a fight on your hands, but it would be easy for you just to tell us where the stone is.'

'I don't think so' she said. She charged again, Serj alongside her. They each grabbed a devil by the head and twisted their heads, breaking their necks. The other devils fought back strong and hard, but they were no match for the extraordinary powers Amy and Serj had acquired. After several minutes of savage fighting, Amy and Serj stood battered but unbowed. Around them, the thirty devils lay on the ground, all dead or dying.

'You will never get the stone!' she shouted at the last two survivors. 'Finish them, Serj.'

'You're the boss' he replied. Seconds later the last devils were dead.

'Ok, let's get ourselves to the airport, I knew we should have just hired a car' said Amy.

'I'm thinking the plane leaves in about twenty minutes and we are about twenty minutes away' said Serj. 'I really don't think we will make it thanks to those arseholes.'

Amy tried Henrik's number again. 'Why can't he answer his damn phone?' she cursed, as he turned on the ignition and drove off.

Leaving the car on the road outside the airport, they ran into the check-in area and Amy ran ahead of Serj to the queue. Everyone moved out of the way to let her get to the front desk. They were mesmerised by her wings.

'Can you tell me if the New York flight has left?' she asked the attendant.

'The last flight is on the runway and taking off this minute, is there something I can help you with? The next flight for New York is not for another two days now, I'm sorry about that.'

'No, no that's OK' Amy sighed as she walked back to where Serj was standing, her head down. 'He's gone' she said. 'He's either going to get murdered by the devils or they will get the stone and we won't be able to get to him in time. I don't know why he can't put his damn phone on'.

'Look, we can try contacting him for when he arrives back home and we can advise him of what to do then' said Serj. 'In the meanwhile we need to get booked on the next flight wherever it goes. Let's just go the long way around, I don't want to stay here overnight waiting.' They made their way back to the flight information desk.

★ ★ ★ ★ ★

Several hours later, after landing in Algiers and waiting for the next flight, Amy managed to get Henrik on the line.

'Henrik, it's Amy, what the hell are you playing at? What have you been doing?

'Look, I thought I could find the stone but I was wrong, it wasn't where I thought it was. I have just arrived home, so I really need to sleep.'

Henrik was lying because he was worried that the phone line had been bugged or that someone nearby might be listening. He wanted to wait for Amy to arrive home before he told her the truth of where it was.

'We have been worried sick about you, why has your phone been off? You should have picked up. We were in Iraq, we came here looking for you and now we are stuck out here and we don't know when we will get back. Anyway, did you hear about the Pope, what is that all about? Does he really think angels will take over his post?'

'Well, all I know is that he was having trouble dealing with the death of the angels and after finding out two of his men were part of the Iblisari, that just topped it off for him. I guess he didn't feel worthy of the post or running the holy world knowing he hadn't noticed that two of his own aides were evil.'

'Right, OK, so what about the stone, do you think it's

somewhere else? How are we ever going to find it?' Amy asked.

'I think I need to do more research, or maybe read the stories over again to find clues. Look, I need to go, Barbell is calling, I will see you soon Amy.' The phone went dead.

'He doesn't have the stone and he is safe' Amy told Serj. 'He said he thinks it is elsewhere and will have to investigate further.'

'My god, did he even apologise for having us run across the world looking for him?' Serj asked.

'No, he seemed really tired. I guess we should just leave it there, maybe just go back to Arguineguin and to the closing meeting and we can let the doctor know what has happened, then go home from there. I know there's a flight heading out there in two hours. There is nothing else we can do here and there is no need to rush home now, is there?'

Soon after the conversation with Henrik, Amy called Dr Konte to tell him what had happened and to let him know they would be making their way back to Argunieguin as soon as they could board a flight. Dr Konte advised them that soon after they had left to find Henrik, the remaining angels had been set upon by many devils; it had ended in many deaths. Half the remaining angels had died, but 60 per cent of the devils had been killed, leaving just over 300 angels and around 30,000 devils. Dr Konte sounded weak and upset, as if he were to blame for not being able to protect them.

He then suggested that Amy and Serj should take a short trip before returning back home. He told them they should stop off at the island of Krobir to get a feel for the place, as it was mentioned in the historical stories of the angels. Amy and Serj accepted his offer to go and visit the small island and within a few hours they had arrived there. They stayed overnight and returned back home the next evening.

CHAPTER FORTY ONE

'Welcome all of you' Vladimir said as the devils congregated in Russian headquarters. 'You have all done well so far and we praise those who have lost their lives trying to win us our freedom.' There were chants of praise ringing through the large room. 'We have only a few men left, but we will fight stronger and harder and we will find the stone. We are here to discuss how we can improve and progress with our powers now that we have discovered there is one superior angel, a female, and we have reason to believe she was last seen in Iraq. She has powers greater than the rest and she is the only one who can get rid of the stone.

'This angel is our target. We must find out who and where she. We also have more news on the old man named Henrik, the one who found out about the angels and brought it to our knowledge by spreading the news to the world. He has information on where the stone is and where the superior angel is. He will be able to lead us to them, I am sure about that.'

'My group and I will make it our priority to find this man and get him to take us to the stone' said one of the leaders. 'We will start looking into this straight away. Wherever she lives we will find her and the old man and we will destroy them if they do not co-operate.'

They spent the next few hours working on their fighting skills and distributing new weapons between them to allow them to have better chances to kill. Little did Vladimir know that the woman he wanted to find lived in the same part of America as he did, and that she was just a working parent who led a normal life.

Least of all did he guess that she was in love with his own son, and his son was in love with her.

CHAPTER FORTY TWO

While Henrik sat in the taxi on the way back home, all he could think of was the stone. All they needed was another meeting or two with all of the angels and a few days to work out a plan on how to defeat the devils. This had to be arranged as soon as possible, because it was only a matter of time before they worked out where the stone was, and it was clear the devils were clever enough to do so.

Barbell was due to leave to see the grandchildren for a few weeks, so when Henrik arrived home she was happy to see him, if only for a short while. He planned to follow her down in a couple of days to join her. She'd told him there was a case packed and ready for him and that he was not to go off to any more meetings, as the family holiday was more important.

After his tea Henrik went out for an evening stroll to the grocery store. On his way back he was approached by a tall man in dark clothing.

'Hand over what you have, old man!' said the figure. Henrik could not see his face.

'What are you talking about?' He stammered.

'You are Henrik are you not? You have the stone and you must give it to me. We know you took the stone from Iraq.'

Henrik realised that his suspicions were correct and the devils were watching him.

Just then he noticed a police car slowly passing by. Quickly and without thinking too much about it, he ran over to it. The devil walked off in the opposite direction. Henrik stopped and spoke to the officers, and as soon as he saw the devil disappear he jumped into a nearby taxi and told the driver to go.

Henrik started to worry even more now, thinking he was still being followed, so he asked the driver to stop off at a shop where he could buy a paper and asked him to keep the meter running. Leaving his payment on the back seat, he jumped out and went into the shop. He ran straight through to the back, out past the back doors and over to the back of a restaurant on the opposite side of the alleyway. He needed to lose whoever was following him.

As he hid he was spotted by the workers in the restaurant, so he ran further through and jumped into another cab on another road and headed toward towards home via the back streets. After half an hour of driving around he decided it was now safe, so he carried on his journey, remaining vigilant of everyone around him. He still felt watched and unsafe. He felt as if he had interfered with things by attempting to take the stone.

Amy wasn't around to advise him on what to do. The only thing he could think of doing was to get home, sleep and get straight out of the house early the next morning.

After the last few hectic days Henrik was exhausted. The moment he got indoors he fell down on the sofa and wrote a note to Amy.

Amy,

As you know I am back home after the last few trips and I plan to leave the country for 3 or 4 days until the meeting next week. I have had to arrange the meeting as I have important information for you all.

I'm afraid I lied to you about the stone. I did find it, but I had to lie to you when we spoke over the phone. I lied because I was worried I was being traced, which I was. They are following me everywhere.

If I wait for you to return, the Iblisari may find me and probably kill me, so I am off tomorrow first thing in the morning.

After finding the stone I decided to return it to its rightful place, which is back in Vuoil, Iraq. I placed it in the first tomb after the last gate in the ruins. The tomb has the numbers XXXVI, meaning 36, which is three twelves, the date you angels appeared.

In a week and a half there will be some construction work at the ruins, but before the work commences the area will be empty and I think that is the right time to go and retrieve the stone. As you know there will be danger there, which is why we need to meet.

I am sorry you wasted a trip over there but I didn't expect they would be watching me. I thought I was doing the right thing. I have definitely put the devils off their tracks because they believe I have the stone here.

I have no doubt they will find out somehow where the stone is soon, but it is secure and waiting for you. Enclosed you will find the keys to the large padlocks on the tomb.

Should I not be around for the next meeting for whatever reason, you must go and attempt to retrieve the stone two weeks from now. Please advise the others so you can all prepare to go over there together. You must know that the Iblisari will be following you and they will more than likely be somewhere close by, so you must all be prepared to fight and kill.

I am writing this as I am worried for my wife and me. They are on to me. Should my trip go smoothly I will see you at the next meeting in 4 days.

Dispose of this letter immediately.

Good luck with everything, I hope to see you soon.

Henrik.

After slipping the letter through Amy's door, Henrik was able to get a few hours' rest before taking a taxi to the airport early the next morning to join Barbell and their daughter Marion with the grandchildren in Mexico. He couldn't wait. The last few weeks had been stressful. He needed time to recover.

In the small hours of the night, Henrik was woken by a sharp pricking sensation in his neck. He opened his eyes to see two figures in front of him in the darkened room. He could only presume a third was behind him holding the knife. One of the devils was the one who had accosted him in the street a couple of days before.

'What do you want?' Henrik grunted.

'We are here for the stone', said one of the devils.

'I don't have any information on the stone, nor do I know where it is. And even if I did I wouldn't be telling you' said Henrik calmly.

Henrik said his prayers in his head. He knew these were his last few moments, but if there was a chance the world could be rid of evil then he was willing to die for it. He trusted Amy would be able to use her powers to get to the stone before any of them.

'Old man, I suggest you advise us of the whereabouts of the stone, it would be in your best interests', the second devil said. 'We have killed before and we will carry on killing until the stone is in our possession'.

'Well I would rather die than tell you where it is. You have killed innocent people to get to it, so you might as well kill me too. I couldn't care less, because you will find there are very strong angels left out there and you will also find it hard to overpower them. You will never get the stone. I have placed it somewhere safe, somewhere far away from here, a place you will never think of.'

'Well then old man, prepare to die, slowly', they said. They hauled him up from the sofa and dragged him over to a dining chair, where they tied him up.

'We will give you another chance to tell us where the stone is' the first devil said. 'We will search your home until it is found.'

'I won't tell you anything', Henrik replied.

The devils punched Henrik in the face, shoulders and chest until he was drifting in and out of consciousness. They took knives from the kitchen and slashed his face and arms with them. Still Henrik did not give in. He was determined to say no more. This infuriated the devils, and they began to cut him deeper and deeper. Henrik could feel his life slipping away and all he could think about was his family and the peaceful world they would be living in soon, once the angels managed to get to the stone.

With one last stab in the chest Henrik was gone. At 70 years old he had seen many things and enjoyed a full life. Seeing angels arrive on Earth had topped it all off.

CHAPTER FORTY THREE

Amy was devastated by Henrik's death. He was one of her best friends, and they had taken his life. She was now worried for her children and Max, even though they had nothing to do with what was going on.

The AAG had arranged two meetings over the next few days in New York to discuss what had happened and what they needed to do next. The plan was for all the remaining angels to go over to Iraq in seven days' time to secure the stone against whatever opposition they met.

Amy had advised the AAG of the letter Henrik had written her and the area where he advised the stone would be but she didn't let the other angels know of the exact place where the stone was, as she thought it best to wait. The devils were sure to be in Vuoil shortly after they all arrived and they all knew they would be fighting, but they had to get it over and done with.

Amy was so determined to get over there and fight for what they had done to Henrik and so many of the others that she felt no fear whatsoever. However she couldn't let Max know what was going on.

The kids had gone off again to San Diego for a few days, so Amy could concentrate hard on what she needed to do. The night before the trip she spent the evening with Max enjoying some peace without the kids shouting and playing loud music.

'Max, I want you to move in now' she said. 'Come and live

with me here, life is just way too short and you're going to anyway so you might as well do it now. What do you think?'

'Well I guess it would be the sensible thing to do, my place is going on the market next week, so OK, why not?' he replied then went over to the fridge to get a bottle of champagne to celebrate and to try cheer her up a bit, although Amy didn't feel much like celebrating after what had happened to Henrik, she was more angry than anything and wanted to just concentrate on destroying the devils.

The morning of the trip Amy woke early to get her things together.

'Why are you up so early? Where are you going?' Max asked as he stretched in bed.

'I told you I have a business trip to go on, how could you forget?'

But Max hadn't forgotten; he had never been told. Amy didn't want him knowing earlier in case he demanded to be allowed to accompany her to protect her.

'I have to be in London in like eight hours' she said. She leaned over him and gave him a kiss on the lips, with a sinking feeling that it might be the last.

Max didn't want to moan at her for leaving him again so quickly after just returning. He knew she was upset about Henrik and might need some space.

'Amy, I hope you're not lying to me and you do actually have a have a meeting over there' he said. 'I'm just worried about this Iblisari crowd. They're evil. They've already killed, and from what they did all those years ago I can imagine they have in mind getting rid of every single one of you. Can't I come too?'

'Oh Max don't be silly, it's a few days of meetings and communicating with the others and finding out what the future holds for us and it will be covered with security. I can't help it if I have been chosen as the leader, I can't change that. And come on, we both know I can take care of myself.'

'Yes I know, and I know you're ten times stronger than me, but I still want to take care of you and look after you. Angels have been killed goddam it Amy, there are barely 300 of you left!'

He pulled her closer to hold her. As she held on tight to him a tear started to run down her face, but she wiped it away and jumped up to carry on with what she was doing not mentioning the fact there were a lot less angels left than he thought.

'Max, seriously you have nothing to worry about' she said. 'We have taken out many of them too, with simple self-defence only. I know there are so many more of them than us, but if we can do that with self-defence then just think what we can do when we put our minds to actually killing them. But as I said it's just a few quiet meetings in London, so just watch those dogs of mine and I'll be back before you know it.'

Amy felt so guilty lying to him, but it was for his own good.

'Max, why don't you just move in while I am away? It's really up to you; you can have a few days here on your own before we all arrive home.'

'I think that's a great idea' he replied, getting excited about it. 'I'll do it as long as you allow me to put the money I have towards paying off the mortgage, that way I can pay my half.'

Amy agreed to the offer and Max agreed to moving in straight away. She gave him one more hug before she set off.

On her way to the airport Amy was starting to feel pumped up ready for the trip to Iraq which could end up changing the world forever.

She just wanted to get out there to fight the Iblisari, but she was also worried about what would happen if all the devils were waiting there for her. They all knew now who she was and how important she was. She just had to make sure she got that stone.

★ ★ ★ ★ ★

In Iraq the weather was hot and clammy with no breeze. The sun shone down so hot on her skin as she walked toward the ruins. Amy was the last angel making the trip. All the others would be there waiting and preparing for the Iblisari to show. The whole area had been shut down to prepare for the construction works the next day.

As she entered the main entrance to the ruins, the place was like a ghost town. Something wasn't right; she should have seen someone by now.

She pushed the doors open and walked into the courtyard. She felt the same as she had the last time when she had been with Serj, but the day was bright and no ghostly figures were visible.

She walked over towards the long corridor leading to the next courtyard. As she arrived at the entrance to the corridor she felt a weird sensation in her bones, a sinking feeling, as if something bad was about to happen.

Opening the gate she walked around another corner and stopped in horror. In front of her lay the dead bodies of many angels and devils, some of them only children. They were scattered along the long corridors and around the entrances. She ran over to the nearest angels and fell to her knees weeping. She recognised many of them.

She tried to pull herself together and stood up, preparing to carry on past them. She desperately hoped she wouldn't find Serj or Christina among the bodies, or any of the other angels she had become close to over the last few weeks.

There were dead angels everywhere, but it looked as if they had put up a fight. The surviving devils had to be very close somewhere in the ruins, and Amy knew she had to be on guard because they would be searching for the hiding place of the stone.

Over the weeks the devils had also been losing their lives rapidly. She calculated that there could only be 5000 or so left now. She stopped and wondered how it had come to this and how there were so few angels left. How were the rest of them going to survive? She needed to find the others as soon as possible so they could take down these evil monsters together.

She said a prayer for the dead angels and walked towards the light at the end, which led to the courtyard. She walked carefully, listening, but she could hear nothing until she finally saw the large courtyard in front of her. She cautiously walked around the pillars and beams in case there was someone watching, ready to pounce and attack her.

Then she heard the sound of fighting. She ran around the corner to see two angels battling with a group of devils. They were surrounded by the bodies of many more devils that they had just killed.

Amy rushed in to help, her wings expanding rapidly, but she was too late to save the last two angels. Even as she stepped in they fell to the blows of the devils' scythes.

There was no time to think. Amy attacked, using her wings, legs and arms to grab punch and kick the nearby devils. She knocked eight of them to the floor, and then turned around to grab one more by the neck. She placed him in a headlock and twisted his head back, breaking his neck.

The other devils surrounded her. 'Where is the stone?' one of them asked her. 'Look around you, we have killed the rest of your friends. Do you want to join them?'

'We won't be giving up this fight' Amy said defiantly. She ran in with her wings at full span, knocking the three of them over. Stamping in the face of the nearest one, she crushed his skull and his head split in half. Then she turned to the other two lying on the floor in pain and walked in between them. She grabbed the collars of their cloaks and picked them both up, throwing them twenty metres across the courtyard into two large pillars.

As she walked off she looked back at the angels who had died and said another silent prayer for their courage. It was a tragic loss, but she had to carry on and fight for them. This waste of life had to have some purpose.

As she walked through the courtyard into the next section she encountered more devils, at least twenty of them, and finished them off too. She started to notice how well her strengths were now working and how easy it had become to beat the devils, but there was always the fear of seeing more dead angels.

Amy had now lost count of how many were left on both sides. In the distance she could hear more fighting, and when she got closer she could see Serj and a group of other angels. When she ran to get closer to him she saw around fifty devils lying face down covered in blood.

'Thank god you're OK' she said.

'Well same to you, I thought you had been taken down.'

Ahead of them three more angels were fighting for their lives. The other angels joined in and a few minutes later the rest of the devils were lying face down on the sandy ground.

'Thank god you guys are all still alive', Amy said as she ran over to them,

'Well we were pretty worried about you' one of the angels replied.

'You do know Amy that it's just you, me and these three left?' Serj told her.

'Just you guys? I can't believe this, and it's getting worse and worse' she said as she put her hand on her forehead. 'We need to stay strong. And the devils, how many do you think there are left of them?'

'From what I have seen I would say fifteen or twenty now at a guess, we've done pretty well.'

'Wow Serj, you must have killed hundreds or thousands within the last few minutes, I'm very impressed' she told him. Serj interrupted 'let me introduce you to these guys.'

'This is Orlando from Spain' Serj introduced him first. Orlando was tall with short dark hair and the fittest body Amy had ever seen. He had perfect tanned skin and stood six foot five.

'This is Elizabeth from Ireland' said Serj. Elizabeth was also tall, with pale skin and long black hair, rosy cheeks and green eyes.

'And this is Adonay from Peru'. The third angel was a stocky, well-built young man with strikingly good looks and beautiful blue eyes.

'Hi' Amy said, 'you guys have done so well, it's a shame there are just the five of us left, we need to tread very carefully.'

'Well the last one I took down said that the next few devils are the strongest ones of all. They include their leader, Vladimir. They'll be the ones we have to save all our powers for', Serj told them all.

Adonay came forward after dusting himself down. 'You know I was really scared before I came here knowing there would be the Iblisari to take on, but since I saw that first devil murdering my friend, that was it! I have taken down at least a hundred and I'm ready to go for more. I know it may end badly and I may not make it out alive, but I will fight and take them down until my last breath.'

'Same here' added Elizabeth. 'We have already wiped out 98 per cent of them. I really think we can do this'.

'Every single one of us here has done so well, from being normal humans just weeks ago and having to deal with the fact we are these special beings with wings' said Amy. 'That's a lot to take in and a lot to deal with. And then to have to take on these evil creatures, well it's a hard thing to get our heads around.'

'I just want to go for it' said Orlando. 'I want to get to those others and I want to drain the blood from every part of their evil bodies, there is no way they are going to get me I can tell you that now. They have taken our friends away from us. We need to work out something so they can't take one more angel.' He started pacing angrily up and down.

'Orlando, we all feel the same' Amy told him, 'but we need to calm down and save our anger for when we fight. We don't have much time. We may bump into them in a few minutes. We need to work out a few tricks before we see them.'

Amy and Serj showed them some extra fighting moves they

could use. Then she gathered them together and prepared to walk towards the entrance of the old palace hall. Amy still didn't tell the others that she knew exactly where the stone was. She wanted to wait for the coast to be clear and for all the Iblisari to be out of sight.

'Now I have an idea where the stone might be' said Amy. 'As you know I am the only one who can hold it and destroy it. If for some reason I don't make it out of here, the only other people able to do this would be Max and my children, but they would not stand a chance. They would have been dead by now if they were here, I just couldn't do that to them.'

'As I told you before, I would have done the same' said Serj. 'We all would have. Please do not think you have made the wrong decision here.' He placed his hands on her shoulders.

'Thanks Serj. Now before we go I need to let you know that when we get the next few devils it should be easier, and I will then be able to tell you where the stone is. She held her arms out to draw them closer. 'When I give you this information you must go to the place, but you must make sure there are no devils in sight or they are all confirmed dead. You should then retrieve the stone and get back to me with it as soon as you can. Whatever you do, do not go near it if I am far away and if there are more than three devils alive here. If that's the case you must leave it for me. But if I am killed and the coast is clear you should take it and hide it. If I cannot destroy it, no one can. However, if I die, then the person who has my heart, Max, will be able to destroy if you take it to him or my children. But the Iblisari must all be killed first. If they cannot all be killed, the stone will have to be kept and hidden from future devils until angels appear on the Earth again in thousands of years' time, and by then the devils and the Iblisari will be stronger than ever.

The most important thing is not to let them get their hands on it. All clear?'

The angels agreed. They all took deep breaths and slowly prepared to hunt for the devils. Suddenly a gust of wind swept by them, and in front of them stood five ghostly figures of angels.

'Jesus Christ!' shouted Elizabeth.

'You have all made such great effort' said the leader of the angel ghosts. 'You have done well, better than we could do all those many years ago. You have all been praised highly from above and we will be watching over you. Good luck!'

Amy stepped forward and bowed down to them, and the rest followed.

'We are sorry for what they did to you so many years ago and what they have just done to our fellow angels' she said. 'We have tried very hard. We will try our best to get the stone and put an end to this, I promise.'

'We know you will try' said the spirit. 'You have already done so well. You have taken some of them from this planet, and that was something we did not have the chance to do. We trust you all, farewell!' The spirits faded into darkness.

The five living angels stood still for a further few minutes to take in what they had just seen. They all felt a wave of energy and excitement. Finally they got themselves together and started to walk to the area where they knew the devils would be waiting. Amy, Elizabeth and Adonay took the lead, followed by Orlando and Serj. They knew the devils could appear from anywhere, so they needed the strongest at the back and front. They also needed to keep Amy safe.

It was not long before they heard the laughter of devils echoing down the passageway. The angels didn't hesitate to show themselves. Adonay and Elizabeth went in straight away and grabbed the necks of one devil each, giving them no time extract their weapons. The devils didn't stand a chance and fell to the floor dead. Then Orlando used his fists to knock out another devil.

Amy and Serj took on two each. Serj jumped over his two and attacked from behind, using his deadly hands like machetes to slice through their necks so that their heads were left hanging on with pieces of skin and flesh. Amy's two devils reached inside their cloaks for weapons, but when Serj and Elizabeth saw this they grabbed a devil each, breaking their necks.

Adonay and Orlando took on the last two, and before the others had time to walk over to help they had finished the devils.

'Well done' Amy said. 'Now we must find the rest.' They walked towards the next part of the courtyard and saw five very large and strong looking devils ready and waiting for them, already with their knives in their hands.

The angels knew this would be a harder fight. Amy and Serj took on the two largest devils and the others took the smaller ones. This fight was the hardest of all, and soon Elizabeth was down on the ground with lacerations to her stomach and neck. Amy quickly jumped up and levitated, grabbing the nearest devil with her feet. She wrung his neck, then stamped on his head to make sure he was completely dead. She then ran over to the devil that had killed Elizabeth and punched him to death with lightning-fast blows.

Amy ran over to Elizabeth, seeing that she was starting to move a little. She knelt down, cradling Elizabeth's head on her lap.

'Elizabeth, listen to me, you stay with us you hear?' she murmured, but Elizabeth was weak and blood was gushing from her neck.

'I'm sorry, I tried' she murmured. 'Leave me here and carry on, you will do this I can feel it.'

'Shh, don't strain yourself' said Amy.

'Amy, I am going, you fight on' Elizabeth replied. As Amy stared at her, her eyes slowly closed and her body went limp.

Amy looked up to the sky with tears in her eyes, but she had to keep strong. She picked Elizabeth's body up and carried it over to a safe place to leave her to rest. Turning around to the others she saw that one of the devils was about to put a knife through Adonay's skull. She ran over, grabbed his arm and twisted it so far back that it came out of its socket. Then she pulled harder, ripping it from his body. The devil ran off screaming, but Amy ran after him, grabbing him and throwing him against the wall, killing him.

The four surviving angels quickly slaughtered the last two devils and left their corpses on the ground. They started to walk on, but Adonay wanted to return to say goodbye to Elizabeth. He ran back before Amy could tell him not to, so she and Serj had no choice but to wait for him at the end of the courtyard. After waiting for over three minutes it was clear that something was wrong.

'Serj, can you go and fetch Adonay, we need to stay together' said Amy. Serj ran back around the corner to see Adonay on the ground, his wings ripped to shreds and his throat slit. 'Fuck!' Serj shouted. He then noticed that one of the last devils they killed was not lying on the ground where they had left him. But he was too late. The devil jumped out from behind a statue and grabbed Serj from behind, holding a knife to his throat. Serj grabbed the devil's arm hard and flipped his body over, slamming it onto the floor and crushing his windpipe.

Serj took a last look at Adonay behind him on the ground and closed his eyes to mutter a quick prayer before running back to Amy and Orlando.

'Guys, I am really sorry, Adonay has gone' he said. 'But I managed to get the last of his killers.'

Amy and Orlando looked at each other with great sadness.

'OK listen' said Amy. 'There are only three of us left and we have been spared for a reason, we are going to survive. We need to be confident. We cannot let them win this.'

'Amy, we need to take a few minutes to sort a plan out here' said Serj. 'You need to be safe, we need to get you into the tomb to get the stone.'

Amy then told them where the stone was, as quietly as possible in case there were devils lurking somewhere close.

'Their leader and at least ten other devils are unaccounted for and there are three of us' asked Orlando. 'How are we going to do it?'

'No one goes near the tomb unless the coast is completely clear' said Amy. 'Firstly we need to find out where the hell they are. Then we will be able to work out how to take them on. If we get to their leader and kill him, we will be able to kill the rest of them easily.'

'Right, so do you think we should split up and maybe spy on them if we see them? Then we can report back here?' asked Serj,

'Yes I agree with that. The devils that are left will more than likely be together plotting as we speak.'

★ ★ ★ ★ ★

A few hours earlier, back in New York, Max had got himself out of bed and jumped into the shower to get himself ready for work. He had a weird feeling that Amy was lying about where she was going and that something bad was going to happen. He found it weird that she had not mentioned it to him. She knew he worried about her safety, especially after what had happened to Henrik.

As he finished his shower he saw a screwed-up piece of paper in the bathroom bin. He trusted Amy with everything else, but not this. He knew she was hiding something, probably to protect him.

He bent down and took the paper from the bin, then walked over to the bed with it, trying to straighten it out so it was clear enough to read. The first thing he saw was that Henrik had signed it and it was dated the night before he was found dead. After reading through the first few lines, Max realised how Henrik had died. He must have posted it through Amy's door just hours before.

Amy had known about this all along. Max now realised where she had gone and what she was doing. Surely she was about to get herself killed.

He paced up and down the room, repeatedly trying her number. She would be at the airport now, about to board the plane. He had to stop her, and if he was too late at the airport he would be getting on the next plane out of there. He knew of the area of Vuoil as he had heard Amy speak of it many times on the phone to Henrik.

Max found the spare key to Henrik's house hanging up on the key stand, so he put his clothes on and ran over there to see if he could find anything. When he arrived he put some gloves on, as the police were still using the area as a crime scene. Searching around, he found a diary with a list of names and numbers in it, one of which was that of Dr Luciano Konte. After further rummaging he found details of the area in Iraq where the angels had previously been slaughtered. He jotted down the number and the address and ran back to Amy's house.

After trying to call her for the eighth time he gave up. He got his stuff together and set out to the airport. She might be physically stronger than him, but she was the love of his life and he was ready to go to any length to save her.

On his way to the Airport he checked her flight to find it had left an hour before, so he left a message on her phone:

'Amy, I know where you are, why did you lie to me? There is no way I am letting you do this alone, you will get killed, please call me ASAP. I am on my way to find you, I can't believe you have gotten involved in this without telling you. I hope you're OK and will see you in a few hours. Love you.'

He ended the call and sat back in the taxi. He was sweating badly with the worry at the back of his mind that something might have already happened to her.

An hour later he arrived at the airport and ran to the desk to book the first flight available, which was in two hours. The flight finally started to board and a few hours later he was about to land at his destination.

Little did Max know that Amy had already arrived at the ruins and was about to begin fighting for her life – and for the future of the world.

CHAPTER 43

* * * * *

With every move she made and every punch she threw, Amy thought of Max and the kids. She just wanted a normal and peaceful life and to have this planet free of evil. That sounded like heaven to her, the idea of people being able to feel safe wherever they went and adults never needing to worry about their children.

As the three remaining angels advanced on the last devils, they pumped themselves up to kill, ready to do whatever was necessary. The devils had congregated around the next corner and were chanting in a small circle with their weapons on the ground next to them. The angels stopped and waited, watching them to see if they could work out the best way to approach them.

As they watched, Amy realised that the tallest devil was the one she wanted to get. He towered over the other devils, his eyes so blue it looked as if he had no irises. He was probably 60 to 65 years old, but he looked strong, fit and very evil.

The three of them decided that they should make their move while the devils all had their heads down.

'Ready guys, we go in now' said Amy. 'I will run in first, and I want you guys to be right behind me. Good luck!'

At her signal, they ran towards the devils in a frenzy. The devils were caught off guard and as they lifted their heads up Amy dragged the nearest one and swung him around, smashing his body on to the wall. Serj fought with two devils, punching and kicking them until he grabbed one and smashed his face into the ground over and over again. The other devil grabbed him from behind, and before he knew it there were three on top of him. But now they had his wings. After struggling for a few minutes they overpowered him and with their knives they ripped his wings to shreds, leaving him rolling around on the floor in pain.

Orlando had done well. He killed the three who had taken

Serj, but after five more minutes and having taken down a couple more devils he was also dead. Amy looked up and saw that at least seven or eight devils had gone missing, including the tall leader. She was now left there alone.

She couldn't bear to look at her friends dead on the floor; she had enough of seeing them like that. She set off to hunt for the devils who had escaped.

Amy was now left to fight the final battle on her own, feeling great sadness at what she just had to endure, losing so many close friends among the angels, as well as Henrik, who had been like a father to her. She now hated the devil creatures with a vengeance. Yet she knew this last battle would be one she would have little chance of surviving. What would the children do without her? But she had to do it for them and Max more than anything else, and that made her stronger and even more determined to kill every last one of them. She could do this. She felt ready to take on the last few Iblisari devils along with their leader, Vladimir.

She was about to enter the area where she knew they would be all waiting for her, the very place where the slaughter had taken place in 2012 BC. She took a last deep breath, held her head up high and walked through the iron gates. She walked past the pillars on either side, not caring if one of them jumped out on her - she was ready. She had anger built up inside her after what had just happened, after the devils had taken all those innocent lives, yet again.

It was a long walk through the yard, but she carried on. This was the way towards the tomb where the stone was. She knew the devils were on their way there, but she was sure they did not know how to find it.

Suddenly she saw a shadow to her left and a devil jumped out in front of her. Amy didn't flinch. She carried on walking and punched him out of the way as if she were knocking aside a drooping tree branch. She heard the cracking sound of its skull against the wall.

'One down', she said as she turned back around. Her piercing eyes stared straight ahead as she carried on walking, waiting for the next one to approach her.

Then she saw another shadow lurking behind the statue of a god. Amy spread her wings and soared to the top of the statue. Then she leaned over to see a further devil hiding behind it waiting to pounce on her. She slowly brought her right wing up, and then with a swipe she sent the devil flying over into the wall. His remains slid down it like dripping paint.

Further down she saw the last gate and she was now only metres from where the stone was. She could see that the tomb was still securely locked, and felt relieved that they had not yet found it. Looking through the crumbling wall, she now saw the lead devil. With him were three other devils, all over six feet tall. Amy didn't hesitate.

'So this is where you are hiding!' she called.

'Ah, we have been waiting for you' growled Vladimir. 'Are you here to die?' He laughed and he stepped out from behind the other devils.

'I am here to kill the rest of you and take the stone and destroy it', Amy said.

'But you are the last one left' replied Vladimir. 'You may be strong, but we will overpower you, with or without our weapons. You may have been able to kill the rest of us, but I guarantee you will not be able to defeat us, and especially me. You will never reach the stone or see your family again. Say your prayers!' Vladimir laughed again.

The sun was slowly going down, but it was still very warm and there was an eerie quietness in the air. Amy knew the angel spirits were hovering overhead, watching her every move.

She pictured the events of the last slaughter. She knew she was in the middle of the area where it had happened. Looking around, she saw up towards the sky the angels laughing and joking with each other, the excitement on their faces. They looked happy and contented floating above her; it was a vision of them moments before their deaths. But then as a dark cloud appeared the angels slowly disappeared out of her sight, and she heard again the screeching and the screams of pain and shock.

Amy shook her head. She did not want to see that picture in her head again. It was disturbing and upsetting, and the devils who had done that were the same as the ones who were now standing within metres of her, looking ready to slaughter her.

Yet she felt no fear. She walked slowly towards them again, not taking her eyes off them. She walked faster and faster until she was just five metres away from them, standing as still as the statues around her.

Vladimir looked familiar to her. She felt she had met him somewhere before. She had no idea he was Max's father.

As they stared at each other, the first of the devils advanced towards her. She lifted up her arm and put her wing around herself, then punched him in the stomach and chest. He came back at her and she bent her legs down and kicked her leg out to trip him over. As he fell she jumped up and placed her foot on his throat. He tried to grab her leg, but she took his arm and twisted it around until he squealed with pain. With her foot back on his neck she kicked him in the temple, causing instant death.

From behind she saw another devil coming at her. He grabbed her by the throat and dragged her towards Vladimir, who was just standing still watching them. He had never seen such strength in a human before. He knew she was the one who had taken so many of his devils, so he needed to be ready to take her on.

Amy put her hands on the next victim's arm, trying to remove it, but this one was strong. She kicked him and then managed to get her mouth down to where his arm was and sank her teeth deep into his flesh. The devil shook her off and she turned around, her wings slamming into his face and knocking him to the ground. As he lay there she struck him a sweeping blow, removing his head from his body. She turned around and looked up to see the remaining three devils.

Amy joined battle with the next two while Vladimir watched them closely. He could see she was getting stronger and that he might have to be the one to kill her. He slowly walked around her as she fought with the two devils, checking out her every move. His devils were getting weak and he knew they could drop at any moment.

He was right. Amy dashed one devil's lifeless body to the ground, then the other. Finally she stood before him, alone.

★ ★ ★ ★ ★

Max was now only three miles away. He had rushed through customs with just a small rucksack on him, still trying to call her every five minutes. He had rushed rushing through every doorway and corridor and within fifteen minutes of landing he was out of the airport and in a taxi and making his way to the temple ruins.

Max had no idea if Amy was alive or not, and wondered how he would be able to protect her against these powerful and evil creatures. She had four times his strength and intelligence, but he was strong and fit and had fighting skills of his own. More significantly, on the way to the ruins he had stopped off to call at a hunting shop. He wanted to have a gun on him, just in case she was in trouble.

As he held the gun he had just purchased he felt his past all come back to him. He hadn't held a firearm for years, and it made him feel weak again. It also brought back memories of the secret cult his father was in. He wondered now if his own father was involved with the Iblisari.

★ ★ ★ ★ ★

Back in the ruins, Amy stood facing Vladimir. 'So here we are, just the two of us' he said. 'I have killed all of your creatures and you have killed all my men.' His eyes narrowed. 'Oh, and I am not stupid. I now know where the stone is. I had someone go through your things just a few hours ago at your home. You should have destroyed the letter the old fool left for you, as he told you to. I thought I would wait for you to be here before I take the stone.'

'You won't be getting anywhere near that stone' said Amy. 'You will be wiped off the face of the Earth within days and so will every other evil person. The Iblisari will be forgotten forever.'

Vladimir laughed. 'I guess we will have to fight to see that, because in the next few minutes I will wipe you from the planet. In years to come we will be bigger and stronger and we will overpower the next set of angels, then you will have no chance!' He laughed at her.

Standing feet apart, they clenched their fists ready for the final battle. Vladimir took two scythes from his cloak and held them out in front of him. Amy started by jumping up in the air. She landed behind him, kicking him to the ground and knocking the blades from his hands. But he was up before she could blink and took a swipe at her with his fist. The blow did no damage.

Vladimir then ran at her and punched her in the stomach and chest. She responded by grabbing his fist and pushing his arm back. She bent it further, forcing him to kneel down. But quickly he pushed her back and managed to throw her against the hard stone wall. Amy hit the wall hard, but her wings protected her and pushed her back up straight away. She soared up and dived down on to him, kicking his head. Vladimir jumped back up, grabbed her head and neck and bent her wings back, causing her great pain. But she managed to recover and threw him against the wall.

Vladimir rose and picked up his knives once again, then began to circle her. She stared hard at him, and without thinking further she levitated herself towards him and aimed a kick at his head. They both fell to the floor. Vladimir quickly jumped up and pounced on Amy, slashing one of her shoulder blades deeply, which weakened her wings. Then he held one of the blades to her throat. Despite her strength she was unable to get herself out from underneath his heavy body as her wing was now damaged. The knife was getting closer and closer to her neck, and she could almost feel the steel about to pierce her skin.

★ ★ ★ ★ ★

Max's driver pulled up 200 yards from the temple ruins.

'I need to get closer' Max told him. 'And why is this area derelict? I thought this was a tourist area.'

'Not today sir, there is important event going on outside town and the ruins are undergoing construction work. The place should just be destroyed, it is way too old.' The driver put his hand out for payment. Max didn't ask further questions. He knew the area was empty because there was something serious going on, and he knew exactly what it was.

Max found it odd that there was no security protecting the area. It was like a ghost town; no people, no security guards and no signs of angels. The whole area was silent.

He walked through the main entrance to the ruins and reached the tall gates leading on to the site. Everything was open and it didn't feel safe, but at the same time he felt as if someone or something was watching over him.

As he took the turning to go to the long corridor that led to the courtyards, looking down he saw the dead angels scattered over the ground. The scene was barbaric. He turned away in shock and put his hand on the wall, heaving. He bent over further to vomit against the wall. He didn't want to look any closer in case he found her among the mutilated bodies. He didn't know what he would do if her saw Amy lying dead, but either way he had to search for her.

He walked by the angels' lifeless bodies scattered over the ground. Somehow they all looked beautifully peaceful, even though they had obviously been killed in the most violent way.

He took out his gun and loaded it. Then he slowly carried on, stepping over more dead bodies to get to the other end. He started carefully checking every corner in case someone or something jumped out at him. He had no idea which way to go, but he presumed if he followed the bodies he would be going in the right direction.

Around the next corner and into the next courtyard he saw more dead angels, but among them there were many dead men and women in dark cloaks. He knew these must have been the Iblisari devils. They looked like ordinary humans, but he could tell even though they were dead that they were evil. Their crushed and twisted bodies gave him a glimmer of hope that Amy and a few more angels were safe somewhere.

★ ★ ★ ★ ★

Still struggling with Vladimir, Amy became weaker and weaker as he held her, the scythe beginning to pierce her skin despite all her efforts.

'You will never make it, I will come back for you', she gasped, staring into his evil eyes.

'You are the last one' hissed Vladimir. 'I can promise you that once you are gone the future angels will never stand a chance. We will be ready and waiting for them. They will not live for even a minute!' he growled back at her.

Amy looked up into the sky. Above her she could see the spirits of the angels, hundreds of them, floating in the air. They seemed to be praying and weeping. Vladimir gave one last push and the knife sliced through her skin and deep into her flesh. Amy took a last breath. Then Vladimir ripped the knife across her throat and jumped up proudly to watch her last moments on Earth.

Amy shook as she looked up at the angels over her.

'Sorry' she whispered to them. It was the only word she could get out. Then she closed her eyes, and all she could see were bright lights surrounding her. The lights seemed to be drawing her towards them, and she could see nothing else. 'This must be heaven' she whispered.

As she floated through the tunnel of light, she finally came to a stop and looked down on to what appeared to be land. The land was empty, but just then there was a flash and she saw four babies lying on the ground. Then from nowhere she saw the misty figure of a man, as if he were floating on a white and gold cloud, above two of the babies. On the other side over the other two babies there was another misty and blurry shape, a man riding what appeared to be dark cloud. She knew immediately that she was looking down at God and Satan.

Amy could see the two, the force of good and the force of evil, lifting up their hands towards each other, driving great strokes of lightning at each other. The lightning strokes clashed and the two beings fought. The lightning between them was becoming bigger and brighter. And then, with a loud bang, a stone struck the ground.

At this point the figures of God and Satan disappeared, leaving the babies alone. She knew that she was looking at Adam and Eve and at Ibli and Sari, the first humans on Earth, the good and the evil.

Amy wondered why this vision had appeared in front of her. Then she suddenly remembered the stone which had been created by the fight between God and Satan. This was the stone that had caused so much trouble in the world; and it all stemmed from Satan's children tampering with it.

As Amy looked down from above, she saw herself lying dead on the ground and wept to think that she had failed everyone. She saw the faces of her children laughing and playing on the beach when they were young, and she saw Max. She could have changed everything, but now she was making her way to heaven.

She began to walk towards the source of the light.

CHAPTER FORTY FOUR

Vladimir felt proud. This was the moment he had been waiting for and true to his promise, even though he was the last man standing, he and the Iblisari had taken down every last one of their enemies.

Chanting to Satan, he walked over to the tomb where he knew the stone was. He used a large rock to open the padlock and after a ten-minute struggle he opened the door up and walked into it, finding his way to the stone. There the pyxis was, in front of his eyes. He stopped to wipe Amy's blood off his knife, ready to open the box with it.

He opened it up, picked the stone out and carried it outside, holding it up in the sunlight. It shone brightly, showing all the sparkles and colours in it. Now that he finally had it in his hands, he would never let it go.

It was time to head back to America with the stone.

★ ★ ★ ★ ★

Max had no idea which way to go. He just kept running past the bodies, more and more worried that he would find Amy among them. He was out of breath, but had no time to stop. He had to try and save her.

Then he heard someone smashing a gate open. He headed towards the next entrance, which led into a courtyard.

A few moments later he saw an angel's body lying on the

ground. He ran up to it, desperately hoping it was not her. Then to his desolation he saw her. It was Amy, and she was lying still on the ground soaked in blood. Max fell to his knees, grabbing her and shaking her lifeless body.

'Amy, Amy, please wake up! Amy, wake up!' he cried. He picked up her bloodied body and held her across his knees. His worst fear had come true. He looked up to the sky, sobbing loudly, then bent down to kiss her. Although she was covered in blood, she still looked as beautiful as ever. He held her tightly for another few moments, unable to let her go, feeling as if he was not meant to leave her. Max felt his whole world had just ended. A sick and empty feeling went through his body.

Then he heard a gate slamming, perhaps thirty metres away. He gave Amy one last kiss and placed her softly back on to the ground. Then he picked up his gun, and with tears streaming down his face he ran towards the noise. He knew it must have been her murderer.

As he turned the corner he saw a tall figure walking back towards the main entrance. The man looked dirty, as if he had just been in a fight. As he got closer, Max could see bloodstains on his hand.

He ran quietly towards him. Then he raised his gun.

'You, turn around!' He held up the gun, shaking and crying. 'You killed her, you killed her, turn around!'

Vladimir thought he recognised the voice. He stopped and slowly turned around, his cloak hood draped over his head. Then he looked up and laughed.

'Max my boy, what are you doing here?' Vladimir asked.

'What the fuck! Pull your hood down' Max shouted. He knew that voice, but he needed confirmation.

Vladimir slowly took down his hood. Max almost choked to see that it was his father. It confirmed all his earlier suspicions that he was part of the Iblisari.

'What are you doing here?' Max shouted, trembling. He

thought back to the times many years ago when he had walked in on his father and his father's friends chanting around a fire or dealing with a body.

'Max, put the gun down' said Vladimir. 'You shouldn't be here, but now that you are you should know that we are safe to carry on now. They are all dead, son. All of those idiot angels have gone.'

'Are you serious? You're a sick asshole! You killed Amy, the woman I love. You're evil and I knew that a long time ago. Why do you think I left you out of my life?'

'Put the gun down son', Vladimir said again.

'You killed my mother, and now you have killed Amy'

'Oh you mean the superior one! Are you telling me you fornicated with a fucking angel? A son of mine, with an angel! Well she was too powerful, she had to go. And your mother was an interfering whore, she deserved it.' He laughed at Max. Then he took the stone discreetly from his pocket and placed it behind his back.

Max flicked the trigger back. 'I am no son of yours' he said. 'You took our mother from us and forced us to live with you and your dark life. Do you think we wanted that? We hated you every single day we lived with you. Why do you think I got Andre away? We knew you were evil but we had to live with it, we feared you!' Max cried at him.

'But that didn't stop you from getting involved and killing people yourself, boy.'

'You forced us into that. Did you think we could get out of it, out of that life we were bought up into? You don't deserve to be here!'

'Max put the gun down. You weren't a very good killer back then and you wouldn't have the nerve now.' Vladimir laughed and turned to walk off.

Max could only think of Amy lying on the ground lifeless. He would never have a normal life without her and the kids. What

236

would he tell them? This was his father's fault. He hadn't only taken her life and the other angels' lives, he had brought pain and misery into the lives of so many people while running the Iblisari and his gangs.

As Max watched his father walk away with the stone in his hand he knew this was his last chance to do something about it, his last chance to repay the world for the bad Vladimir had done over the years. Justice could only be served one way.

'Stop!' he shouted at his father, but Vladimir kept on walking.

Max lifted the gun, pulled the hammer back and fired. The bullet hit his father square in the back. Vladimir stopped and turned around, staring at Max. Max shot at him again, but Vladimir turned back around and carried on walking.

Max ran closer and pulled the trigger twice more, and finally Vladimir fell to his knees. The stone fell from his hand as his whole body hit the floor with a loud thud. He struggled for a few seconds, holding his hand out to his son, blood pouring from his mouth.

Max fell to the floor crying. It was all over.

He finally pulled himself together and stood up. Then he slowly walked over to his father's dead body to pick up the stone. But as he picked it up, Vladimir suddenly came to life. He shot out a hand and grabbed Max's leg.

Max didn't hesitate. He raised the gun again and put the last two bullets into his father's head. He felt a sudden sense of justice for what he had done, and not a trace of remorse. This was for the people of New York and the world.

Max ran back to where Amy's body lay. Holding the stone tightly in his hand, he knelt back down to hold her again once more before letting her go.

'Amy, I love you so much and I'm so sorry I let this happen to you' he sobbed. 'I want you to know I will take care of those kids of yours and you won't need to worry about them. I've killed Vladimir. I have the stone here in my hand and I don't know what to do with it, so I will leave it with you. I'm so sorry it has ended this way.' He kissed her lips for the last time, then said goodbye.

He lifted up Amy's hand to leave the stone in it, but as he was about to transfer it, it suddenly started trembling. He opened his hand to see that it was beginning to crack across. He stood up with his hand still out in front of him, watching it. Was it some kind of egg, and was something about to hatch from it?

He tried to shake it out of his hand, but the stone stayed there. As he carried on watching it, it softened and slowly turned into dust before his eyes. The dust was slipping through his fingers like sand.

Max had no idea what was happening or how he had managed to do this, but he dusted it off his hands, turned away from Amy and carried on out of the temple grounds to alert the police. He still couldn't believe he would never see her again.

Little did Max know that he had just changed the world. Now that the stone had been destroyed, evil humans and people with severe criminal tendencies were disappearing one by one from the face of the Earth. Prisons and high-security mental asylums were emptying all around the world. All those who had evil minds but lived normal everyday lives would also disappear one by one, without a trace and in a few days' time, the world would be empty of them.

Max was the one who had the heart of the superior angel; Amy's heart.

CHAPTER FORTY FIVE

Max arrived back in New York and pulled up outside the house he had only just moved into with Amy and the kids. He stayed in his car for a while, not knowing if he could go inside seeing all of her things, but he needed to be strong. The kids were still staying away with the family, where the news was broken to them that their mother had been killed.

Max had to look after them, as well as getting himself through these early stages of grieving. After half an hour of sitting in the car, he got out and walked up the drive to the front door. He was shaking as he tried to open the door, but as soon as he entered the house he broke down. He saw her shoes, her coat hanging up on the coat peg. Her scent filled the house as he walked through to the sitting room. Wandering around the house, he grabbed a picture from the mantelpiece of the two of them on holiday in Paris. It made him think about the time they had first met, when he had knocked her bag on to the tracks at the station.

Just then the doorbell went. Max had no idea who it might be, so he didn't bother to answer it. But the caller was persistent and kept banging on the door harder and harder.

Finally Max got off the sofa, wiped the tears from his eyes and walked to the front door.

'OK!' he shouted as he opened the door. Two well-dressed men stood there.

'Max, my name is Dr Luciano Konte' said the man on the left.

'I was a friend of Henrik's and I knew Amy. I am from the AAG and this is Peter Wilson from the government. We are both part of the team that discovered the angels would appear in 12/12/12 and all the stories behind it all. May we come in?'

'Well, I am kinda busy' Max told them and started to close the door, but Dr Konte put his foot in the door.

'Max, we are truly sorry for your loss. Amy was a good woman and a good angel, but we do need to speak to you about the good that's come out of this.'

Max was shocked, but he opened the door up for them and allowed them to come into the hall.

'No good has come from this for me' he said. 'This has ruined my life and will ruin the lives of her children. Can you imagine how they feel, being told their mother has been killed, along with all the other angels? So tell me what good has come from this?'

'Max, we know how you are feeling right now' said Konte. 'We became close with the angels, especially Amy, and I've known Henrik as a close friend for many years. Look, I don't know if Amy told you or not, but there were other stories behind the stone that she may not have mentioned.'

'Like what?' Max asked.

'Max, first we need to know if you saw the stone at all?'

Max explained how he had killed Vladimir, without mentioning he was his father, and how he had ended up with the stone in his own hands. Then he explained how it had turned into sand and disappeared into nothing.

'So Max, were you aware that the stone could only be destroyed by the superior angel, or someone who had the heart of the superior angel?'

Max looked confused.

'Max, that was you. When you took that stone and held it, you did more than crush it. You have changed this world. Evil is now disappearing from the whole world. She didn't mention this to you, did she?' the doctor asked.

'No she didn't. I guess she didn't want me involved. She was protecting me, that sounds like her' he told them. 'Well whatever has happened to this planet I'm not sure I care. My whole world has ended without her, so right now I couldn't care less. I would rather the world stayed as it was if it meant her being here right now.'

Max walked back into the sitting room and sat back on the sofa, his head in his hands. 'Look guys I really need some time' he said. 'I have to collect Amy's kids from the airport and sort out her funeral, so I would appreciate it if you could leave me for a few days? I can't take this in right now.'

'OK, we understand and once again we are so very sorry to have bothered to you so soon. We just wanted you to know what a big impact you've been to this planet, you and Amy. We'll speak to you at a later date when things are a little less raw and if you need anything please contact us.'

The two men gave Max their cards and made their way out of the house.

Max lay back on the sofa, and for the first time in two days he fell asleep.

CHAPTER FORTY SIX

Amy's funeral took place one week after her death in the Catholic church just half a mile from her home. Her parents, grandparents and siblings were among the large crowd that gathered in the small church. Max, Jake and Scarlett sat in the front row just three metres from her coffin. Neither of them had spoken since they had left the house that morning. No one who sat in that church took any notice of what was happening in the world around them.

The world had got rid of all evil, and peace and tranquillity had spread throughout the planet as it had before life and the stone existed. There were no murderers, rapists or other evil-minded people lived. The prisons and high-security mental asylums were almost empty. The only people left in them were those who had been forced into a life of crime or were there for petty offences. Thanks to the angels and Max, people could now walk around safely and peacefully.

Max couldn't take his eyes off the coffin, knowing Amy was in there. It had been seven days, but he wanted to open the coffin and hold her. He didn't care what she looked like now; he just wanted to be close to her. He had only known Amy for under a year and the kids for less, but all three of them had changed his life. He had never felt the way he had when he was with them, and even now she was gone he felt he had to be there for Jake and Scarlett. And they felt the same way. They reminded him of Amy, and Max reminded them of their mother. He wasn't about to leave them on their own. He had become part of the family, and it was going to stay that way.

After the deaths of the angels the AAG were there at the mortuary to formally identify all the bodies to spare the families. They were all tidied up and placed in coffins in preparation to be sent back to their home towns and families. Max dreaded this day and wanted it to be over with as soon as possible. It hurt too much seeing Amy's coffin and meeting her parents and family listening to the stories of what she was like growing up. He could hardly pull himself together and accept the fact that his own despicable, evil father had taken her life.

After the service the coffin was taken into a room at the side of the church to prepare for the burial. As the family walked outside to receive sympathies, Max made his way to where Amy's coffin lay.

The undertaker was doing the last-minute preparations for the coffin to go into the hearse when Max asked for a few moments alone.

'Please, could you open the coffin?' he asked. 'I need to say my last goodbye to her' he said.

'Well you do understand she will not look as you remember her' said the man. 'I would advise you to leave her be and remember her as she looked before she passed away.' But Max reached into his pocket and pulled out $200 and handed it over to him.

'Sir I still don't think it is a good idea, but I will leave the key on top of the coffin. You have ten minutes. The hearse is waiting'.

'Thank you, I really appreciate this' said Max, and the man walked out of the room.

Max stared at the coffin and took the key from the top of it, his hands were clammy and he was beginning to shake. Was this really a good idea? But he knew he would never be able to get on with his life until he had seen her just one last time.

Trembling, he slowly guided the key into the keyhole. Then he slowly turned it. He stood back and carefully lifted the heavy coffin lid. He kept his eyes closed as he began to raise the lid, and took a deep breath, remembering the last time he had held her in his arms alive.

Max then opened his eyes slowly to see her for the final time – and jumped back in shock. He couldn't breathe.

The coffin was empty.

But if Amy wasn't there, where was she? What had they done with her body?

Perhaps it was being used for medical research and so on without her family's consent. Max was fuming. How could this happen? But he couldn't go out there and explain to everyone that Amy's body had disappeared. He needed to find out from the guys who had identified the angels' bodies and ask them what they knew and when they had last seen her body.

He closed the coffin, locked it up and handed the keys back to the undertaker, who was waiting outside the door. 'Thanks, I really appreciate that' he said, as he tried to compose himself.

He went to find Dr Konte and found him in the distance talking to Amy's family.

'Excuse me, may I interrupt?' he asked.

'Doctor, may I have a word?'

'Yes of course, what is it?' asked the doctor,

'You know what it is, I have just gone to say my last goodbye to Amy' Max whispered aggressively. 'She is not in the damn coffin! Where the hell is her body? I know you know something about this, where the hell is she?'

'Max, we can't discuss this here, follow me.' The doctor walked towards the rear of the church and through the back door out into the yard and down the path towards the graveyard.

'Where are we going, what is happening here?'

'Max, Amy's body is lying in rest on a small island somewhere in the Arabian Sea near the Indian ocean, an island very few people in the world know of. A handful of angels are buried there according to their own wishes. There are people living on the island and they have taken samples for DNA from the angels for small experiments, nothing big. Amy signed up for this the day before her death, and she wanted me to let you know where she would be buried and how beautiful an island it is and that you should not advise anyone of this whatsoever. It has to be kept a secret. She wanted to help the scientists find out more about the bodies of the angels, how they were so strong and intelligent.

'Max, I am sorry you had to find out her body was not in that coffin, but she wanted this. However she wanted only you to know about it. She requested that you visit the island and her grave along with the children, but they need only think it as a holiday, it is up to you now whether you wish to advise them of this. You do not need to tell them if you think it is best not too.'

Max didn't know what to believe any more, but he knew that if Amy wanted him to do this then he had to give this place a chance.

'So I can take the kids for a so-called beach holiday, and then explain to them where her body is and then go and see her grave?' Max asked. 'How can I let those children cry over their mother's coffin when she is not even in it?'

'Max, their mother's spirit is watching over them, whether her body is near or far she will be right beside them' said Dr Konte.

Max shook his head. 'There just had to be something else, I couldn't just say goodbye to her could I? So where do I go? I will need three tickets booked and I will need details of when and where.'

'We will sort out everything for you, just let us know when you are able to travel and we will have you over there as soon as.'

'Well I want to get this over with and we all need a break, so I want to leave tomorrow or the day after. I have to keep Jake and Scarlett occupied' Max sighed.

'That will be arranged for you Max. I will email you to get

further details and to discuss how to get to the island and who to meet.'

As they walked back to the church, Max gave Dr Konte his email address. Then he rejoined the funeral party with everyone else to say their goodbyes to Amy's soul.

CHAPTER FORTY SEVEN

Three days later, Max, Jake and Scarlett embarked on the nine-hour flight from John F Kennedy airport to Madagascar, where they were transferred again to another small aircraft which took them to an island in the Indian Ocean.

'You will now have to take that boat to your final destination' said the pilot. 'There will be someone waiting there for you.' He pointed to a small boat docked at the end of a tiny pier. They climbed on board and cast off. Another hour passed before they could see the island of Krobir in the distance. It looked bigger than they had imagined.

When they finally arrived in Krobir they found it to be a deserted place with no pier and no dock, just miles of clear white sand and dazzling turquoise ocean. Way beyond the beach the island had a small row of houses and villas in the distance, and further up was a small mountain with the houses of a village scattered up its slopes. It was surrounded by beautiful green trees

They were met by a young Australian girl who introduced herself as Anela. 'Welcome to the island of Krobir" she said.

'Hi, I'm Jake and that's Scarlett and that's Max' said Jake.

'It's nice to meet you all' said Anela. 'I take it you are Mr Grekov?' she was looking over at Max.

'Yes I am, but please call me Max.'

'OK Max. We have a beautiful villa for you, you see the white one over on the far left?'

'Oh yes, I see it' said Max.

'It is the most wonderful villa, the best one on the island I think and you will have a great stay here. I will take you up to the villa and show you around.'

As they walked Anela talked to them about the island. 'Krobir is kind of a part of Australia even though it is miles from it' she said. 'It is the people's own private island and we are not ruled by any country, even Australia. It is like we are in a different world here. It is a beautiful place to be and you will love it here.'

'This place is pretty awesome' said Jake.

'Yeah, it's so pretty' added Scarlett. 'How did you find this place, Max?'

'Oh a friend of a friend' he replied. He hated lying to the kids, especially after what they had been through. He thought that once they were settled in the beach villa he would explain that Amy was buried here and why. What harm could come from that? They had a right to know. It was bad enough not being able to tell her parents.

'So what's beyond the mountains?' Max asked the girl.

'Well the small town you see there is one of four we have on the island. There are only 10,000 people living here and we take pride in looking after our island. You know we are not even on the map' she told him.

'Wow, that's incredible' replied Max.

'Jake are you OK? You seem a little dazed' Max asked.

'Nah, I'm cool' Jake replied, still not taking his eyes off Anela.

'Ah, I see!' said Max laughing. Anela was a beautiful young girl with flawless mahogany skin and long dark silky hair. She spoke with a soft accent which was unrecognisable to them.

'You guys, it's so amazing here!' Scarlett shouted. She did a cartwheel in the sand, and for the first time since her mother's death, she smiled.

Max stopped walking for a minute and for the first time in days he felt a little happiness. Amy must have known they would love this place. He knew they were hurting badly inside, but it was a good feeling to see them happy, even if it was only for a few minutes. Although his heart was in a million tiny pieces and he just wanted to scream and cry out loud, he knew he had to pull himself together for them.

They finally made it to the villa, which was a white, wooden two-storey building with a small veranda overlooking the softly sweeping waves. Inside it had the finest dark wooden floors and a beautiful wooden staircase with white walls and white furniture. It was very stylish, cosy, bright and airy, and there was even a selection of fruit and champagne waiting to greet them.

'Mr Grekov, I am sorry I mean Max, you will find the fridge has been fully stocked up' said Anela. 'If there is anything you cannot find, please give us a call. There are other villas scattered around within walking distance but they are all unoccupied at present, for the next three days anyway, so you should see no one on this beach. If you do you should advise us. You will also find around the front of the house that you have a car with a full tank of gas, so please go and explore the island in it. Eat what you want or sleep for the evening. I'm sure you will have a wonderful stay here. Oh, and before I go I must advise you that there is a party in the village tomorrow evening and you are all invited.'

'So will you be at the party tomorrow?' Jake asked Anela. She bowed her head and smiled, apparently a little embarrassed. 'Yes I will be Jake, I hope to see you there' she said as she waved them goodbye.

'Very smooth Jake, very smooth' Max joked. They all laughed together while Scarlett ran for first choice of the bedrooms.

Later on that evening, after their evening, meal Jake and Scarlett went off to bed, as they had all had a long day travelling. Max thought it would be best to wait until the morning to explain to them what he knew about where their mother was lying, and why.

After wishing them goodnight, he took his bottle of beer out onto the porch to relax. The tide was starting to come in and the moon was bright. He kicked off his shoes and walked down the wooden steps and towards the water's edge. There he sat on the damp sand, looking up at the moon. He thought about his life and why he had been subjected to such heartbreak and sadness. He had lost his mother because of his father, and he had not been there to protect her when she was murdered. And he had not reached Amy in time to protect her either. But one thing he knew – no other person in his life would be hurt by him again.

He wondered how long he would be able to go on without Amy. He bottled his feelings up so much around the kids, just to make sure they were OK. They were the only thing keeping him sane and together. He felt like more of a friend to them than ever now, and knew that in time he would be the one they relied on as their father. He was a very lucky man to have them in his life now.

Max smiled and shook his head, remembering the time Jake had accidentally called him Dad and they had ended up having a play fight. It was just those little things that he had never had as a boy that made him so determined to give these kids what they deserved and what their mother would have wanted for them.

As he rose up from the spot he sat in and dusted himself off, he saw a figure approaching in the distance. It was only a silhouette because of the beach lamp a few yards behind it, but Max knew no one else was staying in the area for the next few days, so whoever it was should not be there.

'Who's that?' he shouted out, but the person didn't answer. Max stood up taller to prepare himself. It looked like a woman. He felt a little scared, which was unlike him, but after what he had been through he had to be vigilant about what was going on around him.

'Hey you're on private property, this is my part of the beach!' he shouted. But when he looked again, the figure had disappeared.

Maybe he had had one too many bottles of beer at dinner.

He went back to the swinging bench on the porch and sat there. After fifteen minutes or so he had started to doze off when he heard a creak from the bottom of the steps that led to the beach. He jumped up from his seat and slowly stepped to look over the edge, picking up a sand shovel on the way.

Then he saw something that made him think he was going mad or dreaming. He stared. It couldn't be!

Slowly raising his trembling body, he poked his head over the wooden balcony to see someone standing at the end slowly walking up.

It was Amy.

'What the fuck? I'm dreaming, I'm dreaming!' he jabbered to himself. But the more he said it, the more it was becoming real. There she was, right in front of him.

'Amy?' he said, walking towards her shaking, tears staring to come out of his eyes. 'Amy, is that really you? Are you a ghost or are you alive? Am I seeing things, what is going on?

Amy spoke.

'Max, please stop talking, it really is me' she said in her familiar soft voice. 'I need to explain what has happened here. I'm OK and I am very much alive, not a ghost.'

Max was trembling as he got closer to her. He reached out and touched her skin, half expecting to find there was nothing there. But she was real, a living, breathing person. Amy, his Amy, was alive. She looked weak and fragile, but more beautiful than ever. Although it was dark he could see her glossy skin and rosy cheeks, coloured by the hot sun. Her hair was flowing freely in the light breeze. She looked wonderful.

'But everyone thinks you're… gone' he said helplessly. She walked up to him and placed her finger on his lips to keep him quiet. Then she pulled him closer to her and wrapped her arms around him.

Slowly Max lifted his arms and returned the hug, the hug that should have been impossible.

'Max, I am so sorry you have had to go through this. Jake and Scarlett, how are they?' she asked, sounding worried. 'I have been watching you over the last few hours trying to work out the best way to approach you.'

'Amy this is too weird, I can't take it in right now' Max said, gently pulling away. 'The kids are fine, but they are torn up inside. Why wouldn't you call or send a letter, anything? Do you know what we have been going through, the hell we have suffered? Amy you were dead! I held you, you were covered in blood, your neck…'

Amy put a hand over his mouth. 'Don't, that's enough' she said. 'I can explain everything, but you need to calm down. We both need to calm down and relax.'

Max walked back up the steps on to the porch area and sat on the chair and Amy followed. In the light he could see a large scar on her neck. Her face was still covered in light bruising. She looked scared and was limping slightly. Max was ecstatic to see her, but the shock had overwhelmed him.

They looked at each other with an awkward silence, then Amy gave him her hand and they walked back down to the sea together.

'OK, I'll explain. About an hour after the fight I regained consciousness. No one was around and I was in serious pain. My injuries would have killed a normal person, but angels have exceptional strength, as you know. It did nearly kill me, in fact I think I did die, but I just wasn't ready to go I guess. Anyway, I could hear shuffling, as if there was someone else struggling, so I dragged myself up to see who was moving, and around the corner I saw Serj. He looked worse than I did. His arm was hanging on by a piece of skin and the only way I recognised him was his black curly hair. He had dragged himself a long way to look for me. We then saw that Vladimir was dead.

'Then we heard voices, but we were so weak and thought it

might be the devils back to finish us off, so we had to play dead. But as they got closer we realised it was Dr Konte and Mr Wilson. They managed to call some people and they took us to a hospital. Then they scoured the place to see if there was life anywhere else and managed to find a few more angels, badly beaten but still alive. They also looked for the stone, but it was not in the place Henrik had said. They presumed it had been taken by a devil because the tomb looked as if it had been broken into, but after searching all the devils it was clear that none of them had the stone.

'The four of us spent the next couple of days in the hospital. Serj lost his arm, but other than that he'll be ok. By the end of that time the world already seemed different. Evil was steadily being removed from the world, so we all realised someone must have found the stone and destroyed it. After Dr Konte and his team did some investigation they found out that this person was you!

'When you destroyed the stone, everything in the world changed. As you now know, you have made history by freeing the planet of evil. While this was going on we had to be taken to a safe place where no one could track us, especially as the devils were angry, their leader had been killed and they would have come after us. We didn't know they were all dead. That's why we had to lie and pretend we were dead. In fact fifteen of us survived, but we had killed all of the members of the Iblisari. And look what's happened, we won and you had a big part in it.

'Within a few days we had started to regain our strength, and we were brought to this beautiful island. The AAG told us about it before and it sounded so amazing, they showed us pictures of it. They knew this would be the place we should retire to and that's why they bought us here, so we would be able to decide whether we wanted to see if our families would come here or not. It was only planned after the great battle with the Iblisari. It was a hard time being without you and knowing what pain you must have been going through, but it had to be done quietly. This is an unknown island and although the world is a safe place to be in now, we have been advised that to carry on a simple quiet and happy life we should stay here forever, because if we go back to the real world we will never be left in peace. We would still be angels, and with only fifteen of us left we wouldn't have a moment's peace. We have been here less than a week and already we feel safer and more relaxed than we ever did. All we needed was our families.'

Amy looked down at her hand, still clasping Max's.

'It took a lot out of me from the day I had turned into an angel and in the following weeks I almost died. This life here is completely different and it's what I think I need right now. But of course all that matters is you and the kids, so at the end of the day I will do whatever you guys wish.

'I know you don't want to leave the life you had in New York Max, and I understand you will not want to come and live here with me, and Jake and Scarlett will probably feel the same, so if you all want to go back home after this trip I will suffer the consequences and come with you, for I would rather be dead than without you guys.'

'I need to tell you something, Amy' Max said, looking scared. 'The man who attempted to kill you, Vladimir, well I killed him. I knew he had just killed you and that he had the stone. He told me himself that he had just taken your life. Amy, that man was my father.'

'He was your *father*? Oh my god Max! Now I understand how your life growing up must have been so difficult. He really was a powerful and scary man. I can't believe you had to live with that, I'm so sorry.'

'Yeah. I didn't want to have to use a gun ever in my life again and I didn't know how I would do it, but it was easy. Killing him was such a relief for me, just the fact that he was no longer part of this world. Amy, I just can't believe you are here, after the heartbreak, holding you dead in my arms. I'm sorry I greeted you like that and I understand now why you had to do it this way. Looking at you I cannot tell you how happy I am!' He pulled her closer to him and held her tightly as they both wept.

Just then they heard the floorboards creak and jumped up to see Jake and Scarlett at the doorway, staring in shock. Max walked forward.

'Oh guys, this will be explained to you! Please be calm, this is real, you're not dreaming, your mom is here, she's alive and well.'

Amy stepped forward, holding her hands out for them. They stood there speechless. Then they slowly walked towards her to touch her hands. Once they knew they weren't dreaming they put their arms around her and started sobbing tears of shock and happiness.

'Careful guys, she is really fragile, she has been in hospital' Max told them.

'Oh sorry Ma, but what the hell is going on, how come you're alive?' Jake asked.

'I can't believe this Mom, you're really here!' said Scarlett.

'I knew you weren't dead, I could feel it' said Jake, as they all cried and cuddled each other again.

Max then let her explain what had happened to the children as he went inside to get a well-earned drink. After a while, Jake came into the house. 'Max, can I talk to you?' he asked, motioning to Max to follow into the dining area.

'Yeah of course Jake, what's up?'

'What do you think about staying here on the island? We wanna stay here, we don't care about going back home, we can visit America whenever we want, we can even go over there for college if we want, but we wanna stay here with her, you wanna stay too, right?'

Max paused. 'Listen, I am happy to stay here, I would do anything for you guys, but what about your school, your friends, your lives back in New York? Are you sure you want to do this? I need to know you guys are one hundred per cent happy with being here. This will be a real quiet life for you guys, so you need to take time and be sure.'

'I don't care what life I have back there, we can get flights over whenever we need to' said Jake. 'I am staying here to look after my mother. Losing mom was the worst feeling ever, she and Scar are the most important things to me. And apparently there is a quicker and easier way to travel other than the way we got here. I want a happy family life, and I don't want Mom to go through any more stress. Dragging her back home is not an option.'

Max gave Jake a hug. 'I am so glad to hear you say that' said Max. 'I won't be leaving you at all. I think we'll be happy here.' They walked back into the house to join Amy and Scarlett.

So it was agreed; they would make their home together on the island. Amy told them she would need to return to collect her things from where she was staying on the island, which was two miles from the villa.

'Amy, there is no way I am letting you out of my sight, we will drive you there' said Max. 'You can collect your things and we will drive back here. The last time you went off without me you almost got yourself killed!'

'Yeah Mom please don't leave us again, we can all go then come back here and chill out, watch a film like we used to' said Jake. Scarlett agreed.

'OK you guys, remember I'm not an invalid' said Amy, and they all laughed. 'But you're right, we will all have to stick together from now on. I promise you all we will have a wonderful life out here, and kids, in a few years' time I want you out travelling the world, I want you to go to the best colleges. I don't want being here to hold you back.'

'Yeah, we got you Ma,' they both said at the same time.

'Oh and I can't wait for you guys to meet Serj, he is so cool, you will love him. He's the lead singer in a metal band.'

Amy took a walk outside while she waited for Jake and Scarlett to change from their pyjamas. She took a deep breath as she looked at the black ocean and the dark sky filled with stars. She felt so lucky to be here. And as Max walked over to her and put his arms around her, she knew they would be happy and safe forever.

THE END

ND - #0466 - 270225 - C0 - 203/127/23 - PB - 9781861510426 - Matt Lamination